WHEN IN DOUBT

What Reviewers Say About VK Powell's Work

Line of Duty

"Ms. Powell is an expert at writing police procedurals, and with this book, she also shows us just how talented she is at combining that with a lovely romance."—*Rainbow Reflections*

"I love a sexy butch cop, and Finley Masters was everything I needed. Not only was she damn hot, but she was a tormented soul, and that, my dear friends, just made her even sexier."—*Les Rêveur*

"I find myself wanting to reread the book, because the path each character takes is unique. The series of moments where their beliefs are tested and transformed are both big and small. I loved the pacing and I enjoyed that nothing ever felt like filler. ...I like to think of reading a story as entrusting yourself to the pilot of an airplane. You're in highly capable and talented hands here. I am already looking up other VK Powell books to buy."—*Lesbian Review*

Second in Command

"I love the family at the centre of the Fairview Station series, and their various careers in and around law enforcement and other public service professions. ...I greatly enjoyed the scenes involving the whole Carlyle family and was cheered to see various of the more peripheral members find their own place in the scheme of things."
—*The Good, the Bad and the Unread*

"I enjoyed the storyline and felt like the plot twisted more than once and made turning the page more exciting. The secondary characters in this book (and *Captain's Choice*) were excellent, and I thoroughly enjoyed every time the Carlyle family get around the dinner table."—*Les Rêveur*

Incognito

"[F]ast paced, action packed and keeps you glued to the page."
—*Lesbian Reading Room*

"*Incognito* by V.K. Powell is the kind of intrigue/thriller novel that I enjoy. ...If you enjoy a good mystery with interesting characters and a bit of romance, then try this book."—*Rainbow Reflections*

"Well written main characters with plenty of chemistry. A good supporting cast as well that provide some good laughs and emotional feels. A fun read with enough action and romance to keep you interested."—Kat Adams, Bookseller (QBD Books, Australia)

"The strongest part of the book was the interplay between leads. ...Both women learned to keep people at arms' length, Frankie with her abilities to become almost anyone, and Evan with her almost obsessive need for rules and order. They clash, because Frankie's often mischievous behavior is so out of what Evan thinks she needs. But they are attracted to each other, and it does blow up their world view a bit."—Colleen Corgel, Librarian, Queens Borough Public Library

"If you're in the mood for a fast-paced romantic intrigue novel with action, romance and humour, this might be one for you."
—*C-Spot Reviews*

"[T]his book is exciting and fast-paced and the chemistry between the two main characters is great."—*Jude in the Stars*

Take Your Time

"The last book in the Pine Cone Romance series was excellent, and I reckon VK Powell wrote the perfect book to round up the series. ...If these are the sex scenes VK Powell can write, then I have been missing out and I will definitely be checking out more because WOW! All in all... Fantastic! 5 stars"—*Les Rêveur*

Captain's Choice

"VK Powell is the mistress of police romances and this one is another classic 'will she won't she' story of lost loves reunited by chance. Well written, lots of great sex and excellent sexual tension, great character building and use of the setting, this was a thoroughly enjoyable read."—*Lesbian Reading Room*

Deception

"In *Deception* VK Powell takes some difficult social issues and portrays them with intelligence and empathy. ...Well-written, enjoyable storyline, excellent use of location to add colour to the background, and extremely well drawn characters. VK Powell has created a great sense of life on the streets in an excellent crime/mystery with a turbulent but charming romance."—*Lesbian Reading Room*

Side Effects

"[A] touching contemporary tale of two wounded souls hoping to find lasting love and redemption together. ...Powell ably plots a plausible and suspenseful story, leading readers to fall in love with the characters she's created."—*Publishers Weekly*

About Face

"Powell excels at depicting complex, emotionally vulnerable characters who connect in a believable fashion and enjoy some genuinely hot erotic moments."—*Publishers Weekly*

Exit Wounds

"Powell's prose is no-nonsense and all business. It gets in and gets the job done, a few well-placed phrases sparkling in your memory and some trenchant observations about life in general and a cop's life in particular sticking to your psyche long after they've gone. After five books, Powell knows what her audience wants, and she delivers those goods with solid assurance. But be careful you don't get hooked. You only get six hits, then the supply's gone, and you'll be jonesin' for the next installment. It never pays to be at the mercy of a cop."—*Out in Print*

"Fascinating and complicated characters materialize, morph, and sometimes disappear testing the passionate yet nascent love of the book's focal pair. I was so totally glued to and amazed by the intricate layers that continued to materialize like an active volcano...dangerous and deadly until the last mystery is revealed. This book goes into my super special category. Please don't miss it."—*Rainbow Book Reviews*

Justifiable Risk

"This story takes some unusual twists and at one point, I was convinced that I knew 'who did it' only to find out that I was wrong. VK Powell knows crime drama, she kept me guessing until the end, and I was not disappointed at the outcome. And that's not to slight VK Powell's knack for romance. ...Readers who appreciate mysteries with a touch of drama and intense erotic moments will enjoy *Justifiable Risk*."—*Queer Magazine*

"*Justifiable Risk* is an exciting, seat of your pants read. It also has some very hot sex scenes. Powell really shines, however, in showing the inner growth of Greer and Eva as they each deal with their personal issues. This is a very strong, multifaceted book."—*Just About Write*

Fever

"VK Powell has given her fans an exciting read. The plot of *Fever* is filled with twists, turns, and 'seat of your pants' danger. ...*Fever* gives readers both great characters and erotic scenes along with insight into life in the African bush."—*Just About Write*

Suspect Passions

"From the first chapter of *Suspect Passions* Powell builds erotic scenes which sear the page. She definitely takes her readers for a walk on the wild side! Her characters, however, are also women we care about. They are bright, witty, and strong. The combination of great sex and great characters make *Suspect Passions* a must read."—*Just About Write*

To Protect and Serve

"If you like cop novels, or even television cop shows with women as full partners with male officers...this is the book for you. It's got drama, excitement, conflict, and even some fairly hot lesbian sex. The writer is a retired cop, so she really writes from a place of authenticity. As a result, you have a realistic quality to the writing that puts me in mind of early Joseph Wambaugh."—Teresa DeCrescenzo, *Lesbian News*

"*To Protect and Serve* drew me in from the very first page with characters that captivated in their complexity. Powell writes with authority using the lingo and capturing the thoughts of the law enforcers who make the ultimate sacrifice in the fight against crime. What's more impressive is the command this debut author has of portraying a full gamut of emotion, from angst to elation, through dialogue and narrative. The images are vivid, the action is believable, and the police procedurals are authentic. …VK Powell had me invested in the story of these women, heart, mind, body and soul. Along with danger and tension, Powell's well-developed erotic scenes sizzle and sate."—*Story Circle Book Reviews*

Visit us at www.boldstrokesbooks.com

By the Author

To Protect and Serve

Suspect Passions

Fever

Justifiable Risk

Haunting Whispers

Exit Wounds

About Face

Side Effects

Deception

Lone Ranger

Take Your Time

Incognito

When in Doubt

Fairview Station Series

Captain's Choice

Second in Command

Line of Duty

WHEN IN DOUBT

by

VK Powell

2021

WHEN IN DOUBT

ISBN 13: 978-1-63555-955-2

This Trade Paperback Original Is Published By
Bold Strokes Books, Inc.
P.O. Box 249
Valley Falls, NY 12185

First Edition: June 2021

Credits
Editor: Cindy Cresap
Production Design: Susan Ramundo
Cover Design By Tammy Seidick

Acknowledgments

First, to Len Barot, Sandy Lowe, and all the talented and insightful folks at Bold Strokes Books, thank you for allowing me to transform my law enforcement experiences into stories of survival, the struggle to balance love and livelihood, and the fight between good and evil. I am grateful for the opportunity and for the guidance you continually provide on each project.

Cindy Cresap, many thanks for your time and attention on this manuscript. Your perspective and insights were invaluable. The steady doses of humor didn't hurt either. Hopefully, I learn something new with each book.

To my beta readers—D. Jackson Leigh and Jenny Harmon—you guys are the best. This book is better for your efforts, and I am truly grateful.

And last, but never least, to all the readers who support and encourage my writing, thank you for buying my books, sending emails, and giving shout-outs on social media. Let's keep doing this.

Chapter One

Jeri Wylder strapped the equipment-heavy gun belt to her waist and glanced around her ranch-style house, wondering when it would truly feel like home again. After reclaiming the family residence, she'd expanded the living, kitchen, and dining rooms into an open-plan space with a more modern feel, but renovation couldn't fix everything. Now, silence echoed off the walls. The friendly banter over breakfast, sharing highlights of her day with her parents while making dinner, and creating a bedtime jingle with them before sleep were only memories.

The first few years back, she'd tried to fill the void by burning through every online dating site and friend referral for the right woman to share her home and possibly even start a family, but no one felt quite right. No one excited her physically, made her need and feel needed, and grounded her after a day of negotiating domestic disputes and chasing criminals. Megan, her current flavor of the month, wouldn't be happy with that thought. She breathed a sigh of frustration mingled with loneliness and headed toward her car in the driveway.

A tiny yelp drew her attention to her neighbor's front porch and an energetic wire-haired terrier. "Toto, what are you doing outside at dinnertime, boy? Did Mrs. Doyle forget you again, or were you chasing some bitch around the neighborhood?" She patted him and received a vigorous shake of his tail. She could've sworn he grinned at her. "I'm guessing the latter. Let's get you inside before your mom panics." Mrs. Doyle had become a surrogate grandmother when Jeri moved back, and they spent hours sharing stories and dissecting the problems of the world. Often when Jeri came home at night, she'd find leftovers on her front porch from Mrs. Doyle's latest cooking binge—steak and Guinness pie, Irish stew, or scones.

She found her neighbor's key on her ring next to a four-leaf clover Mrs. Doyle had given her, eased the front door open, and scooted Toto inside. "Good boy." She'd normally stay and chat, but when they started talking, it led to rounds of sherry or Jameson's and stories about Ireland, and Jeri couldn't be late for work. On the way, she thought about her lovely elderly neighbor and her scrappy little dog. She'd asked Mrs. Doyle once why she named him Toto. Her answer still made Jeri smile.

"Think about it, girl. A story about a quest to the Emerald City, which had to be an Irish pub. And the Scarecrow, Tin Man, and Cowardly Lion, no doubt ossified punters, who saw Munchkins, witches, flying monkeys, and different-colored horses. I just imagine me boy Toto doing the same on his nightly prowls."

"I do love the Irish," Jeri said as she parked and sprinted to lineup.

Her zone partner, Randy Mardis, and his best friend, Carl, held court at the back of the room near the bulletin board filled with wanted posters, and the rest of the squad huddled around. Carl was telling a story and suddenly whipped his ASP from the holder, flicked the expandable baton open, and simulated sword fighting. He was a testosterone-fueled asshole who'd probably wet himself at the first sign of real trouble or shoot first and ask questions later— exactly the kind of person the department didn't need. A few of the guys laughed at his antics, most didn't. The sergeant waved for quiet as he entered, putting an end to the hijinks.

Randy joined her at their usual table near the front, and she nudged him with her elbow. "Your boyfriend is on a roll today. I swear you two could be brothers. Hell, you even dress alike." She pointed to the sleek Italian leather gloves he and Carl wore on duty every day, summer and winter. "Should I be jealous of this bromance?"

"Fuck off, Wylder. You know we grew up together in NoHo."

She'd heard his story of two inner-city kids from Weehawken, New Jersey, a town parallel to Midtown Manhattan and separated by the Hudson River, who fought their way through school and drug wars together. "Yeah, but still, if you'd prefer him as a zone partner, I'd be okay with it."

He shook his head. "I'm good."

After the daily briefing and zone assignments, Sergeant Bruce waved his officers out of the room. "Okay, studs, get out there and police the city. And don't get into any shit I'll have to write up tonight. I'm not in the mood."

Jeri pocketed her notepad and followed Randy toward the patrol car lot. He lumbered side to side as if his bulky muscles overburdened his frame. She loved working with him because his size alone deterred most suspects, and he was always good for a laugh, but tonight he seemed unusually reserved—no snarky comebacks to the sergeant and not even a joke about the scraggly ginger fuzz Carl was trying to coax into a respectable beard. "You all right, partner?"

He clicked the lock of the patrol car and popped open the trunk and doors. "I guess."

She leaned against the car and studied his eyes that were usually alive with mischief. Tonight, they were flat and vacant. "Your mom?"

He nodded. "Things aren't looking good." He searched the back seat of the patrol car and trunk before stepping closer. "I wouldn't mind checking on her before it gets too busy. She was having a lot of trouble breathing when I left."

"Do it. I'll cover the calls. Just shoot me a text when you're clear."

"Thanks, partner," Randy said. He slid the driver's seat of his patrol car back, climbed awkwardly inside, and then waited while she checked her vehicle, loaded her equipment, and got in before he stuck his hand out the window and counted down. "In three, two, one." They blasted one quick warbling yelp of their sirens at the same time. The daily ritual was a parting nod and, they both agreed, brought luck.

Jeri grabbed the mike. "Car Eleven-thirteen, ten-forty-one. Badge One-five-two." Checking on duty gave her a rush every time, and she held her breath, waiting for that first call.

"Ten-four, Car Eleven-thirteen." The telecommunicator acknowledged but nothing immediately followed.

"O—kay," Jeri breathed. Maybe Randy would have time to check on his mom and get back to their area before the calls started. She rolled her window down and inhaled the cold night air, loving the chilly tingle in her nostrils and down her throat. Unless it was pouring rain, her window was always open. She needed to see, smell, and hear her surroundings. Cocooning herself in a patrol car like some officers denied her senses and felt like a liability.

She cruised her zone—the central business district and outward past the University of North Carolina Greensboro—checked the hotspots and waved to shopkeepers who stayed open for the first Friday celebrations of each month to catch the crowds. The CBD swelled during office hours with suited businesspeople but spewed them out at five o'clock in favor of trendy college-aged kids and a different level of vitality.

Everything was quiet for the moment, but drink-and-sex-fueled fever would take over eventually and transform peace into chaos. Jeri loved the energy and challenges of night shift and had volunteered to continue on the least-favored schedule her entire seven-year stint on the Greensboro Police Department. Randy thought she was crazy because late shift seriously cut into his extracurriculars, but she didn't really have a social life, unless casual dating counted. And night shift proved a good excuse for distancing. She glanced at the dash clock. Randy had been off grid for almost two hours. She reached for her phone but was interrupted.

Her MDT chirped with the familiar call signal before the telecommunicator said, "Car Eleven-thirteen. Prowler, possible B&E in progress. Madison Building on Fisher Avenue near Elm. Car Eleven-fourteen assist."

She pressed the acknowledge button on the mobile-digital terminal and added a verbal response, which she only did on serious calls. "Eleven-thirteen, ten-four."

Randy acknowledged, and then her phone chimed. She glanced at his text.

Problems at home. Stage and wait for me.

"Eleven-thirteen, I'll advise on assist. I'm almost there." She hoped to give Randy a few more minutes, but a burglary in progress could mean someone was inside the residence or nearby and possibly at risk. Waiting equaled more danger. Waiting wasn't her. She cut her lights, parked on a side street, and crept through the shadows toward the address. A tall Leland cypress beside the Madison provided perfect cover, and Jeri wedged into its spiky limbs to scan the area.

A white male dressed in black with a hood swung a dark container back and forth as he walked around the perimeter of the building. The heady smell of gasoline bombarded Jeri's nose as she inhaled, and she grew lightheaded. Her nose itched, and she stifled a sneeze in the crook of her arm.

The suspect tossed the container toward the street, reached in his pocket, and pulled out a box of matches. He cursed under his breath as several of the short sticks fell from his shaking hands. Gasoline vapors hung thick in the air. If he struck even one tiny spark, the whole place would go up and probably her with it.

Jeri forced her way through the prickly limbs of the tree and ran. "Police. Stop." She anchored her left arm against her body, charged, and drove her shoulder into his chest. Matches scattered, and the suspect hit the ground with a thud. She straddled him, her fist cocked.

He raised his hands, gasping for air. "I give up."

"On your stomach." He rolled over without resistance, and she plucked her handcuffs from her belt, locked them in place, and stood. Adrenaline flooded her system, and she hopped from foot to foot shaking her arms to calm herself. She glanced around. Two patrol cars pulled up, but not Randy, and she hoped nothing serious had happened with his mother.

"Where's your partner?" Carl scanned the area and chuckled. "Slacker. Is he hiding in the bushes letting you do all the work?" When Jeri didn't respond, he asked, "Want me to transport him to jail?" His northern accent reminded her so much of Randy that she smiled.

"Yeah, and call the fire department to hose down the gas. I'll talk to the complainant and see you at the magistrate's office."

❖

From her penthouse on the fourth floor of the Madison, Simone Sullivan smelled the heavy odor of gasoline. She'd seen someone creeping around outside and called the police, thinking it was another graffiti artist hoping to tag the wide expanse of naked brick on the east side of the building. She hadn't expected an episode of *Cops* to unfold right outside her window, but she'd been unable to look away.

The officer burst from the tree next door, curled himself like a projectile, and charged the suspect headfirst. In seconds, he had the man handcuffed and then did a victory dance before the other units arrived. The adrenaline rush of battle or fear made a person feel invincible and often led to impulsive actions with regrettable results, at least she'd found it so in her line of work. She was still at the window when her buzzer sounded, and she rushed to answer. "Yes?"

"This is Officer Wylder. Did you call about a prowler?"

Simone smiled at the sound of a sexy female voice. Not what she expected. "I'll be right down, Officer." She quickly changed from pajamas to jeans and a V-neck sweater before taking the stairs two at a time. Maybe watching the arrest had spiked her adrenaline as well, or was it the realization that a woman had come to her rescue? "Seriously, Sullivan?" She chastised herself for succumbing so easily to a stereotype and took a few breaths to calm her pulse before opening the stairwell door into the lobby.

"Officer Wylder, I'm Simone Sullivan." She offered her hand and gazed into eyes an unusual shade of bluish-gray that swept her body before making steady contact. The officer's palm heated hers, and Simone shivered from the warmth of it.

"Are you okay, Ms. Sullivan?"

And perceptive too. "Yes, you have warm hands. Mine are usually so cold." She stepped back. "Sorry. I tend to be too blunt. Professional habit. But you have questions. Shall we?" Simone motioned toward a two-seater bench in the entryway, and Officer Wylder waited until she sat before joining her. Chivalry. Bonus.

"Can you tell me what happened tonight? For the report."

Wylder's uniformed leg pressed against hers was hot and muscled, and Simone started to shift but settled into the contact instead. When she did, the tightness along Officer Wylder's thigh eased as well. "I was getting ready for bed when I heard a man's voice from the courtyard below. Sound carries around here, bouncing off the houses and overpass funneled toward us like a wind tunnel. He was cursing and mumbling, nothing I could make out. When he moved closer to the building and I couldn't see him anymore, I called. I couldn't tell what he was doing until I smelled gas. He was going to torch the place." It wasn't a question. She just didn't understand why, and why was an important part of her makeup, personally and professionally.

"He's in custody now. Do you have any idea why someone might want to burn the building?"

Simone shook her head. "I was wondering the same thing. We've had a few acts of vandalism the past few months, mostly graffiti, nothing serious. I can't imagine."

Officer Wylder asked all the necessary questions to fill out the report and then placed her hand over Simone's. "Don't worry. Arson is usually a crime with a specific motive. We'll get to the bottom of it."

Simone rolled her hand over to squeeze Wylder's fingers between her own. It wasn't professional for either of them, but at the moment, she didn't care. As much as she believed she could handle anything, having someone douse her home in gasoline rattled her. "Thank you. You've been very kind, Officer Wylder."

"Jeri. We're holding hands, so you should at least know my first name." She smiled, and her teeth sparkled from a face tanned golden bronze. Jeri started to say something else, but the stairwell door opened, and Mrs. Robertson and her Boston terrier headed toward the exit.

"What's going on out there, Simone? Are we safe?"

"Of course, Mrs. Robertson."

"I smell gas. Are you sure?" Mrs. Robertson picked up her dog and cradled her in a protective hug.

Jeri rose from the bench and approached Mrs. Robertson. "Is it okay if I pet her?" When she nodded, Jeri stroked the animal behind her ears and cooed soothingly before addressing Mrs. Robertson. "You're perfectly safe, ma'am. Where did you get your Boston?"

Mrs. Robertson straightened and grinned widely. "Nix Kennels. Vita is the absolute best breeder of Bostons in the state, possibly the country."

"I totally agree. You're lucky to get one of her pups."

"Tell me about it. I was on her waiting list for almost two years." The puppy wriggled in her arms. "Guess I better go for that walk before it's too late."

Jeri gave the puppy a final stroke and said, "Don't let her drink or lick anything around the building until the fire department clears. I wouldn't want her to get sick."

"Thanks, Officer."

Simone watched the exchange with interest, sensing genuine compassion and tenderness from Jeri. Greensboro officers were usually cordial and accommodating, but she'd gone out of her way to reassure Mrs. Robertson and to pet her dog. Not every officer would've taken the extra time. "That was very nice of you." She stood beside Jeri, surprised and pleased that she barely came to Jeri's shoulder. "Careful. Your humanity is showing, Officer."

"What can I say? Dogs bring out the best in me, especially Bostons."

"I can't believe you know Vita Nix," Simone said. "A couple of my friends are on her waiting list for puppies now. She's won so many championships I can't remember them all and she's been to Westminster. Just excellent." Jeri grinned, and the bronze of her cheeks deepened. "Did I say something wrong?"

"It's just...she's my best friend, so I'm a little prejudiced. We've been friends—" Her cell phone buzzed, and she dug it from her pocket. "Excuse me." She glanced at the message and the laugh lines around her mouth tightened and her brow furrowed. "Sorry. I should go. I have a suspect to process." She reached into her shirt pocket and pulled out a business card. "I'll put the incident number on the back, in case you need a copy of the report."

"Thank you, Officer. Jeri." Their business finished, Jeri headed for the door. Simone should let her go. Imaginary red flags popped up all over Jeri's body. *Cop* stood out prominently above her head warning of the whole mentality and blue line thing. *Low pay* peeked from her back pocket. *Weird hours* preceded her out the front door. And a *notoriously promiscuous* bright crimson tag flapped comically at her crotch. Add the chorus of family and friends yelling, *"Don't do it,"* and Simone stifled the invitation on the tip of her tongue.

Jeri paused at the front door and stared at Simone with those eyes. "I don't usually do this, but would you like to have coffee sometime, Ms. Sullivan? I mean, after work one day. If you're not busy. Or attached."

All the red flags disappeared, and Simone grinned, enjoying Jeri's bumbling and the touch of color on her cheeks. "I'd like that very much. I've got a soft spot for Boston terrier fans."

Jeri winked. "Lucky me. I'll text you soon."

Simone hadn't felt even a flutter of interest in anyone in ages, but Jeri Wylder stirred a whirlwind of questions, challenges, and possibilities. Simone rushed to the window and watched Jeri swagger back to her car. Simone leaned against the windowsill, her heart racing and her mouth dry. *Oh my.*

Why had she asked Simone Sullivan out? There was nothing special about the strawberry-blonde's appearance, but something about her interested Jeri. Maybe it was the way she settled so easily at Jeri's side on the bench, the certainty with which she accepted Jeri's invitation, or possibly her refreshing candor and the maturity it implied. Whatever the reason, Simone was at least worth a cup of coffee Jeri decided as she pulled into the bay at the jail.

Randy's face was strained, his jaw tight when he opened her car door. "Why didn't you wait for me?"

"I was practically on top of the place when the call went out. And it's a good thing I didn't. The guy was about to torch the building."

"Okay. Sorry. I'm a little wired." He fell in beside her as she walked toward the entrance. "So, you're charging this guy?"

She softened her tone. He'd been worrying about his mother for months, and tonight must've been particularly hard or he wouldn't be jumping her case for doing her job. "Of course, I'm charging him with attempted arson. He was trying to strike a match when I tackled him."

"He's stoned out of his mind. I looked in through the glass. He was all over the place."

"Still, gas and matches, not a good thing, especially if you're stoned. I've got to relieve Carl and file the charges. Catch up with you later?"

"Sure." He started to walk away but stopped. "Hey, you still hitting that paralegal, what's her name, Mary?"

"Megan. Yeah. Why?"

"Why don't the six of us go out soon. I need to blow off some steam. Maybe Carl can find a date, but with that fucking fungus all over his face, I don't know." He laughed.

"Sounds good." She waved and keyed in the code to the magistrate's office.

Carl handed over the arrest paperwork and nodded toward a corner out of earshot of the suspect and magistrate. "You sure about this? The guy is totally fucked up. You might have trouble proving intent. Just saying."

"What's with you? He doused the place in gasoline and had matches in his hand when I tackled him. Sounds like intent to me. If the magistrate disagrees, I'll knock it down to something else." She waved the paperwork. "Thanks for bringing him in."

"No problem." He started out but turned back. "Randy says we're going for drinks."

"We'll see." She wouldn't. Couples' outings fell under the heading of things to be avoided until she found the right woman. Married and partnered friends wanted their single mates to be as miserable or as happy as they were, but she handled the former well enough on her own by darting from woman to woman and wasn't sure the latter would ever happen. She'd devoted her dating life since coming out to finding someone she could trust who meshed with her personality, but most seemed to only match her sexual appetites. That had been enough until recently. Her thoughts returned to Simone Sullivan. Could she be a possibility?

CHAPTER TWO

When her last patient left, Simone kicked off her shoes, turned so she could look out the window and prop her feet on the sill, and thumbed through her appointment book. The rest of the week was jammed with clients, good for business but bad for a coffee date with a gorgeous cop. She'd anticipated Jeri's call for the last two days, but instead of the real thing, she'd replayed the feel of Jeri's leg pressed firmly against hers and the unfamiliar surge of arousal it produced.

She wasn't sure why she'd been so attracted to Jeri, but the pull had been powerful, almost unsettling. Her training as a psychologist told her it was some old unresolved issue bubbling up, but she refused to analyze her excitement to death. For the first time in ages, she chose to feel.

Her cell vibrated across the desk, and she glanced at the caller ID. "Hi, Erica."

"Charlotte and I are going to Zeto for wine. She has a VinoMatic card full of credit she's dying to cash in. Come with."

She glanced at her watch. What were the chances Jeri would call at seven o'clock? Fantasizing about a woman she didn't know and who might never call was one thing but wasting her life waiting was another. Her friends were a sure bet, and she needed a break. "I'm there."

The brisk walk to Zeto from her office in the night air erased the litany of client problems and almost made her forget about

Jeri…almost. When she opened the door, Charlotte and Erica called from the back, already seated with a flight of wine in front of them and a third waiting for her. The ambiance of the cozy wine shop closed around her when she stepped inside. Posters touting wines from around the world hung on every wall, and bottles cradled in racks and displayed on barrels surrounded small tables making them feel more intimate. "You girls rock."

Erica rose and gave her a big hug, followed by Charlotte. They'd been roommates at Duke and sorority sisters in Alpha Delta Pi. Late-night bonding, secret rituals, and the privilege of living in an incredible house on Duke's campus had cemented their friendships, with only one significant rift through the years.

"ADPis unite," Charlotte said. "Hope you like what we chose."

"Since I don't see whiskey, I'll take anything with alcohol." She settled and raised the first glass to toast. "Here's to no more problems tonight."

"Amen, sisters," Erica agreed, clinking her glass to the others. She swept her other hand through bouncy black locks and grinned before downing the wine with a single gulp. "Yum."

Charlotte shook her head. "Our sister never takes life slowly." Unlike Erica, she tasted delicately and studied Simone as she slowly sipped. "And you…always taking the middle road."

"That's why you both love me. I bring moderation to your extremes." Erica—emotionally volatile and shamelessly vocal—was the total opposite of Charlotte—soft-spoken and introspective, but they were both fiercely loyal and devoted to their friendship.

"Absolutely," Erica said. "Have we all decided on a date for the Guilford Green Foundation's gala?" She glanced at Charlotte before focusing on Simone.

"I'm not sure I'm going." Simone raised her second glass and sniffed the contents. "If I'm supposed to be able to tell what's in this, I'm a horrible wine connoisseur."

"And a worse deflector," Erica said. "Of course, you're going because we're going, and two ends without the middle never works. If you don't have a suitable date, we'll find one."

"No!" Simone sucked wine down her windpipe and coughed. "The last time you fixed me up, she was like Velcro. I almost filed a stalking report." The mention of a police report revived the image of Jeri—tailored uniform, salt-and-pepper hair short on the sides with a longer swatch swept to the right, and those eyes. She sighed dreamily, and Charlotte and Erica caught her.

"Okay, who is she?" Charlotte asked.

"Who's who?" Simone drank again, stalling for time to compose herself.

"Whoever is making you blush like a teenager," Erica said. "We both know *that* look."

"No one, really." Was that true? They'd just met but dismissing Jeri as no one so easily felt wrong. Still, she hesitated. Neither Charlotte, Erica, nor her family would consider a police officer a suitable date for the GGF gala, or any other occasion. "It's…the police officer who responded to my call the other night."

Erica and Charlotte turned toward her totally engrossed, wine forgotten. "You've been out with her?" Charlotte asked.

"Not yet, she asked me to have coffee sometime."

"And you accepted?" Erica knocked back her second wine sample, and Charlotte twisted a strand of her long blond hair around her index finger, a nervous tell she'd developed in college. "Of course, she knows you own the Madison."

"It didn't come up. Besides, what does that mean anyway?" Simone asked, not sure she wanted to acknowledge where this conversation was heading.

"Don't be naive, Simone. It wouldn't be the first time one of us has been targeted by someone hoping to improve their situation. And besides, you *never*, and I do mean *never* go out with strangers. You're way too—"

"Cautious," Charlotte supplied.

Erica nodded toward Charlotte. "What she said."

"I know, but there was something about her." Simone rolled a glass between her palms. "I can't explain it." Erica shook her head, and Simone preempted her. "You're about to point out that she's 'not like us.'" She finger-quoted the phrase she'd heard so many times that it left a bad taste in her mouth. She sipped more wine to wash it down. "I have no idea *what* she's like, but she's been vetted by the Greensboro Police Department so she's not a criminal."

"Like that's a favorable recommendation these days. You *have* seen the quality of officers being hired nationwide. Right?" Erica screwed up her mouth like the wine had gone bad. "I can't imagine anyone in our circle working as a police officer for community service, so we have to assume she's *not* one of us. I don't mean to be petty, but it just saves time and heartache if we stick with what and who we know."

Charlotte shrugged. "I mean, really, Simone, they make practically nothing and risk their lives. Do you want that? I couldn't handle wondering if every time I saw her would be the last."

"Char, it's not like we're dating, much less serious."

"Okay." Erica waved both hands in the air. "I get the animal attraction. Cops are kind of hot with the uniform, handcuffs, and dominance thing, and they're notoriously thirsty. If it's just a sex thing, I say go for it, just don't get carried away."

Charlotte nodded. "Yeah. Anything serious and you're asking for problems. Remember what happened with Kay."

Erica zinged Charlotte with a seething glare. "Did you *have* to bring her up? None of us wants to be reminded of *that*."

The memory jolted Simone, and her throat tightened. She'd never forget Kay or how their relationship had been sabotaged by friends and family. Simone had withdrawn from everyone afterward, refusing contact for months, unsure if she'd ever trust anyone again. She'd almost lost her family and dearest friends, but in the end had chosen numbness over isolation.

"Are you okay, Simone?" Erica asked.

"Yeah, I'm good." She'd ridden the wave of privilege all her life, mostly adhered to the unwritten rules, and colored within the lines of what her family and friends considered acceptable behavior. But it had been years since she'd met someone worth the inevitable backlash and conflict. Could Jeri Wylder be such a person?

Simone struggled between cursing them for bringing up painful memories, thanking them for their limited approval of a tryst with

Jeri, and delivering a much-needed sermon about their classism and elitist attitudes. Since seeing Jeri might never materialize, she kept quiet and chugged her third sample while her friends stared. This one tasted bitter. Was it the wine or their conversation?

When Simone crawled in bed that night, the memories they'd stirred resurfaced. She clutched a pillow to her chest, tossed and turned, and tried to rationalize why she'd lived so long without loving someone as she'd loved Kay. Sleep finally came and so did her darling Kay.

Kay's belief in love and her innocence had been destroyed by her first girlfriend. She was shattered and needed comfort. Whatever the reason, for however long, Simone would give Kay anything she wanted—a truth that had burned inside since their first day as college roommates. And now, Kay reached for her.

She stroked Simone's face, and passion burned and hungered through her. Gooseflesh and heat trailed Kay's touch. Knots in the pit of Simone's stomach melted. Tension evaporated, replaced by euphoria, the softening of years of denied yearnings.

"Oh my God, Kay."

She waited, anticipation turning to pain, as Kay brought their lips together. Kay's tongue seemed to caress her mouth and clit at once. With a single kiss, Simone's life changed forever.

"Touch me. Please, Kay." It was all going too slowly.

Kay skimmed her fingers along Simone's arms and up her back, increasing the pressure between her thighs. She palmed Simone's breasts through the thick fabric of her bathrobe and massaged in torturous circles. Simone felt simultaneously obsessed and possessed.

Kay peeled the bathrobe from Simone's shoulders, knelt in front of her, and placed her head against the dip of Simone's naked stomach. "Say you'll love me forever, Simone. Say it."

"Forever and beyond." She hugged Kay to her. She meant every word. If they ever parted, her heart would surely turn to stone.

Kay guided Simone backward onto the bed and devoured the fullness of Kay's breasts, her erect nipples, and the curve of her hips. "You've wanted me for a long time, haven't you?" Kay's self-satisfied grin curled the corners of her luscious mouth.

Simone spoke from the heart. "Yes."

Kay stretched her body alongside Simone and nestled her head between Simone's breasts. "My God, you are gorgeous. Can I touch you...down there?"

"If you don't, I'm going to die." Simone felt the possibility of her words deep inside.

Kay trailed her fingers slowly up Simone's thigh and into her silky wetness, and Simone opened for her. She moaned and rocked forward against her sliding fingers.

"Do you like this, baby?" Kay looked teasingly up into her eyes.

"Yes...please don't...stop." Simone's breath sputtered from her lungs. Anything detracting from pleasure was wasted energy.

Kay cupped Simone's pubic mound and expertly manipulated her clit, and Simone thrusted her hips, begging for more, faster contact. Her lust built like a tightening spring.

"Breathe, baby," Kay whispered and plunged a finger deep inside.

"I can't...oh my God!"

She tightened around Kay's finger, all her energy focused on that one pulsing, aching bundle of need between her thighs. She bucked, begged, and cried. When Kay leaned forward and sucked a breast into her mouth, tremors started in the tips of Simone's fingers and toes and charred a path toward her center. The closer it got, the more it intensified.

"Let go, baby, just let go." Kay panted.

"Kay, oh God, Kay!"

The coiled tension in Simone's pelvis snapped and jerked her time after time toward release. Liquid heat oozed from her and into Kay's hand. Kay's lips covered hers in a demanding kiss, and Simone opened, stroking and sucking Kay's tongue in time to the tiny aftershocks between her legs. Their hot flesh connected at every dip and swell, as if they were made for each other. When her *contractions subsided, Simone was numb and totally satisfied. She'd finally been really touched physically and emotionally. Completely.*

Simone woke wet with sweat and tears. Why hadn't she seen the trouble brewing? After only six months together, Kay vanished and searching produced no clue as to why she'd left or where she'd gone. A year later Simone learned the awful truth and those responsible for Kay's disappearance. Would she ever feel that connection, that passion again?

CHAPTER THREE

Jeri sat in lineup the next evening and debated sending the text she'd typed on her cell. Three days since she'd met Simone, and every one Jeri had thought about contacting her but chickened out. The more time that passed, the easier it was to discount the invitation and Simone's eagerness. Was Jeri being professional by not calling, playing hard to get, or just plain scared? Whatever the answer, it was time to act or forget Simone Sullivan. Today, Jeri had chosen her least worn uniform and shiniest shoes to make a good impression but was losing her nerve again.

"Wylder," Sergeant Bruce said. "Earth to Wylder."

"Sorry, sir."

"Good job with the arsonist. The detective said he's still not talking, but it won't matter. You caught him in the act. Not much wiggle room there. Well done."

"Thanks, Sarge." She glanced sideways at Randy waiting for the celebratory fist bump they always exchanged after a significant arrest, but it never came. He tapped on his phone, and when the sergeant dismissed them, he bolted for the door. She tried to catch up, but he jumped in his patrol car and peeled out of the lot. Maybe he'd gotten an emergency text from his mother's caregiver. She'd talk to him later.

Carl nudged her shoulder on the way to his car. "All right?"

"Yeah. Any idea what's eating Randy?"

"Nah. Probably didn't get laid last night and has blue balls."

"Thanks for that visual, Carl." Jeri checked her vehicle, pulled her phone out, and hit Send. *Ready for that coffee?*

Simone responded quickly. *Definitely. Six? Where?*

Green Bean on Elm.

Jeri slid her phone back in her pocket and fist-pumped the air. She'd had tons of dates, so why was she acting like a teenager with a crush? This was just one more first date...or maybe Simone really was different. Special. *Just go with your gut, Wylder. You've got this.*

She tested the siren, hoping that skipping her and Randy's lucky ritual once wouldn't make a difference. "Superstitious much?" She headed toward her zone with two hours to kill and plenty of time to practice describing her current dating situation. She and Meg weren't exclusive, but they'd been seeing each other for two months. In the lesbian world, some would consider that practically engaged, but not in Jeri's. When she found the woman who inspired trust and monogamy, she'd know it. Something about Simone said she wasn't fling material, and the thought made Jeri uneasy as she cruised her area checking for possible problems.

After work hours on weekdays, the central business district could be a ghost town, and with schools on winter break, even more so. She'd only answered one call as the six o'clock hour approached, and she hoped her luck held long enough to get a better sense of Simone Sullivan.

Jeri parked on the street, waved at the owner as she entered Green Bean, and secured a small table in the back with a clear view of both exits. The café felt intimate with its low ceiling, black-and-white retro tiled floors, and muraled walls. The only natural light filtered in through the large front bay windows with sconces providing ambient light throughout. Her back to the wall, she scanned, sorting patrons by threat potential until satisfied with the safety of her surroundings. She focused on the front door again as it opened.

Simone Sullivan glanced around the room, made eye contact with Jeri, and stopped briefly before heading her way. She wore leggings and a V-neck sweater that accented her curvy assets. Jeri's mouth dried and she reached for a drink, but she hadn't ordered yet. Damn. The closer Simone got, the quicker Jeri's pulse thrummed.

"Is this seat taken, Officer?"

"Yes. I mean no. It's yours." Jeri rose and pulled out the chair beside hers. "Please." Simone casually touched Jeri's hand as they settled, and the heat coursed up her arm. She wasn't used to casual touch feeling so personal and intimate.

"I was glad to hear from you. I thought you'd forgotten me." Simone's smile was open and inviting.

"Is that even possible?" She pressed her lips together. Where the hell had that come from? She'd thought it, believed it, but it wasn't something she'd normally say while trying to be cool on a first date.

Simone's smile widened and the pupils of her green eyes dilated.

"Sorry." Jeri fumbled in her pocket for money to take her focus away from the way Simone stared at her like she was something to eat. "What would you like to drink?"

"Decaf mocha latte. If I drink the hard stuff this late, I won't sleep all night." Simone reached for her purse, but Jeri waved her off.

"Be right back." Jeri placed their orders and waited at the counter, taking the opportunity to observe Simone more closely. She extended her legs under the table and raised her arms over her head in a deep stretch. Her torso was long, legs short but firm, and her full breasts strained against the stretchy fabric of the forest-green sweater. Twisting from side to side, she breathed heavily and then straightened again. Her movements were easy, almost sensuous, and Jeri moaned.

"One decaf mocha latte and one latte no foam extra shot," the barista said.

"Thanks." She paid and slowly walked to the table, careful to control her breathing and the direction of her gaze. She wanted to stare at Simone, imprint her image in her mind, and trot it out as her idea of a perfect female body. Add her reddish-blond hair and green eyes, and Jeri could easily get lost. It had to be that Irish thing.

"Here you go." She set the coffee in front of Simone and took her seat. "Back problems?"

Simone smiled. "Aren't you the observant one?"

"Occupational necessity."

"I was a gymnast in my early days and still have aches and pains to prove it. A low center of gravity is a plus for the sport. I loved it too. Vaulting, floor exercises, beams, bars, and pommel horse. What's not to love about that, right?"

"If you say so." Jeri laughed, envisioning Simone performing each exercise as she named them. "I was more a basketball and volleyball girl myself. Height is a must."

"And you wear it well, Officer Wylder."

Simone smiled again, and Jeri lost herself in the warmth of it. She read people every day, homing in on facial tics, breathing rates, eye movements, and body language. All of Simone's nonverbal cues registered as sincere, inviting trust. How rare, especially in Jeri's line of work. "Are you flirting with me, Ms. Sullivan?"

"Depends. Would it bother you?"

"Nope." Jeri's heart raced again. "Not at all, but before we go straight to the public table dancing part of the program, tell me a little about yourself. You already know what I do for a living." She waved a hand down her uniform, and Simone's gaze followed, her eyes wide.

"I certainly do, and if you don't mind me being totally blunt and somewhat of a cliché, I find it quite a turn-on. I mean, really, who doesn't like a hot woman in uniform?"

"You really don't mince words." Her cheeks grew warm, and Jeri tried to deflect. "You have family here?"

"Parents, who are diplomats and travel for work most of the year, and an older brother and his wife. We've lived in Greensboro all my life, and I love it. You?"

"Just me. It's a long story that I'd like to tell you, but it'll take more than a cup of coffee squeezed between calls." She'd really just said she'd *like* to tell Simone her story. A first. "Suffice it to say I built my life from the ground up and became a cop because I believe in the work."

"And based on what I've seen, you're very good at your job." Simone gave Jeri's hand a squeeze before releasing and lifting her coffee mug.

Jeri squirmed, growing increasingly uncomfortable being in the spotlight for so long. "So, what do you do when you're not flirting with police officers who respond to calls at your home?" Simone laughed, and the sound of it rolled through Jeri in pleasurable waves.

"Guess."

Jeri leaned back in the chair, balanced it on two legs, and studied her from head to toe with exaggerated interest. The longer she stared, the redder Simone's face turned.

"I'm not sure I'm up for such close scrutiny."

"You should be because I'm guessing model."

Simone laughed again. "Hardly. Too heavy in some areas, too light in others. Try again."

Jeri rested her chin in her hand and stared at Simone's lips. "Professor of something."

"Why professor?" Simone cocked her head to one side, interest sparking in her eyes.

"Because I'm imagining impressionable college students enthralled with your voice and the sexy way you lick your lips when you talk." Simone's face reddened again. "Too much?"

"Just unexpected. Are you flirting with me now, Officer Wylder?"

"Undoubtedly. So, am I right?"

"Opted out of academia. Too restrictive, and as you've so astutely pointed out, too many forbidden temptations."

"Good move," Jeri said. She drummed her mug with her fingers. "Nurse?"

Simone shook her head.

"Medical doctor."

"Nope."

"Okay. I give up."

"I'm a—"

"Cars Eleven-thirteen and Eleven-fourteen, respond to a possible drug deal in progress. Abandoned building at Six-twelve Morehead Avenue."

Jeri jumped from her seat. "I'm sorry. I'd hoped for more time, but duty calls. I've always wanted to say that. Thanks for meeting me." She pushed her chair in and started to walk away, but Simone caught her hand.

"Can I see you again?"

"I'd like that. I want to explain my...situation. Be in touch." Jeri brushed the back of Simone's hand with her thumb, released, and hurried to her car. A woman like Simone Sullivan didn't come into Jeri's life every day. She was used to younger women she met in bars or through friends who were interested in expensive dates, great sex, and superficial conversation. Simone asked about her life and feelings, challenging Jeri to be honest and authentic. Maybe that was why she was so excited and terrified about seeing Simone again.

Simone nursed her coffee for an hour after Jeri left and reviewed their interaction from a therapist's perspective. Jeri had been vague about her family, possibly because of trust issues, but had apparently had difficulties she'd overcome to better her life. A cop's life, her friends would argue, with no inheritance or valuable society connections. When she measured Jeri against the things her friends valued, they seemed trivial and irrelevant and only intensified Simone's interest. Another question surfaced. Had Jeri's focus on rebuilding her life included a partner or lover? Maybe that accounted for the pain she'd seen in her eyes when she spoke of the past. She shoved her chair back, left a big tip for occupying the table so long, and walked home with the burning question. What was that *situation* Jeri wanted to explain?

When she turned off Elm Street onto Fisher, some of her neighbors were gathered in front of the Madison Building. One of them spotted her and waved her over.

"They've done it again," Larry Caswell said, scratching his balding head and pointing to the east side of the building. He lived on the second floor with his mother and made Simone's life miserable with constant complaints about noise and anything else that didn't suit his militarily-regimented liking. "When will this stop?"

The graffiti caricature of her blended blues, reds, and greens in an artistic rendering that would've been flattering if not for the words "Get out, bitch" bisecting her face in bold black letters.

"I wish I could tell you, Mr. Caswell."

"They're trying to scare us out of our homes. Isn't that why they attempted to burn down the building?" He stepped closer, gesturing angrily toward the Madison.

"I don't know. The police arrested a man and are investigating the incident. We should have answers soon."

"Why are you protecting them?"

"I'm protecting our residents, Mr. Caswell. Speculation about a connection to redevelopment or the contractor without evidence won't help us."

"Speculation? We're not the only ones being terrorized by these people. The entire community has been victimized, subtly and overtly. You know what they want. My mother is eighty-five and can't handle the stress of moving from her home."

"We're all stressed, Mr. Caswell, but please let the police do their jobs." She pulled out her cell, snapped a picture of the wall, and dialed the painter who'd handled the last three incidents of graffiti. When she hung up, she turned back to the gathering. "Please, go back to your homes and be patient. We'll get to the bottom of this. Believe me, we won't be driven out."

Simone climbed the four flights to her condo, poured a short shot of whiskey, and opened her computer. Caswell was right about one thing. There had been too many incidents of burglary, vandalism, and graffiti in their neighborhood recently. She regularly checked the Police to Citizen website and too often lately had filed reports herself. When the P2C site opened, she clicked on the reports section and filled out the all too familiar form and attached the photo. She was tired of filing reports and waiting passively for others to do something. Tomorrow she'd contact an attorney to investigate the recent code violations leveed at the Madison. And she'd do some snooping of her own about the history of the building. She might even have a chance to talk to Jeri again since she worked this area. She liked that idea, maybe a little too much.

Chapter Four

The abandoned property at 612 Morehead abutted the Freeman Mill Road overpass and attracted youngsters looking for an out-of-the way place to use drugs or have sex. If Jeri approached from the front of the house, they'd scatter through the dense underbrush on a series of concealed paths that led to downtown and vanish before she got out of the car. She stopped a block away, double-tapped her body camera to activate it, and walked toward the columned front porch.

A dim stream of light from inside swayed back and forth like the beam of a flashlight or cell phone and oozed between missing boards. She flattened beside the front doorframe and peered around the corner but saw no one, pulled back, and checked again. The faint sound of voices, and then the light went out. Slowly, she made her way toward the sound, clearing each room she passed. The place reeked of stale beer and urine, and she swallowed hard to keep from coughing. At the last room, she stalled outside the door and listened.

"I found this thing under the house," a male voice said. "It could fly us to the moon or vanquish our enemies. Who knows?"

"You're talking crazy. It looks dangerous. Get rid of it," a female replied.

"No way. It won't hurt you. We'll get high first and give it a try. When I tell you, just pull the pin and throw it. Could be the fireworks show of the century."

"I don't want to," the woman said.

"Don't be such a pussy, just do what I say."

Jeri craned her neck around the doorframe for a visual of the subjects and the scene. Whatever she missed the body cam would catch, but she needed to know what she was facing now. The couple were silhouetted by moonlight streaming in behind them, which meant when she stepped out, she'd be the visible one and at a disadvantage. She had to take them off guard.

She moved into the room and pointed her weapon with tactical light in the direction of the voices. "Police. Show me your hands."

"Fuck," the male said. "An invasion."

"I gi...give up," the woman replied, her voice trembling.

The two stumbled to their feet from an old mattress in the corner, swaying from side to side. Both were neatly dressed, definitely not homeless. The male waved a Pabst beer can in one hand and stared at her wide-eyed. "What the fuck? Get out of our place, dude."

"What you got there?" She nodded toward the female's hand, trying to keep her voice calm and level while sounding non-threatening.

"I don't...know." Her voice quivered and she extended the gadget toward Jeri.

"I found it under the house, man," the male said. "Just gonna shoot off some fireworks later. Light up the world. You know, fucking around."

The device had a pull ring and compression handle, longer and more cylindrical than a traditional oblong, ridged grenade. Flashbang. Still dangerous, possibly lethal. "I need you to put that on the floor for me, please. Gently. We don't know how long it's been under the house in the elements. It could be highly volatile."

"How did you know—" The male dropped the beer can and reached behind his back.

"Keep your hands where I can see them," Jeri commanded. The stress in her voice made it sound higher, and sweat formed under her vest despite the cold wind whipping through the broken window. Where the hell was her backup?

"Do what she says," the female said. "Don't get us killed."

"Shut up and pull the pin."

The guy tugged a long shiny object from his belt and moved closer. He was moving so fast that she only caught a glimpse silhouetted in the moonlight. A knife? "I said stop. Now. I *will* shoot you. Stop." Jeri stepped back, praying he'd comply.

"Fuck that." He charged, and the female pulled the pin on the flashbang and flung it at Jeri's feet.

A blaze of bright light and an ear-piercing explosion left her blinded and her ears ringing. She wobbled sideways, disoriented by the blast. Her flashlight created only glare in the thick smoke and blinded her further.

"He's got a knife," the woman screamed.

Jeri flailed her arms to disperse the smoke and stumbled. Her sight and hearing were compromised, so she retreated, staggered, and then heard a distinctive sound. The discharge of a weapon. Had she fired? A noise drew her attention to the right and she turned. Searing pain and then only darkness.

❖

"Hey, partner, wake up."

Randy's voice sounded far away. Jeri tried to open her eyes, but every time her head throbbed and her stomach roiled.

"Can you hear me?" His voice held the frazzled pitch of immediacy and concern.

"Y…yes," she whispered. "Wh—what happened?"

"You really gave that dude—"

"Shut up, Carl. Don't worry about that right now, Jeri. Can you sit up?"

She shook her head and immediately regretted it. Her stomach churned. "Oh crap."

"Okay. Stay down. EMS is on the way."

"Randy, what happened?" She slowly opened her eyes to dim moonlight and glanced around. A man's body slumped against the wall on a bloody mattress, and a scrum of officers surrounded her like a protective shield. "Did I do that?"

"You don't remember?"

"No." Bile rose in her throat, and Jeri turned to the side and threw up. "Am I injured? Did he stab me?"

"What do you mean?" Randy trained the beam of his flashlight over her body and then around the room. "I didn't see a weapon, but you're okay, except for that goose egg on your forehead."

"The guys and I will check," Carl said and made a circling motion with his index finger.

"Randy." She grabbed his shirt and pulled him close. "Find the woman."

"What woman?"

"Yeah," Carl said, "what woman?"

"I feel—"

When Jeri opened her eyes again, she didn't recognize her surroundings. Uncomfortable bed, white linens, flowered curtain, and wall-mounted TV. An annoying beeping sound and the pungent smell of disinfectant assaulted her senses. Hospital. She raised her head, and the beeping machine went berserk.

"Hi, hon." Her best friend, Vita Nix, rose from an uncomfortable looking chair in the corner and came to her.

"Wat—er." The word croaked from her parched tongue and lips. "Water."

"No water right now. This will have to do." Vita spooned crushed ice from a Styrofoam cup into Jeri's mouth and she sucked greedily.

"Thanks," Jeri said. Vita's eyes were bloodshot and ringed by dark circles. She'd been worrying, and it was all Jeri's fault. "I'm sorry, Vi."

"What have you got to be sorry about?"

"You shouldn't have to deal with this. You look tired. How long have you been here?"

"Don't talk craziness. We're family. As soon as Randy called last night, I came." She placed the cup back on the side table and tucked the blanket around Jeri's shoulders. "It's cold enough to hang meat in here. How do you feel?"

"Like somebody hit me with a brick. Did they?"

"Randy said you fell and hit your head. Don't you remember?"

"Not really." Jeri remembered receiving the call, doing a partial premises search, and coming to the last room. Everything after that was a blur.

"Guys in plain clothes came by last night, but the police union rep told them to go away. I'm not sure what that was about."

"Detectives or internal affairs." Detectives meant a serious crime had been committed. Internal affairs presence implied an event requiring administrative investigation. "Wait. Did I shoot somebody?" That would explain both.

Vita stared at the monitoring machine several seconds before making eye contact. "That's what Randy said, but I don't know any details. Nobody would tell me anything."

"Is he—" Her whole body tensed, and the word stuck in her throat. "Dead?"

Vita nodded solemnly. "I'm sorry, honey. I can't imagine how hard that must be to hear."

Jeri sucked in a sharp breath and slowly tried to blow the ache out of her chest. *I killed someone. He had a life, a family, dreams. How can I ever come back from that?* "Who, who was he? What was his name?"

"Hon, do you really think you—"

"Please, Vi, don't shut me out. Tell me his name. I'm sure it's been on the news." Jeri clutched the sheet with both hands until they ached, praying she'd wake up from this horrible nightmare.

Vita leaned closer and whispered. "Calvin Vanoy, white, twenty-nine years old."

Jeri tried to pull a face from her foggy memory to go with the name but came up as empty as she felt. "How could I forget shooting someone? Have they given me drugs?"

"I don't think so. They thought you had a concussion and were worried about a brain bleed. That's why they kept you overnight."

"Oh, God, Vi. I can't remember what happened."

Vita took her hand. "Don't think about that right now. Concentrate on feeling better and going home in the morning. You need rest. I'll be right here keeping the vultures away."

"Thanks." But she couldn't stop trying to remember. If she'd killed someone, how could she *not* remember? Too much adrenaline or nausea? Shock? A family was mourning a dead loved one because of her. She needed to apologize, to make amends. Even if she recalled the incident, the department would never let her make contact until the case was investigated and finally closed. It could take months. She eased back against the pillow and closed her eyes, willing herself to make sense of what happened. Drug call, clearing an abandoned house, one last room, and then nothing.

Chapter Five

Two Weeks Later

Tunnel vision blurred Jeri's surroundings, but she was acutely aware of the minutia of her body. A sharp wind from the broken window sliced her thin uniform and pricked her with splinters of cold. Her teeth clicked together uncontrollably. Sweat pooled under her vest leaving patches of gooseflesh. Bad smells and pain.

Moonlight. Two silhouetted figures. She raised her arm, heavy and disjointed, as if by a puppeteer's string. Words ran together in her mind. No. Don't. Stop. But she made no sound. Her nose burned, and sourness rose in her throat making her retch. She squinted through foggy haze but couldn't focus.

Smoky air swirled around her. Each gulp choked as she pulled for breath. Someone lunged toward her. Jeri tried to back away but stumbled. She grew light-headed, sweating, and shaking. The bitter taste of fear settled in her mouth.

Someone screamed. "He's got a knife." Was it her?

Jeri marshaled her strength and lunged toward the spinning light. "Stop!"

"Jeri, wake up."

Jeri bolted upright swinging her arms, fear griping her like an ardent lover. A distant voice called to her. She struggled to focus on the sound and her surroundings.

"Babe, you're having another nightmare. Wake up." Megan shook her hard.

Megan's apartment. Bed. "I've…asked you not…to shake me…" Jeri rasped, her breath coming in long pulls.

Megan stared at her, wide-eyed and sleep ruffled.

Jeri's T-shirt clung to her, sticky and wet, and she shivered. "What time is it?" Her whisper was barely audible.

Megan glanced at the clock. "Three o'clock, as usual."

"Sorry I woke you. Again." Jeri pressed her fingers against her temples.

"It's going to be okay." Megan stroked Jeri's hair and reached to pull her closer.

Jeri flinched, afraid of, or not wanting, her touch, but she wasn't sure which. Megan immediately withdrew. "When, Megan? When will it be okay?" Megan had suggested Jeri stay at her place after the incident, and she'd agreed, hoping company would help chase away the nightmares and the terrible knowledge that she'd killed another human being, but it wasn't working. She refused Megan's attempts at comfort and didn't understand why. "I'm having the same dream over and over." She raked trembling fingers through her hair. Was she going insane? She'd never been so confused about her life, her job, or uncertain of herself.

Megan turned on the bedside lamp and cupped Jeri's chin, stroking the slight cleft with her thumb. "Maybe you need to visit Dr. Cleaves more than once a week for a while."

Jeri jerked away, shaking her head. "Don't start. You know how I feel about that."

"Actually, I don't. All I know is that you won't even discuss it."

Jeri rose and paced at the foot of the bed. "It feels like the only thing we *do* talk about anymore. The only reason I'm going is because it's mandatory."

"Jeri, you experienced something every cop prays will never happen. If you can't get past it, maybe you should consider another line of work."

"Not happening." Jeri raised her palms toward the ceiling. She didn't want another argument with Megan about therapy or her job.

Her work had been a sore spot since day one. According to Megan, it wasn't good enough for Jeri, and the pay was always an issue. They'd only been dating a couple of months, but already Megan sounded like a demanding harpy.

"We could start fresh, away from the memories. Get a house, decorate, make new friends. That's all I'm saying."

"But I love my job. It's who I am." Lately, she wasn't so sure. The initial grilling by detectives, and subsequently internal affairs, when she told them she couldn't remember had made her question everything about that night and herself. Was she withholding information because she'd done something wrong as they suggested?

"It's a job, Jeri, not a very good one, and certainly not who you are. You've been having these dreams for two weeks. Every night. I'm not sure how much longer either of us can go on if you don't get some real help."

Jeri stopped pacing and glared at her. "Is that some kind of threat?"

"I feel like I'm on the verge of a nervous breakdown myself, being awakened nightly, feeling like a zombie at work, and trying to understand what's happening when you won't even talk to *me* about it."

"You wouldn't understand, Megan."

"Okay, here we go. The cops' code of silence bullshit again. If cops are such elite and highly evolved individuals, why can't they help you with this? Talk to one of them already."

"It's not that simple." The code of silence had nothing to do with it. Cops didn't like to talk about weakness or fear. They were supposed to protect others from those things. How could she tell the guys she'd been so scared that night she'd shaken violently, killed a suspect—she wasn't sure which came first—and then forgotten everything. She was the first woman involved in an OIS in the department. They'd think she was a wimp, or worse, a coward unfit to return to the field.

"Jeri, you shot a man who was trying to kill you for God's sake. Even a lowly member of the public like myself understands that. I don't really care who you talk to, but you need to do it. Soon."

Megan rose, walked to Jeri's side, and put her arm around her waist. "Babe, we need to have fun again. You stay cooped up too much, thinking about things you can't change. Maybe if we got out a little, went dancing, relieved the stress, you'd feel better."

"Will dancing help me remember or make these dreams go away?" Megan dropped her arm from Jeri's waist, and she resumed pacing.

"I don't know, Jeri." She raised her hands in surrender. "Just trying to help." She climbed back in bed and pulled the covers over her head. "I'm going back to sleep."

"I'm sorry. I know you didn't sign on for this when we started dating. I wouldn't blame you for walking away." She moved to Megan's bedside and slid the covers back. Her young face, framed by blond hair and accented by dark blue eyes, broadcasted impatience and frustration. Jeri bent to kiss her good-bye, but Megan pulled away. "I think I'll go for a run."

When Jeri turned to go, Megan said, "Remember we're having dinner with Andy tonight. Six o'clock at Smok'd on Elm Street. I'll ride with him from work. His sister's joining us."

Jeri suppressed a groan. Spending the night in the company of strangers was not her idea of a fun or relaxing evening. "Tell me again why we're having dinner with your boss?"

"We never go out anymore, and besides, his wife is out of town and he's lonely. So, play nice and please try to be on time for a change."

Jeri started to defend herself, realized there was no defense for the truth, and left well enough alone. At least Megan was off the topic of Dr. Cleaves.

"And if you don't like Cleaves, find somebody else."

Was there no end to this? Their months together before the shooting had been sexually charged and emotionally rocky, but the weeks since had been almost unbearable as the nightmares worsened and Megan grew more intolerant. No relationship could survive these conditions for long, especially not a new one, and she didn't have the energy to fight two battles at once. Jeri pulled on a pair of department-issued sweats and grabbed her off-duty Walther PPK .380 from the bedside table and tucked it into her ankle holster.

On the short walk to the park, Jeri considered breaking it off with Megan. She wanted and deserved more, and Jeri was tired of their constant bickering. She'd perfected the art of dodging her lover, often to avoid another fight. And if she was honest, another reason for avoiding Megan was Simone Sullivan. She couldn't stop thinking about her, but after the shooting, couldn't imagine seeing her again either. Jeri felt like her personality had changed along with her life and she had nothing to offer anyone right now. She should probably take the high road and end it with Megan.

Jeri went back to her house after her run and collapsed on the sofa. When the phone woke her at four o'clock in the afternoon, she checked caller ID and let it go to voice mail. Vita. She was the only person Jeri would consider talking to right now—because Vita would track her down if she didn't—but couldn't bring herself to answer.

Vita was a lot like the Boston terriers she loved, running ninety miles an hour, bouncing off the walls with hyperactivity but sharp as a surgical instrument. She believed life was too short to be stupid or waste time on unnecessary words. Her friendly advice often struck home with marksman-like precision. Jeri usually loved her honesty, but today the inevitability just made her anxious. When her cell pinged with the message, Jeri listened.

"I'm going to keep calling until you answer." Vita barked a command at one of her dogs in the background and added, "Don't make me have to track you down."

Jeri reluctantly called back. "What's up, Vi?"

"Well, I've got a bitch in heat, and a stud that's humping everything but her. Besides that, not much. When can we get together? Is tonight good for you?"

"I can't. Megan and I are having dinner with her boss. Why, I don't know since she sees him eight to ten hours every day."

"Tomorrow then, that's as long as I can wait to find out what's going on with you. Cop Out. Five thirty. Happy hour."

"I thought you hated that place." Jeri couldn't suppress a smile, thinking of her genetically monogamous friend cruising for the perfect mate in a pool of serially polygamous lesbians.

"I do, but it's the only place in town I'm certain to meet a butch dog lover. Besides, everybody knows female cops are either whores or dykes. At this stage, I need both."

"See you then and give my best to the black-and-white units."

"Wait a minute, hon." Vita turned away from the phone, "Ranger, get off my leg, you little pervert, and go hump that other bitch in heat." She returned to Jeri. "You, my friend, have got to be an aberration. A lesbian who doesn't have a dog. There's something unnatural about that. I might have to call in some help breeding these two." In typical fashion, Vita's attention shifted as often as her Boston terriers'.

"I thought you were a dog trainer. Anyway, isn't that like second nature?" Jeri mashed the TV remote control double time and waited for an explanation she'd rather not hear.

"You'd think, but he usually gets a hand job." Vita chuckled.

"Stop."

"I've been shipping his high-powered jizz all over the country, and I have to catch it, bag it, tag it, and send it overnight. He's not used to performing for real."

"Oh my God, Vita, that's way too much information. I'll see you tomorrow night."

"Bye, hon. Love you."

As Jeri hung up, she heard Vita's high-pitched laugh emphasized by her trademark snort at the end. She was probably already barking commands at one of her champion Nix Kennels terriers. Seeing Vita would be fun, and a drink always sounded like an excellent idea.

If she hurried, she'd have time for one before the obligatory dinner. The thought of facing a couple of hetero strangers for an evening of lawyer talk was unacceptable without fortification. She showered and changed into a plaid flannel shirt, faded jeans, and her signature green Army jacket. At the hallway mirror, she finger-combed her wet hair and let the thick layers fall naturally.

On the short walk, her tight jeans worked against her crotch and desire flashed through her. When was the last time she and Megan had sex? Definitely before the shooting, beyond that she couldn't say. Megan wanted a deeper emotional connection, and Jeri just needed release, a precious few minutes of sweaty, mindless sex followed by orgasm-induced sleep. She couldn't be in a relationship right now. Serious emotions were beyond her grasp.

"Jeri, the usual?" The short, bleached-blonde nodded toward Jeri's favorite spot at the end of the bar when she entered the club. Casey, retired from the NYPD, understood cops and didn't ask a lot of unnecessary questions. She'd mentored Jeri after college, rented her the small apartment over the club, given her a job as bouncer, and guided her in the direction of the police department.

Jeri gave her a thumbs-up. "Got to meet Megan and her boss for dinner." She pulled up the stool, sat with her back against the wall, and scanned the bar, reviewing every feature she'd previously committed to memory. An antique call box that hung on one side of the entry was balanced on the other by a heavy metal section from the renovated jail. The paneled walls and ceiling sported remnants of a bygone law enforcement era: old handcuffs, walkie-talkies, slapjacks, wooden batons, holsters, hats, badges, and even uniforms. Cages from the back seat of police cars served as dividers between booths, and safety cones with flags separated the dance floor from pool tables.

Thirty minutes from now the work crowd would pour in for happy hour and to spin the roulette wheel of potential evening partners. The ambiance satisfied both her need for familiarity and anonymity, and the sameness of it all comforted her, especially when the rest of her life seemed in chaos. Jeri dropped her shoulders, and the knot in her stomach loosened.

Casey placed the vodka tonic on a napkin and scooted it down the bar in front of Jeri.

She raised the glass in an air toast. "Thanks, Casey." She took a gulp. The icy concoction burned her throat and landed heavily in her empty stomach. Warmth spread quickly as the blessed numbness coursed through her exhausted body. The struggle to remember, cope with killing a man, and to feel like herself again, slowly subsided.

"So, how's it going, Jeri? You look a little pooped." Casey leaned against the bar and sipped a glass of ice water.

"Okay I guess." Jeri avoided Casey's questioning stare. The things she hid so easily from Megan and other civilians wouldn't escape Casey's attention.

"You know, it's none of my business, but if you ever need to talk, I'm here. Listening is the real reason God created bartenders, not serving drinks."

"I appreciate it, Casey." Jeri drained the glass and pushed it back toward her. "Can I have another?"

By the time Jeri finished the second drink, slid her tab to Casey, and started the walk to the restaurant, her steps felt lighter, more confident. Even if it was false courage, she needed it badly. At least we won't be talking about the looming *it* tonight. Therapy.

CHAPTER SIX

Jeri arrived at the restaurant fifteen minutes late, and Megan puckered her lips in a tight line and rolled her eyes when she walked in. Jeri thought about leaving, but the man with Megan waved her to their table. The woman sitting with her back to Jeri had wavy, reddish-blond hair pulled back and woven into a sexy French braid. As Jeri came within earshot, the redhead's voice cut with irritation as she exchanged words with Megan. They stopped talking when Jeri got closer.

"Good evening, everyone, sorry I'm late." Jeri took Andy's extended hand.

"Jeri, I'm Andy Sullivan. It's nice to finally meet you. I've heard so much about you from Megan." His blond hair and smooth features gave him the appearance of an innocent boy, but his sharp blue eyes inspected her too closely.

"Thanks for the invitation."

"Babe, this is Andy's sister, Simone Sullivan." Megan motioned to the woman beside her and squirmed uncomfortably in her chair. "Simone, this is my partner, Jeri Wylder."

Jeri tensed and avoided looking at Simone until she was sure her expression wouldn't betray her. Simone. Here. And Megan said "*my partner.*" Totally not what she'd call their rocky association.

"Your partner," Simone said. "I see."

Jeri finally faced Simone, hoping to convey with her eyes that the partner comment was not true, but the moment she looked at Simone, words failed. Those warm green eyes bored into her soul, and Jeri's breathing hitched. Simone's smile lit her face, parenthesized the corners of her mouth with laugh lines, and crinkled her freckle-spattered nose. Rust-colored threads woven throughout her turtleneck highlighted golden flecks in her eyes and hair. She was gorgeous and as surprised as Jeri. The anxiety over Andy's assessment vanished in a wave of warmth and calm, which she attributed to the vodka. She continued to stare until she realized Simone's hand was extended toward her.

"Nice to see you again, Jeri."

When they touched, Simone's slender fingers folded gently into Jeri's larger hand and rested there. The tiny hairs on Jeri's body rose to attention, and her mouth dried. The light scent of gardenia floated past, and she inhaled deeply. My God, she was just as beautiful as she remembered. All she could say was, "You too."

"You know each other?" Andy asked.

"Jeri answered a call to the Madison a few weeks ago," Simone said.

"You never said." Megan looked at Jeri as if she'd hidden some dark secret.

"I had no idea Simone was related to your boss. How could I?" Jeri realized she was still holding Simone's hand and released it before sitting across from her. She needed something to take the spotlight off her, so she waved a waiter over and ordered a vodka tonic.

Megan asked, "Are you sure that's a good idea?"

Careful to keep her tone civil, Jeri replied. "Actually, I think it's a great idea." Being across from Simone Sullivan unnerved her in a deliciously stimulating way. But damn, she should've explained her dating situation over coffee that day. Now, thanks to Megan, she had the wrong idea.

"I'll have another Bushmills straight up, please." Simone smiled at the waiter and handed him her empty glass.

While Andy and Megan finished a conversation about work, Jeri watched a female couple beside them laughing and obviously enjoying each other's company. The brunette peeled a shrimp, leaned across the table, and offered it to her blond companion. Taking the delicacy into her mouth, the blonde licked the other woman's fingers and smiled. How easily the women transformed an ordinary gesture into an erotic experience.

When she returned her attention to the table, she caught Simone's eye just as she glanced away from the same couple. Her lids were heavy, and her cheeks slightly flushed. Their gaze held and neither looked away until the waiter appeared with their drinks. Whatever had ignited between them at their first meeting and sparked over coffee still smoldered between them. Too bad she couldn't do anything about it now.

Andy raised his glass, exchanged a sheepish grin with Megan, and cleared his throat. "I propose a toast to friendship and to friends helping each other."

They all clinked glasses, and Simone raised the Irish whiskey to her full lips and sipped. She closed her eyes and sat perfectly still as if welcoming and savoring the strong ambrosia. Jeri was content just watching her, simultaneously calmed and excited by Simone's presence.

"So, Jeri, how are things at work, with the investigation? Have they cleared you yet?"

Jeri recoiled, jolted too quickly from her appreciation of Simone and thrust back into the hell that had become her life. She willed her expression to remain neutral and looked from Andy to Megan in disbelief. "I can't talk about that, Andy."

"I imagine the interviews with detectives and internal affairs are hard." He didn't let up, coming at her like she was a witness on the stand. "And when they release your name, the publicity will be brutal. Megan said you're having nightmares, not sleeping, and losing weight."

"Really? What else has Megan said?" She shot Megan an I-can't-believe-you-did-this look. Her stomach roiled, and she wanted to be anywhere but here facing *these* questions.

Megan reached for Jeri's hand, but she withdrew from the touch. "Babe, I was desperate. I don't know what to do anymore. I needed to talk to someone. Andy's just trying to help." Megan wouldn't look at her, a sure sign she knew just how big a betrayal this was to Jeri.

Simone's gaze hadn't left Jeri during the tense exchange. Was she in on the conspiracy? While she remained silent, Jeri knew from years of sizing people up that Simone was absorbing and evaluating every word, expression, and nonverbal cue. The softness in Simone's eyes gave Jeri a feeling of comfort she hadn't expected and, at this point, didn't want. She needed to hold on to her anger, but in spite of herself, the bundle of nerves in her stomach relaxed slightly.

Jeri took a deep breath and faced Andy again. "I appreciate your concern, Andy, but there are criminal and internal investigations pending. I not only can't talk about it, but I'm not going to. Besides, I came here to have dinner and relax, not talk about work. So please, drop it."

Simone raised her glass toward Jeri. "I couldn't agree more. This is a social occasion." Then to Andy and Megan she added, "Give the woman a break, sounds like she could use one."

Jeri nodded to Simone in appreciation. Her response was a quick wink.

Megan looked at Simone. "But I wanted you to—"

"Let's order. I'm starving." Simone motioned for the waiter. "I haven't eaten all day and I hear this place is a carnivore's paradise."

The remainder of the evening passed with a meat smorgasbord, talk about interesting cases Andy and Megan were working, and tales from the Sullivan travelogue spent with their diplomat parents.

Simone regarded her brother with obvious affection, and Jeri wondered what it would be like to have siblings to reminisce with about your childhood. "I could always depend on my big brother. He has a heart of gold and always looks for the good in people."

Andy pointed at his sister playfully. "Simone got into more mischief than anyone I've ever known. We were supposed to be the example, the ambassador's kids, but Simone never quite understood that. She was too curious and independent. Fortunately, our parents were supportive and encouraged us to spread our wings."

"Up to a point," Simone said, barely above a whisper, and Jeri wanted to ask what she meant, but the sadness in Simone's eyes stopped her.

"It must be nice to have that kind of bond." Jeri was as surprised by her comment as the others apparently were. She'd obviously had too much vodka because she sounded like an episode of True Confessions. Or maybe Simone brought out her innermost thoughts, whether she intended to or not. Jeri wasn't sure how she felt about that.

Simone leaned across the table, their eyes met, and Jeri felt she'd been physically touched. A quick intake of breath caught in her throat, and tears threatened. She quickly looked away, reverted to cop mode, and scanned the room. What was happening to her?

"So, Jeri, do you know anything about plans to redevelop the area around the Madison Building in Fisher Park and convert the property to high-end condos?"

"Just that the issue is controversial. I understand the current owner isn't anxious to sell, but the developers and the city think the conversion will help downtown revitalization on the north end." Andy and Simone exchanged a look. "What have I missed?"

"Simone owns the building," Andy said. "A dozen tenants will be homeless if the proposal goes through, and one of them is my baby sister. The whole Fisher Park neighborhood is in an uproar."

"I'm sorry, Simone. You didn't mention it when I took the report." Simone blushed. Was it the attention or the implication of wealth that embarrassed her? Either way, Jeri found it endearing.

"They say you can't fight progress or city hall, but I'll try," Simone said. "We're having a meeting at the Madison with the planning division and the developer day after tomorrow. If I don't sell, they might try to have the building condemned, which is ridiculous since I renovated only three years ago and brought everything up to code. I've retained an attorney to represent my interests."

Jeri was suddenly more interested. "I'll be at that meeting too. The department likes to have a police presence at any potentially controversial community meetings, and since I'm on limited duty and it's unlikely I'll have to do any actual police work, I got the assignment." Jeri smiled at the thought of seeing Simone again under any circumstances.

"At least there'll be one friendly face among the piranhas. If I eventually end up with no home, I guess I could sleep in my office until the landlord finds out."

"You know that's never going to happen, sis. You're always welcome in my home." The two exchanged a look of mutual admiration, and Simone patted Andy's forearm in appreciation.

Jeri drained her glass and remembered the warm, comforting touch of Simone's hand while they talked over coffee. She wanted to know more about Simone, a lot more. "Where's your office?"

"It's downtown near the police department in a beautiful location. Aside from being terribly cramped, it wouldn't be bad at all until one of my clients or the other docs saw me showering in the restroom or sleeping on my sofa."

She'd guessed doctor over coffee, and Simone said no. "You *are* a doctor then?" It fit her perfectly—the gentle touch, inviting eyes, soothing voice. Of course, she was a doctor.

"Not an MD—"

"Jeri, we need to go. It's getting late." Megan reached for her purse and pushed back from the table.

The urgency in Megan's voice set off an alarm, and Jeri ignored the suggestion. "What kind of doctor?"

Simone looked deliberately from Andy to Megan before locking on to Jeri. "Psychologist, a PhD."

Jeri stared into Simone's unwavering eyes and searched for some flicker of a smile, any indication this might be a joke. Seeing none, her temper flared, but she kept her tone even. "You mean a therapist—a *mental* therapist? The sudden dinner invitation makes sense now." Jeri scowled at Megan. "You're right about one thing. It is time to go." Her anger was so close to the surface the harsh taste of it burned her throat.

Jeri rose, looked around the table, and shook her head in disbelief. "It was interesting to meet you, Andy. Next time feel free to inform me of the agenda along with everyone else. Good luck with your housing situation, *Doctor* Sullivan." She placed a wad of cash on the table and walked out of the restaurant.

Simone's voice echoed in her head to the pounding of her footsteps. A psychologist. PhD. How could Simone betray her like that? How could Megan? She should've known it was a setup when she walked in and everybody stopped talking, but her instincts were off.

"Jeri, will you slow down?" Megan struggled to keep up with Jeri's long, determined strides. "Do you want me to apologize for trying to help?"

Jeri stopped in front of the Cop Out. "Blindsiding me with a couple of strangers? That's your idea of help? I want you to apologize for disrespecting my privacy and for setting me up with people who have no idea of who I am or what I'm going through."

"Well, it'd be hard to find anybody who *does* know what you're going through from your perspective. If a trained professional can't help, I give up."

Several people peered out of the club as their discussion became louder and more heated.

"Does that mean you want out? If you do, just say so." Jeri gauged her feelings about the possibility and found nothing. Megan stood close enough to touch her but didn't, and Jeri sensed them drifting further apart as the conversation deteriorated. Again, she felt nothing.

"It means I don't know anymore, Jeri. I've been trying to really connect with you from day one, but since the shooting, it's been impossible. I can't do it alone. You're always too tired, too drunk, too angry, or too absent to care. What am I supposed to do?"

"Whatever you want, Megan. Life's too damn short to do anything else."

"I'm not the enemy, Jeri, contrary to what you might think. It's not weakness to let someone help you."

Jeri's insides knotted. Then why did it feel exactly like weakness? Trust was not her friend. When she was young, she'd learned the hard way to take care of herself. Now was no different. And if she was perfectly honest, she didn't believe she or Megan were committed enough to the relationship to make it through these difficult times.

Two hours of cooling off and a hot shower later, Jeri crawled into bed and snuggled up to Megan's back. Maybe she was being unfair. Maybe she should try harder to give Megan what she wanted. She cupped Megan's full breasts and nibbled her neck. Her own nipples puckered as she massaged the smooth skin of Megan's abdomen and thighs.

"Jeri, don't." She pushed Jeri's hand away.

"Come on, baby, I'm sorry, and you wanted to help." Jeri teased and resumed stroking Megan's breasts. "This is your chance. You know how I love sex with you."

"Not lately."

"Well, I want it now." Jeri stroked again. "And it might help if we reconnect."

"I said no." Megan turned to face Jeri. "I want you to make love to *me*. I'm not one of the barflies you fuck until you're exhausted enough to sleep. Can't you see what you're doing?"

"What are you talking about?"

"You're playing dumb right now?"

Jeri was too exhausted for another round of bickering. She threw the covers off and jumped out of bed. "Fine. You want me to need you and when I try, you push me away."

"I want you to need and trust me emotionally, not just as a physical diversion."

"Sex helps with the feelings." Orgasm broke down her walls for a few seconds, let her breathe a peaceful breath, and momentarily forget, but it never brought real connection. She'd never trusted anyone enough to let that happen.

"All we do is fight anymore. I need space." The words spilled out before she could stop them. She stalked to the spare bedroom and climbed into the cold bed. She hated being awake and alone right now, but the last thing she wanted was to be questioned about her feelings and criticized for her shortcomings. She did enough of that on her own.

Chapter Seven

Simone left the restaurant, seething about being set up and conflicted about seeing Jeri again. She'd never be able to sleep with the clashing emotions inside her, so she pulled out her cell and pushed one on speed dial. "Char, are you busy?"

"Never too busy for you. I'll get the whiskey out." A few minutes later, Charlotte buzzed her into the front entrance of the high-rise and up to her twelfth-floor condo. "Get in here." She handed Simone a rocks glass with two fingers of amber liquid and guided her to the sofa overlooking the eastern skyline.

"I love this view. You're lucky."

Charlotte settled beside her but didn't look out the floor-to-ceiling windows. "Yeah, it's nice, but sometimes I'd like someone to share it with." She sipped her wine, and they sat quietly for a few seconds before Charlotte spoke again, her wistfulness now gone. "Why are you upset?"

"I'm not real—"

"Let's not do that, okay? We know each other too well, and Erica isn't here, so you don't have to check yourself."

Simone squeezed Charlotte's hand. "And that's why you're number one on my speed dial." She took a hefty gulp of whiskey and said, "I had dinner with Andy; his paralegal, Megan; and her girlfriend tonight. When we got to the restaurant, Megan dropped the bomb that she wanted my professional opinion about her girlfriend."

"Can you say setup?"

"Exactly. I refused to be involved in an ambush and told her a public confrontation in front of strangers would only contribute to her girlfriend's problems and hurt their relationship. I thought I'd gotten through, but she did it anyway. Plain and simple manipulation of both of us."

"That's pretty insensitive, not to mention irresponsible."

Simone nodded and glanced at the twinkling lights across the city, avoiding the worst part, unsure she wanted to share.

"And? What you've told me so far is Megan and her girlfriend's problem. You're too good at compartmentalizing to let someone else's drama upset you like this."

"Damn, you do know me." She fiddled with her glass before answering. "Megan's girlfriend is the police officer I had coffee with." Simone paused. At this point, Erica would've been demanding an immediate end to further contact and scolding Simone for being so careless.

Charlotte held her gaze, eyes soft and compassionate. "You had no idea."

Simone shook her head. "Jeri, that's the cop, didn't mention having a girlfriend, but she did say she wanted to explain her *situation* next time we spoke." She swirled the whiskey around in her glass. "I wondered why she didn't contact me again, because we really clicked."

"So, you don't think she was intentionally misleading you?"

"No. She got a call and had to leave, so we didn't finish our conversation. But the Jeri I saw tonight was very different from the one I had coffee with. Her features were gaunt and drawn. The shirt she wore hung loosely from her shoulders, and her jeans sagged below her hips. Dark circles ringed her eyes. Even her confident, positive energy has shifted to something darker and angrier."

Simone had heard the news accounts of the shooting, but the officer hadn't been identified. Even without details, Simone would know Jeri had been through a trauma. When Jeri's gaze had rested on her, Simone was drawn in with an unexpected jolt. The intensity in her eyes could easily deceive a casual observer, but Simone recognized the sorrow. Her heart ached with the same pain she'd sensed in numerous clients but never felt so acutely.

"What's happened to her?"

"She killed that guy in the abandoned house a couple of weeks ago, the same day we met for coffee, but you can't tell anyone, Char. Her name hasn't been officially released yet. I didn't know until tonight, so it was a double-whammy moment. Jeri killed someone and has a girlfriend."

"How horrible."

"Andy throttled her with questions about the investigation, her nightmares, and everything. I could tell she was on the verge of snapping, but she was courteous and respectful even though her emotions and self-control have to be so very fragile right now."

"Do you have feelings for her, Simone?"

Did she? They'd only seen each other twice before dinner. "I think I'm mostly concerned about her. I can't imagine what it costs her to function daily with the guilt and uncertainty hanging over her." An empathic ache pulsed in Simone's chest and grew into anger at Megan for backdooring Jeri by using Andy. She attributed it to Megan's youth and frustration.

"It gets worse." Simone scooted closer on the sofa and rested her head on Charlotte's shoulder. "The death knell came when Jeri found out I was a therapist. She felt betrayed, and I couldn't blame her. We didn't talk about my profession at the café, and being set up wasn't the best way to tell her. She has classic signs of post-traumatic stress disorder and desperately needs to trust someone right now."

"Sounds like she's in a bad way. Doesn't she have friends, family who can help?"

"I'm sure she has friends, but she saved my building from being torched. This might sound crazy, but I feel I owe her." She felt more than gratitude but couldn't identify exactly what. "I don't know how far she's fallen in the downward spiral, but according to her friend Megan, Jeri is drinking excessively, angry all the time, and who knows what other risky behaviors are probably keeping her going."

"What can you do? Sounds like she needs professional help." Charlotte soothingly stroked Simone's hair.

"I can't do anything except pray she's getting what she needs through the department."

"I'm so sorry, Simone, but keeping your distance right now is probably best. Even if you're interested in each other, she probably can't deal with anything else right now, especially something as complicated as emotions and a relationship."

Simone's chest tightened. Charlotte was right. "I know."

But something else about Jeri niggled at Simone's mind, refusing to budge. Was it her compassion and empathy for Jeri's dilemma, her professional impulse to fix it, or the seed of real feelings? She visualized Jeri across from her at dinner—her tanned complexion, thick hair, and the sexy dip in the center of her chin. Jeri's androgynous good looks went beyond attractive, but she was also a woman in desperate need of help. Simone was simultaneously relieved and disappointed that she wouldn't be the one to provide it. She couldn't allow professional passion to influence personal desire or vice versa. The combination was a dangerous one.

CHAPTER EIGHT

J eri pretended to be asleep when Megan eased the door open and looked in on her before leaving for work. Her head pounded after a night of too much vodka, an uncomfortable single bed, and Simone Sullivan's admission about being a psychologist. She wasn't sure which hurt worse, Megan's betrayal or Simone's. Though she and Simone never actually discussed her profession, her participation in the ambush felt duplicitous.

She pulled on her shorts and T-shirt and followed the welcome aroma of freshly brewed coffee. A yellow Post-it with Megan's neat handwriting rested against the coffee pot. *Be home late.* Since when did Megan refer to her place as home? The assumption and the question bothered Jeri. Her cell vibrated on the counter. "Yeah?"

"You coming to work today or did the personnel sergeant and I both misplace your vacation slip?" her sergeant asked.

"Work?"

"Yeah, the thing you pretend to do and the city pays you for every month."

Jeri grabbed the calendar stuck to the refrigerator. "Damn, Sarge, I'm sorry. I'll be right there." Working days on administrative leave screwed with her head and her schedule.

"Take your time, just see me in the office when you get here." The line went dead.

Jeri quickly showered, pulled on a pair of khakis with a white cotton shirt—her light-duty version of a uniform—and grabbed her favorite green Army jacket on the way out. She tossed Mrs. Doyle's newspaper on her front porch and filled Toto's bowl with water. How long had it been since she'd taken the time to really visit with her neighbor? The past two weeks had blurred together in a haze.

When Jeri entered the sergeant's office, he looked up from a stack of paperwork. He studied her closely, raked his fingers over a Marine-style buzz cut, and directed her to close the door. "What's going on with you, Wylder?"

"I lost track of time, Sarge." Totally lame. She buried her hands in her jacket pockets.

"Lost track of time?" His lips tightened, a tell Jeri recognized as an attempt to control his temper. "You might lose track of your car keys, your cell phone, or even your girlfriend, but a cop doesn't lose track of when he's due at work. This isn't the first time you've been late recently, but it is the first time you haven't shown up at all."

"It won't happen again." Jeri hoped she was right.

"When the personnel sergeant told me you hadn't reported in, I told him I'd take care of it. I know you hate being a desk jockey, but we don't have a choice. Try to remember this administrative assignment is only temporary. When it's over, you'll come back to my squad, so don't make me look bad."

"Yes, sir." Jeri's head pounded harder as she recalled the other times she'd been late for work recently. Temporary memory loss was no excuse for rookie mistakes. "Is that all, Sarge?"

"For now. Internal affairs is expecting you for a follow-up interview in ten minutes."

Jeri's head snapped up and her mouth flew open. "Crap."

"Did that slip your mind too?" But he didn't need a verbal response. "Go take care of this thing so you can get back to work. And don't give the personnel sergeant any more grief."

"Thanks, sir." Jeri had never felt so professionally inept. How could she forget something as basic as coming to work? Not even rookies were that slack, and if they were, they paid dearly. She was making careless errors and asking for consideration. She felt her career being siphoned off bit by humiliating bit.

As she reached the conference room door, the sergeant called after her, "Don't forget you've got that community meeting at the Madison after work tomorrow. And don't come anywhere near the station. The chief is releasing your name, and there'll be a big demonstration in your honor. Be grateful the department's letting you do something besides ride a desk. Let me know if there's a problem at the meeting."

Tomorrow. Simone Sullivan. A bright spot. But she still had to get through today. The vision of Simone's face lifted Jeri's mood until she remembered her profession. It was easy to see how people could talk to her. She'd done the same thing over coffee...before she knew she was a shrink. Jeri shuffled toward IA in no hurry to begin another inquisition.

Sergeant Dan Williams, the internal affairs supervisor, met her in the reception area. His beady eyes and narrow lips were stereotypical of the "vile henchman" she'd seen in comic books as a child. Williams had a reputation for presuming officers guilty until proven innocent, earning him the nickname of Hatchet Man. But everyone who'd dealt with him agreed he was fair, just tough as hell. He was totally dedicated to culling out the bad apples and devoted to a department that served the community with integrity and pride. She respected that.

Williams nodded toward his office. Jeri wiped her sweaty palms on her pants and followed him in. He punched the intercom button on his phone and without greeting barked, "Smith, get in here." He disconnected without waiting for a reply.

Luke Smith, a light-skinned African American investigator, entered the office within seconds. Smith had been in internal affairs for several years and maintained the respect of field officers in spite of the unpopular assignment and his guilt by association with Williams. Unlike his boss, Luke believed in giving officers the benefit of the doubt and following the evidence, which made them a powerful investigative team.

Luke took a seat and nodded to Jeri as Williams dictated the date, time, and members present into his mini recorder. Then he turned to Jeri. "We're here to conduct a follow-up interview regarding the shooting at Six-twelve Morehead Avenue. For the record, Officer Wylder has been unable to provide a complete chronological account of the incident thus far due to temporary memory loss. Therefore, periodic interviews are required until the necessary information is obtained to close the internal and criminal investigations and forward the latter to the district attorney. Do you understand the purpose of these proceedings, Officer Wylder?"

Jeri clasped her damp palms together and squirmed in her chair. "Yes, sir."

Williams nodded to Luke, who pulled a small card from his pocket and read the Garrity warnings. She partially listened until he reached a particular section. *You will be asked questions specifically, directly, and narrowly related to the performance of your official duties or fitness for office.* The sentence registered in the pit of Jeri's stomach, and her heart pounded frantically. She'd heard the words many times, but today they threatened *her* livelihood and *her* personal integrity. Even though the warnings included assurance that her participation was voluntary, it never felt that way.

Luke concluded with the standard line, "Do you understand these rights as I've explained them to you, Officer Wylder?"

"Y…yes, I understand." Every nerve in her body sizzled. She steadied her hand, signed the waiver, and then waited for the barrage of questions.

"Can you tell us what happened the night of this incident, Officer Wylder?" Williams squinted over the top of his reading glasses, his voice cold and hard.

Jeri sat perfectly still, closed her eyes, and willed herself to remember. "The call was dispatched to myself, Car Eleven-thirteen, and my zone partner, Randy Mardis, Car Eleven-fourteen. I was downtown, so I took Spring Garden Street to Cedar, turned left, and then left again onto Morehead. I parked a block away and walked to the abandoned house."

"Had your assist arrived?"

"No, sir. I saw a light from inside when I arrived, so I started clearing the house, room by room. As I got closer to the last one, I heard muffled voices, at least two, male and female."

"Did you announce yourself?"

"No. I hoped to catch them in the act if they were dealing drugs."

"Go on," Williams said.

"The male was talking crazy, nonsensical stuff. I stepped into the room and...I'm sorry, sir, that's it. My next memory is of waking up in the hospital the next morning." The knot in her stomach tightened.

"You don't remember asking Officer Mardis if you'd shot someone at the scene?"

"No, sir."

"What about telling him to find a woman?"

"I remember a woman's voice, but not asking Randy to find her."

Williams gave Luke an almost imperceptible nod.

Luke slid closer and put his hand on the arm of Jeri's chair. "This is probably the most important question you'll answer in your law enforcement career, and it's not going away. Think carefully and be absolutely honest. What *really* happened that night?"

Jeri leaned forward, placed her elbows on her knees, and rested her face in her hands. She walked herself through the call again but came up with the same scenario. "I've told you everything I remember. The dispatch, travel route, arriving on scene, going inside, hearing voices, and then waking up in the hospital. That's it. I honestly can't remember anything else. Believe me, if I could get this over with right now, I would, but I can't give you something I don't have."

Williams jumped from his seat and slapped his hands on the desk. "The truth is you don't want to give us the information because it won't look good for you. Isn't that right? The truth of the matter is you acted inappropriately and now you're trying to bullshit your way out of it. Isn't that also right?" His face turned bright red and veins popped on his neck and forehead. He leaned toward her. His dark eyes bored into her, and in their depths, Jeri saw anger and accusation.

"No, sir, that is *not* the truth, none of it. The body cam footage would show exactly what happened. Have you seen it? If you'd let me look at it to refresh my memory, you'd know I was telling the truth."

"That's not an option right now," Williams said.

"What about the other officers' footage?" Williams and Luke exchanged a look Jeri didn't understand nor like. "What am I missing?" She'd asked to see the recordings before but been denied without explanation. "You make it sound like I shot an unarmed man."

"So, you do remember," Williams barked.

"What?" Jeri's insides churned. "No. He had a knife. Tell me you found the knife." But she hadn't said anything about a knife until this moment. Where had that come from? She gripped the arms of her chair.

"What knife? You didn't mention a knife in your original statement. Can you produce a knife?" Williams was on his toes beside her chair.

Jeri tried to decide if she should answer. "I...think I dreamed it."

"You *dreamed* it? Did I hear you correctly, Officer Wylder? You dreamed about a knife? Well, we can certainly take that to the bank, can't we?" Williams snorted in disgust.

Tears burned her eyes, but she refused to give Williams the satisfaction of seeing them. What a nightmare. This couldn't be happening. They actually thought she shot an unarmed man. Then she felt a chill as if someone opened a freezer door. What if she did?

The inquisition continued with Williams ranting and raving around the office, pounding on furniture and throwing papers while Luke tried to comfort and encourage her. No matter what the approach, Jeri was no closer to remembering.

Time crawled, and at five thirty, Williams closed the case file and stared at her. "These investigations should've been over by now, but we've been going slowly to give you time to remember." His tone was quieter with no hint of his earlier rant, a total Jekyll and Hyde transformation. "Until we have a coherent, verifiable statement from you, we can't close either of them. You can go for now."

"Yes, sir." Jeri stood and started toward the office door.

"By the way, Wylder, are you still seeing the department psychologist?" Williams asked the question, although Jeri was sure he already knew the answer since they got a weekly report from Cleaves.

"Yes, sir, once a week until he thinks I'm FFD."

"You might consider doubling up until this memory thing clears. We'll have to keep doing this dance until it does." Williams dismissed her with a wave of his hand.

Jeri's body shook as she walked out of the office. Fear coursed through her like a drug—fear that she could've killed an unarmed man, fear of losing her job, fear of having to see a shrink forever, fear that no one was on her side, and finally, fear that her whole life was about to implode because of one incident that was over in seconds but continued forever. She blundered out of the building and onto the sidewalk, her gait mechanical as she attempted to stifle the impulse to run toward the club and some sort of relief.

❖

Vita's shrill whistle penetrated the blare of music when Jeri opened the door of the Cop Out. "Well, damn, hon, I was about to gather a party of drunk lesbians and search for you. I've already got a buzz." She lifted her signature Three Olives martini and yelled to Casey, "Vodka tonic for my friend, and I'll have another one of these. And how about some chips and dip, please? If I'm going to be cocktailed, I need to be appetized."

Jeri dropped into the booth across from Vita and swore the retro police vehicle cages surrounding them closed in on her. She took a few deep breaths to calm the anxiety. "Sorry, Vi, I got hung up with internal affairs."

"You look horrible. Obviously, it didn't go well."

"Never does. Let's talk about something else."

"I'm glad you made it. I've missed you something awful. It seems like I haven't done anything but change woogie pants on a bitch in heat and try to coax a male into screwing her. Have you ever heard such nonsense? Most males would shag an open wound. It's just my luck." Casey placed their drinks on the table, and Vita said, "Thanks, hon," and offered a huge smile. "I'm supposed to be on this damn gluten-free diet. Thank God alcohol is still okay."

When Casey returned to the bar, Jeri asked, "Are you actually flirting with Casey?"

"Why not? She's a hot butch, likes dogs, and isn't attached."

"You found all that out over your first drink?"

"I don't waste time."

Jeri sipped her drink and listened to Vita's stories of playfully interrogating Casey and her latest canine escapades while the stress gradually lifted.

"Watching all this doggie business is making me horny," Vita said. "I might just take Casey on. It's been almost nine months since I've bumped uglies with anyone."

Jeri tried to remember the last time she and Megan had sex but failed. "She's good people, just don't mess her over. I only know cops, and you've already made it clear you don't want anything to do with them." Jeri gave her a grin and raised her palms in resignation.

"If we're just talking about a quickie, I might be willing to consider anybody."

"Me too," Jeri mumbled under her breath.

"And what exactly does *that* mean?"

Vita leaned closer, her facial expression neutral. She knew how quickly Jeri turned on and off when it came to personal revelations. The slightest negative response would send her into retreat mode when what she needed desperately right now was to talk, about anything except the investigations. "Things are getting worse at home, if that's possible." Saying it aloud felt like a relief and a betrayal. "All Megan talks about is my job, moving into a new house together, and signing me up for a lifetime commitment with a shrink."

"You think she could be right, about the shrink?" Vita popped an olive in her mouth, sucked on it, and waited.

"Who knows? My life is so upside down right now I can hardly keep up with day and night. I even forgot to go to work this morning, Vi. I actually forgot. And, I can't remember the shooting."

"Hon, I hate to admit this, but for once I agree with Megan. I'm worried about you too, and if a shrink can help, I say go for it. You're not your usual chipper self. I feel a lot of negative energy—anger and fear if I had to guess."

"I don't like Cleaves, Vi. I don't trust him."

"You don't trust most people, hon, and especially not shrinks." Jeri nodded. "I should be able to handle this myself. I should be…stronger."

"We all need help sometimes, Jeri. Maybe this guy's just not the right one for you. Find somebody else."

Jeri thought about Simone and smiled. *Why do I like this woman?* She tried to hide the grin, but Vita was too quick.

"You're holding something back." Vita took a big sip of her martini and eyed a young butch passing by their table.

Jeri debated saying anything about Simone, but Vita would never let her keep a secret, much less one involving a woman. "Well, actually, I met someone—"

"As in someone you're interested in, as in a therapist, or both?"

"She's both." Jeri signaled for another drink. This called for more fortification.

"Tell me everything." Vita grabbed Jeri's hands and wiggled her eyebrows conspiratorially.

"I met her on a call a few weeks ago, and we had coffee once. Turns out, she's the sister of Megan's boss, and she's a shrink." Just thinking about Simone made Jeri smile again, even though she was still upset about the dinner thing and finding out she was a therapist. Vita noticed the grin, of course.

"Is she family?"

"Yep." The memory of their flirty banter sent pleasurable waves spiraling through Jeri. "She's gorgeous, nice, and…it doesn't matter. When I found out she was a shrink and I'd been set up at dinner the other night, I got the hell out." Vita evaluated her for several minutes as Jeri's cheeks burned, and she stared at the floor.

"You haven't sounded so taken with anyone since college. And that smile speaks volumes. You must've liked her. Maybe she could see you."

"I don't know, Vi. It feels creepy now, the Megan-Andy-Simone thing, and the two of us having coffee. Besides, I don't want to be her patient."

"So, you're not going to see her again?"

"She'll be at a community meeting in my area tomorrow night, but I'm having trouble getting past the dinner setup." Not for the first time, Jeri wondered if Simone had known about Megan's plan in advance and admitted she didn't want to believe it.

"Don't jump to conclusions until you know the whole story. And in the meantime, try to figure out what's going on with you and Megan. Whatever you decide, I'm with you. Now I hate to drink and run, but I promised to pick up a puppy I'm going to show on my way home and it's getting late." Vita gave Jeri a hug and stopped by the bar to talk with Casey on the way out, leaving Jeri alone with her discordant thoughts.

CHAPTER NINE

After Vita left the Cop Out, Jeri finished her third vodka tonic and watched women on the dance floor in varying stages of vertical foreplay. They casually touched, tested, and finding no resistance, lingered and became more demanding. The sights stirred pangs of arousal and subsequent loneliness that she had no outlet for.

Jeri always struggled between the desire for a heart connection and the physical need for release. Sex was easy, an act she didn't need to explain, but giving her heart was another matter. Trust hadn't come easily before the shooting, but no one would understand this new dark side of her. She'd always coped with her problems through work or exercise, but neither helped anymore. She needed intense physical engagement, obliteration of thought. She needed to feel pain, deserved it after what she'd done. The unnerving thought sent a shiver through her.

Jeri slid her hand down the length of her outer thigh and back up to rest at her crotch. A blonde on the dance floor ran her tongue over a potential lover's earlobe, and Jeri licked her dry lips. When the brunette pressed her crotch against the other woman's thigh, Jeri squeezed her legs together.

"Quite a show isn't it?" a whispered voice from behind asked. In her preoccupation, Jeri hadn't heard Tom, her occasional hookup, approach.

"Yeah."

Tom extended a leg under the table and placed her bare foot between Jeri's legs. "I can help with that itch." Her flimsy blouse was partially unbuttoned and revealed firm breasts with erect nipples. "I'd really like to."

Tom was a classic blue-eyed, blond-haired fem and very much Jeri's type. For a second, the red reflected light off the bar made her hair look like Simone's, but not her features. Simone was more... something.

"Where you been, woman? All right?"

"I guess. Nightmares are the most vivid and real thing in my life right now. How pathetic is that?"

"It's not pathetic, Jeri, just reality for the moment. It will get better."

She and Tom met one night after the bar closed and talked until the next morning when Casey came downstairs to let the cleaners in. Tom was a veteran suffering from PTSD and the only person Jeri had been able to talk to since the shooting. Tom understood. The sex started shortly after, intense, rough sex that obliterated everything but the physical. Exactly what Jeri needed.

"Let's fix you up, soldier," Tom said with a smoldering look.

"Not a soldier."

"What you're fighting right now makes you a soldier regardless of the cause." Tom pressed her foot firmly into Jeri's crotch and said, "Are we doing the cat-and-mouse thing tonight where you run and I chase?" She massaged the spot that minutes before burned under Jeri's touch.

"Is...that...what you want?" Her breath came in gasps as Tom's foot pressed and grinded. Jeri reached around the table and urged Tom to her side of the booth.

"We enjoy it. You're conflicted and pretend to resist, and I'm relentless in winning you over. Eventually, we both get what we want." She teased Jeri's ear with her teeth and then dipped her tongue inside. "Or do you need to talk tonight?"

Jeri shivered and felt her crotch grow wet. "No talking."

"Perfect." Tom kissed Jeri lightly, pinched her nipple to the pleasurable threshold of pain, and slid off the seat. "I'll meet you in the parking lot. Sixty-one vintage Lincoln Continental, Sultan White."

Jeri watched Tom exit through the back door before going to the bar. She leaned closer so Casey could hear over the music. "Another vodka tonic and whatever Tom's drinking."

Casey gave her a skeptical look. "O—kay." She mixed the drinks and slid them toward Jeri. "I hope you know what you're doing."

"Don't worry. I got this."

"Last time you two ended up in my office. Don't pull that shit again."

"Roger that." Jeri took the drinks and started to follow Tom, but Casey caught her arm.

"Look, Jeri, I'm not your mother, your conscience, or your girlfriend, so I don't ask questions. This place is like Vegas. What happens at the Cop Out stays at the Cop Out as far as I'm concerned. You two hook up. That's fine. Just remember you're not exactly yourself right now." Casey patted Jeri's hand and wiped her way down the long mahogany bar.

Jeri opened the back door, and a cold wind almost blew the door shut in her face. She shoved again and stepped out. Tom leaned against a white old-model Lincoln with suicide doors with one foot cocked on the running board of the back seat. Her thin blouse ruffled in the breeze, but her legs were encased in tight black leather. Jeri's center throbbed as she walked closer and tried to concentrate on something else. "Great ride."

"Thanks. Family heirloom."

"Here." They chugged their drinks, smashed the glasses against the side of the building, and whooped a couple of primal screams like they were going into battle. "I'll have to pay for that juvenile behavior," Jeri said.

"You're going to pay for more than a couple of stupid glasses before this night is over." Tom slid her hand under her blouse and stroked her breast in a circular motion. "I'd enjoy this more if you did it. Stop ogling my car and get over here."

"I like it when you tempt me into doing something I'm pretty sure I shouldn't."

Tom grinned. "I prefer to call it teasing until you can't help yourself or giving you permission to do what we both know you want to."

Tom reached for her, but Jeri backed away. "I have a girlfriend, and—"

"Yeah, I know about your little vanilla lover. You told me the night we met. You're nothing if not honest, but I satisfy your *other* needs." Tom placed her forefinger against her lips and then sucked it in and out of her mouth.

Jeri swallowed hard, and her clit hardened. "Yeah, you do."

Tom grabbed the front of Jeri's shirt, pulled their bodies together with unexpected strength, and covered her mouth with a rough kiss. She turned their joined bodies toward the car and shoved Jeri down onto the back seat.

"Wait...I don't—"

"You don't like to be dominated. You need to be in charge. You don't like rough sex. You have a list of conditions, and I remember them all...and usually ignore them. This isn't our first time. But for once, would you shut the hell up and let me fuck you?" Tom pinned Jeri's arms over her head and jammed her knee against her crotch. "You want this as much as I do."

Jeri struggled, but Tom trapped her arms against the door. Tom was much stronger than she looked and majorly hot when she took charge. A total turn-on. "Tell me—"

"No talking. Your rule." Tom lowered herself on top of Jeri and looked up at her. "I won't do anything you don't like, and I do remember what you like. Your safe word is cheese."

"Seriously? I feel like I'm in an X-rated cartoon."

"But it's about to get real." Tom tugged the tail of Jeri's shirt from her jeans with both hands and peeled it over her head. "I love that you don't wear a bra and under these jeans is only flesh." She shucked Jeri's jeans just low enough for access and to confine movement. "You're already hot. I smell you." Jeri tried to respond, but Tom kissed her hard again, and then lowered her mouth to a puckered nipple, licked until Jeri moaned, and then bit down.

"Fuck. That hurt." The pain also drove a charge of arousal through her so powerful that she bucked, writhed against Tom's thigh, and lost all rational thought. "Damn." She pressed Tom's head back to her breast. "Again."

She stared up at a sputtering streetlight and blocked everything except the erratic flickering and the painful pleasure in her body. When Tom eased at her nipple, Jeri struggled, unsure if she wanted freedom or more.

"That's right, baby, fight me. It makes you feel alive, doesn't it?" Tom chuckled and cupped Jeri's sex with her hand. "You're so wet."

Jeri's body throbbed with a wave of primal desire. She parted her legs as far as her jeans allowed. "Touch me. Now." She ripped the flimsy fabric from Tom's shoulders and clutched the hair at the nape of her neck. She yanked and sucked Tom's breasts hard and fast.

"Oh yeah. That's it." Tom gasped as she worked Jeri's clit between her fingers.

When Tom jerked Jeri's pubic hair, sharp needles of pleasure-pain shot straight to her clit and her sex flooded again. "Yesssss."

"Bite me, baby," Tom pleaded.

"I will when you fuck me like you mean it. Make me feel it." Who was this person inhabiting her body, begging a stranger to take her, make her feel something—anything? Even pain was better than the shroud of numbness she'd worn since the shooting.

"You don't do things the easy way," Tom purred. She inserted her fingers one by one into Jeri and then closed them into a fist.

"Do it," Jeri begged her. When Tom plunged her fist into Jeri, she felt she'd split open from the girth and force of the thrust, but the pain fanned out, sparking pleasure and the need for more. "Harder." She covered Tom's nipple and sucked in time to her pumping. There was no tenderness between them, only the need to be completely possessed and pleasured by a stranger who asked no questions and required no explanation.

"Faster. Almost there." Jeri shuddered and tightened around the hand that fisted inside her. She arched her back and clutched Tom to her, convulsing and whimpering in pleasure and pain. The climax ripped through her with an intensity she didn't recognize, leaving only the physical release she craved and the vacuum of euphoria. And she felt powerful and strong again.

Tom withdrew her hand, and Jeri sat up, bringing Tom across her lap. She reached between Tom's leg and entered her forcefully. "Let me have you."

"You've got me." Tom threw her head back and watched as Jeri pumped into her. After a few long, unhurried strokes, Tom tensed and then collapsed against Jeri. "My God, woman, you are hot." Tom's body shimmered with perspiration and the flushed heat of satisfaction. A red bite mark on her shoulder was the only standout to her otherwise flawless skin.

Jeri's stomach lurched. "I did...that?" Her voice almost failed her.

"Don't apologize. I enjoy the pain as much as the sex, just like you."

"But I've never injured you before. I'm so sorry." Jeri stared at the angry-looking mark and tried to get in touch with the part of herself that could intentionally harm another human being, the part that needed this to feel again. She and Tom had agreed on what they wanted the first time they had sex—physical connection, power play, release, and a few moments of blank space in their heads without war or killing.

"It's all good, Jeri. Really. I got exactly what I needed."

As if by spoken agreement, they both reached for their clothes and started dressing. "Thanks, Tom. Take care of yourself."

"You've got my number if you need to talk...or anything."

Jeri climbed out of the car and finished pulling on her clothes as she hurried toward the street. Unfortunately, her respite ended too quickly, and the worrying thoughts returned. Why was she still with Megan when she so clearly wasn't in love with her? Would she ever remember the shooting and get back to her real job? And what did she want from Simone?

She crept into the house, tiptoed unsteadily to the bathroom, and stripped her clothes to shower away the evidence and memories of tonight. Her raw skin burned, and her nipples ached and almost bled from bite marks. Fifteen minutes ago, she'd begged for more, but now she felt only confusion. How could she explain her life right now to Megan, Vita, or especially Simone? If she told Simone she'd been violently sexercising her demons with strangers, she'd probably dismiss her as a potential friend, much less a girlfriend.

She toweled off as much as possible and eased into the master bedroom and found it empty. Same in the guest room. Who could blame Megan? She deserved better than this. Jeri checked her cell. Three missed calls and one voice mail from Megan. She punched in her password. Megan's voice was flat with an undercurrent of anger.

"I've gone back to my place. I'll see you tomorrow, if you're around. We need to talk."

Chapter Ten

Riding a desk in personnel, answering the phone, and monitoring occasional community meetings were Jeri's punishment for doing her job and her idea of hell. Her feelings fluctuated between fear at having too much time to think and anger at being restricted from the field and the answers she needed about the shooting.

"What's up, Wylder?" Carl and a couple of other officers from her squad stood in the doorway. "You going to milk this cushy job forever?"

"I sure as hell hope not. The past weeks are a blur of endless days in IA and the shrink's office." She didn't add, and nights at the bar. "I'm not sure if the criminal and administrative investigators are trying to clear me or find a way to nail me for murder. Trust me, I want out of here ASAP. You guys can't carry my load all by yourselves."

"In your dreams, Wylder." They laughed and waved as they headed for lineup.

"Hey, Carl, got a second?"

Carl scratched his sparse beard and leaned against the side of her desk. He reminded her a bit of Randy with his weightlifter's physique and macho swagger, but that was where it ended. "Yeah?"

"I was wondering if you'd do me a favor?" When he nodded, she continued. "I think there was a woman that night—"

"Stop." He raised his gloved hands and backed away. "Are you trying to drop me in the shit? You know we can't talk about the shooting."

"It's not exactly the shooting." She was splitting hairs. "I just want to find the woman. I'm hoping she can support my side of the story. Please, Carl."

"Did you talk to Randy?"

"He's looking, but another pair of eyes can't hurt. I'll owe you."

"I'm not saying I will." But he nodded and walked away.

She was tired of feeling helpless and waiting for others to prove her innocence. Investigations be damned. She clicked into the records database and typed in Calvin Vanoy. If he had a criminal record, maybe the woman had been an accomplice, associate, witness, or victim at some point. When Vanoy's mug shot popped up, Jeri cringed at the big red letters stamped across his face. *DECEASED.*

She'd see this face every day for the rest of her life and feel guilty for killing him, but that would never compare to what his family would suffer. She squinted at the picture trying to mine anything from his expression or the set of his jaw that might spark her memory. Nothing. She scrolled through his criminal history and felt another pang of guilt for dredging through Vanoy's life after ending it. Did she have the right? Maybe not, but she needed answers and paged down to known associates. Four men, but then… Melony Wright.

Jeri checked the woman's history sheet. A few petty larcenies in her early teens, a couple of marijuana possessions in her twenties, and a cocaine bust nine months earlier. The same date as Vanoy's last arrest. Bingo. She sent a picture of Wright's mug shot to her phone and signed out of the system.

She glanced at the time. Damn. Cleaves in ten minutes. On the walk to his office, Jeri thought about her messed-up relationship with Megan, the liaisons with Tom at the bar, and her apparent potential to inflict pain. Was there a theme? What would Dr. Sullivan say about her behavior? Jeri grinned when she thought about Simone, and then felt depressed. Her actions probably were cries for help, because none of them felt right in hindsight, like the Jeri before the shooting. Maybe everyone was right, and she did need intensive therapy. Cleaves would be happy about that.

She arrived a few minutes early and stood outside the gray stone building, pretending to be engrossed in the directory beside the entrance. As she mindlessly scanned the list, she stopped at the name on the top floor. Simone Sullivan, PhD, LPC. At dinner, Simone had said her office was downtown near the police department. It hadn't occurred to Jeri that Simone might be in the same building as Cleaves. Jeri glanced around, not sure if she wanted to see Simone or avoid her. She'd ghosted her since the dinner, unsure what to say.

She checked her watch and climbed the stairs to Cleaves's office. Why did she dislike him so much? Was it because she was compelled to visit him? The guys she knew didn't like or trust shrinks because cops wanted to be in charge and never admit failure. Maybe she felt guilty about her uncharacteristic behavior and didn't trust Cleaves enough to share it with him. More likely, admitting she needed help made her feel weak. Besides, therapy never helped before.

Cleaves opened his office door and extended his hand. "Good afternoon, Jeri."

The gangly man's expression reminded Jeri of the therapist she'd seen briefly after her parents died. He'd meant well, but she'd been raised not to show weakness, so she'd never opened up. And she was young and angry at the world for the unfairness of her situation.

"Right on time. Go in and have a seat." He motioned to the leather recliner she usually chose because it was farthest from him and offered a view of the outside. He flipped open her chart and poised his pen over the empty page. "So, how have you been?"

Jeri bit her tongue to keep from making a smart-assed comment. "I still can't remember anything about the shooting." She waited, not about to volunteer anything she didn't have to.

"Are you still having the dream you mentioned last time?"

"Yes."

More silence ensued as Cleaves slowly placed the pen on the desk and steepled his fingers. "Jeri, I'm still sensing resistance to this whole process. If we're going to make any progress, we have to work together."

Having a stranger rummage through her life and decide if she was fit to return to work didn't feel like working together to her. "I told you I don't remember any more than I did last time I was here. And yes, I'm still having the same dream over and over and over. What else can I say? You're beginning to sound like the internal affairs guys. I'm not hiding anything."

"I'm not suggesting you are." Cleaves's forehead crinkled in that ah-ha kind of expression Jeri had come to dislike. "Why don't we talk about something else?"

She clenched her jaw and dug her fingernails into the leather covering the chair arms. "I have to be here to talk about the shooting, nothing else." The words had a flat finality that made Cleaves's small eyes open a bit wider.

He scribbled for several seconds before asking, "So how is the limited duty assignment?"

"It pisses me off not being on the street. That's how it's going. How would you feel if your whole world was falling apart because of something you can't remember?"

"I'm sure I'd be as frustrated as you are."

The words stunned Jeri because she hadn't expected him to agree with her about anything. For a few seconds, she couldn't think of anything to say. She should probably tell him she was struggling to cope—drinking too much, not sleeping or eating properly, having rough sex with Tom, and thinking about cheating on her girlfriend with yet another woman—but none of that came out. If she told him any of it, she rationalized that her business would be all over the department by morning.

She jumped to her feet, rage and helplessness making her unsteady. She couldn't stand the thought of anyone with the power to judge whether she was fit to return to work. "I can't take any more of this crap. And you can write that down verbatim for all I care. I'm done here."

Jeri bolted from the office and down the exit stairs two at a time. At the bottom, she straight-armed the emergency release bar and barreled into the lobby almost knocking a woman down as she came toward the stairwell. "Who does that pants-shitter think he is anyway?" she mumbled to herself.

❖

Simone stumbled backward from the impact and dropped her lunch on the tiled floor. The paper bag split and ejected a plastic container of pimento cheese that squirted across the toes of her shoes. She glanced at the woman whizzing past and called out, "Jeri? Are you all right?"

Jeri whirled toward her like she was ready to strike. When their gazes met, the anger in Jeri's eyes turned to horror. "I...it's..."

Simone forgot her lunch scattered in clumps throughout the lobby and moved to Jeri's side. She touched Jeri's arm and felt her shaking. "Can I help?"

"I don't think so." Jeri looked around her. "Sorry about the mess."

"Don't worry. I wasn't excited about pimento cheese anyway." Simone carefully guided them toward a more secluded alcove away from the prying eyes of passersby.

"I'm sorry about your lunch too. I'll take care of it...and your shoes." She reached into her Army jacket and pulled out her wallet.

"Jeri, really. It's okay." The pulse at Jeri's throat throbbed quickly, and her skin flushed. She was upset, and Simone had to be careful what she said next. The tiniest thing might elicit an angry outburst or a bout of tears, neither of which should be witnessed by strangers. "I'll call maintenance when we get upstairs. Come with me." Taking Jeri's hand, Simone led her to the express elevator for occupants and keyed her floor.

Once they were safely inside her office, Simone closed the door and pointed to the small refrigerator in the corner. "Help yourself to a bottle of water while I call maintenance." To her surprise, Jeri complied without comment. While Simone completed the call, Jeri paced. Something had set her off, and Simone feared the cause was two floors below in Robert Cleaves's office.

When Simone got off the phone, Jeri said, "Nice office. Comfy furniture, live plants, and soft music. Perfect for head shrinking, right?"

"Helps my clients feel comfortable and open up."

Jeri scoffed. "Maybe you should give Cleaves pointers."

Simone propped on the corner of her desk and studied Jeri. "Do you want to talk?"

"No." Jeri took a sip of water and smiled at Simone, giving her a stare that made Simone's insides melt. "You're just as gorgeous and thoughtful as I remember. I'm sorry we didn't get to spend more time together before…everything. You wouldn't like me much now. Hell, I don't even like me. I'm not sure I know who I am any more. But unfortunately, you're just as much a shrink as the one I just blew off, so I can't talk to you either."

The comment stung after the lovely compliment, but Simone let it slide. Jeri was hurting. "You don't have to say anything. You can wait in the outer office until you're ready to leave if you'd like. You won't be disturbed. I have some time before my next client, if you decide you want to talk." Simone held her breath, hoping the hands-off approach was the right one. She'd had clients wound as tightly as Jeri before, and anything or nothing could send them further into withdrawal and further away from help.

Jeri stopped pacing and looked at Simone. "Okay." When Simone sat down at her desk and pulled a file from the drawer, Jeri added, "Thanks."

"You're welcome." She kicked her stained shoes off and slipped into a spare set she kept under her desk. Jeri watched her movements, and a look of confusion furrowed her brow. Simone wished she could read what was behind those intense eyes.

"That's it? But isn't it your job to make people talk, whether they want to or not?"

"Sounds like interrogation. I only listen when someone decides talking might be helpful."

"You should definitely give Cleaves lessons. He's probably a decent therapist, but we're just not clicking. Maybe it's my own prejudices, who knows?"

Cleaves was less than stellar in Simone's opinion, but he was a peer, and she wouldn't malign him to a client.

Jeri dropped into the chair beside Simone's desk.

Simone pretended to read the client chart she held but her focus was entirely on Jeri. She wanted desperately to say something to help but didn't know her well enough to be certain of the right approach. The small clock on her desk ticked off the seconds. It felt like hours before Jeri finally spoke.

"I'm tempted to stop seeing him, but I signed the paperwork saying I would and that he could report the results of our sessions to the department. What was I thinking?"

Simone assumed Jeri's question was rhetorical and kept quiet to encourage her to say more. She willed her expression to remain impassive, her fear confirmed. Roger Cleaves wasn't working for Jeri. Sometimes doctors and clients didn't mesh, and it was best to refer and move on.

"If I refuse to see Cleaves again, the department can probably demand it, order me to. Do you think they'd actually fire me?"

Jeri's stare burned into Simone. Nothing but the absolute truth would do at this moment. "I don't know, Jeri. I'm not familiar with all the police department's policies. I'd only be guessing, and you don't need that right now. You need answers."

Jeri's eyes pooled with tears and she blinked repeatedly to keep them from spilling over. She swallowed hard and said, "Thank you."

"For what?"

"Your honesty. I haven't gotten much of that lately…or given much I'm afraid."

The pain on Jeri's face was palpable. Simone could only imagine what she'd been through since the shooting. "You've been on the force for a while, so if there's someone you trust, ask them about it. My guess is the department wants the same thing you do, and if their psychologist isn't working, it's in everybody's best interest for you to see someone else."

Jeri rose and moved to the window behind Simone's desk and stared out silently for several seconds. In an almost inaudible whisper she asked, "And what if I can't do it, Simone? If I can't talk to him, or if I do, and it solves nothing? I tried therapy before and felt weak for needing help and like a loser when it failed."

Hearing Jeri speak her name and the agony that accompanied her confession drew Simone from her seat. She almost touched Jeri's shoulders to comfort her but stopped just in time, unsure if she should. She wasn't prepared for the warmth that radiated from Jeri and urged her closer. She took a deep breath and refocused her attention to the more pressing issue. "You've endured weeks of hell since this happened. You can do anything. I know it."

"Maybe." She turned and stepped back quickly. "I didn't know you were so...close." Her pupils dilated and the pulse at her neck quickened. "I should go. You have clients."

"Before you leave, I'd like to say something about dinner the other night, if you don't mind. I left a couple of voice mails."

"Sorry. I wasn't sure what to say, especially after how I left. I've never had much luck with shrinks and finding out you are one was a surprise. If it had just been us, I'd have talked to you about it. I think. At least I would've before...before the shooting. But the pile-on was a bit overwhelming."

"I understand." Simone didn't want to cause any more distress, but she had to make sure Jeri knew she could be trusted. And she needed to be honest without seeming judgmental or disapproving of Megan. She'd been in the middle with couples and friends in therapy before and it never turned out well. "You felt ambushed."

"You think?"

Jeri's tone was harsh, but Simone understood why. "I wasn't there as a psychologist. I thought I was having a nice dinner with my brother and his coworker. When their purpose became clear, about the time you arrived, I strongly argued against blindsiding you and thought I'd gotten the message across. And...I had no idea you were Megan's partner."

"Partner is a stretch. We've only been dating a couple of months and not exclusively. And before you ask, yes, she knows I see other women. I was going to explain our situation to you the next time we met."

"Thank you." Simone recognized her relief at hearing Jeri's relationship wasn't serious and she'd intended to be honest with her. She moved closer, eager for Jeri to believe her. "I don't ambush people, and I certainly wouldn't have done that to you, especially after our coffee chat. As I told you then, I'm often too straightforward. Besides, I was looking forward to getting to know you better."

Jeri avoided eye contact and scuffed the carpet with the toe of her boot. "You understand that can't happen now, not *right* now. I have to get my life back on track."

"Of course." Intellectually, yes, but emotionally, she hoped they could eventually find their way back to each other to explore the feelings she couldn't vanquish.

"I have to deal with Megan. My job is at risk. When the chief releases my name to the public later today, I'll be ridiculed, hounded, and second-guessed until the truth comes out, and I'll have absolutely no privacy. Criminal charges could be filed against me and possibly a civil suit as well. And there's the constant guilt of having killed someone. I've never felt anything so intense and debilitating. I'm just a mess, no good for anyone. Drinking and random sex are my two new pastimes and coping mechanisms. You should stay as far away from me as possible." Jeri headed for the door. "Take care, Simone."

"Wait." She plucked a business card from the holder on her desk and scribbled her cell number on the back. "Take this, just in case." She placed the card in Jeri's hand, careful not to touch flesh, unsure if she'd be able to stop touching her once she started.

"I already have your number. Remember? Arson call? Incident report?"

"Oh, yeah." Simone's mind blanked when they stood so close, and she tuned in to the chaos radiating from Jeri and how drawn she was to her. "Okay. See you later."

Jeri stopped at the door. "Later?"

"The community meeting?"

"Right. And thank you for this." She waved her hand between them. "And for not letting me make a total fool of myself in a public lobby."

When the door closed behind Jeri, Simone said, "My pleasure." A pleasure and a total heartbreak. She'd seen Jeri's desire in the dilation of her pupils and the rapid pulse at her neck, but she prayed Jeri hadn't seen hers. Adding another emotional component to Jeri's life right now would be the equivalent of striking a match near gunpowder.

Chapter Eleven

A fter work, Jeri hurried to the Madison Building for the planning meeting and slipped into a metal folding chair in the community room seconds before the board chairman called everyone to order.

"Good evening and welcome. I'm Ben Brown with the planning board. Our goal tonight is to hear comments and concerns about proposed residential changes in the Fisher Park neighborhood. If you'd like to speak, please give your name and address to the clerk before coming forward to the podium."

Jeri scanned the room and spotted Simone two rows up dressed in a navy blue suit with her hair hanging loose past her shoulders in waves. A residual stab of embarrassment from earlier evaporated in an unexpected surge of excitement. Simone tugged at Jeri in a way no woman ever had, but in her current state of lunacy, she couldn't indulge her curiosity or impose herself on Simone. As if life wasn't lopsided enough, now she had to sacrifice getting to know the only woman who'd truly interested her in years.

"Before we hear from the gallery, I'd like to introduce a few people you should all know and become familiar with during this process." The chairman continued. "Dr. Simone Sullivan, Mr. Tim Adams, Officer Wylder, and Mr. Anton Finelli, would you please stand?"

Jeri hadn't expected to be singled out nor did she foresee her involvement past this evening's meeting, but she reluctantly stood.

The sergeant told her to attend, report back, and keep a low profile, especially today, nothing about long term.

"As director of the City Planning Division, I'll represent the interests of the city in this endeavor. Tim Adams owns Capstone Management Group, and Anton Finelli is the project manager. Dr. Simone Sullivan owns the Madison Building in Fisher Park and will represent both resident and community issues associated with the issue. Officer Jeri Wylder works the downtown area, and the Greensboro PD has assigned her to us until we reach an agreement about how to proceed."

Several members of the gallery began whispering among themselves. They'd probably seen the chief's news conference earlier that named her as the Morehead Avenue shooter. She felt them gawking, wondering, and accusing. Jeri slumped in her chair, wishing she could disappear, but the stares and speculation were just beginning.

Simone glanced back at Jeri and mouthed, *sorry*.

"We also have representatives of the local Preserve Our Historic Legacy group, although I wasn't aware of any historic considerations in this project. Nevertheless, thank you all for being here and for agreeing to work with us."

A steady stream of speakers made their way to the podium to have their say about the possible demolition of the Madison in favor of high-end condominiums. Larry Caswell, a middle-aged gentleman whose mother lived in the building, talked for ten minutes, growing progressively more agitated, and suddenly pounded the podium. His voice was shrill, and his face flushed as he enumerated the ethical, economic, and emotional reasons the development should be blocked.

If things deteriorated further, she'd have to intervene. Caswell struck the lectern again, shook his fist at committee members, and then started toward Mr. Adams, the Capstone owner.

Several people at the back of the room raised *Preserve Our Historic Legacy* banners and chanted. "Save our legacy, save our legacy."

Ben Brown rapped on the tabletop. "Order. Let's have order please. Everyone will have a chance to speak at some point in the process. Please be respectful." He scanned the room and made eye contact with Jeri.

She wanted to disappear in the crowd, but it was her job to keep the peace. But she wasn't supposed to take police action while on administrative leave, and she didn't need any additional attention. Ben Brown kept staring. She finally stood and started forward, but at the same time Simone rose and joined Mr. Caswell at the podium. She glanced at Jeri and shook her head, and Jeri diverted to the back of the room. Simone simply looked at him, intent on what he was saying, until he stopped.

"Larry, you're exactly right," Simone reassured him. "There are definitely many things to consider on this issue, especially as it pertains to the elderly who will be affected. Your mother, the other residents, and I appreciate your efforts. I'm sure the committee will take your concerns into account. Thank you so much for your valuable input."

"Thank you." Caswell inhaled a deep breath, looked around the room, and nodded at Simone before returning to his seat.

How had Simone done that? Maybe it was a certain look she gave him, her tone of voice, or the words she chose. Whatever the method, the effect had been immediate and quite impressive.

A collective sigh of relief sounded throughout the room. The chairman recovered his composure and addressed the gathering. "Considering the hour, I think it best we adjourn for the evening. I realize there are others who didn't get an opportunity to speak, so we'll meet again in two days, same time and place. We're adjourned."

Jeri stood back while the room cleared and endured the sideways glances and whispered comments about her involvement in the shooting. When the last attendees filed out, she headed toward the exit. Simone caught up and fell in step beside her. The combination of her closeness and the memory of her kindness this afternoon sent a quiver through Jeri.

"Sorry you were singled out in there. You must hate that, especially now," Simone said.

"They've all seen the news." She stuffed her hands in her coat pockets, looked into Simone's eyes, and then quickly looked away. With a glance, she could probably read Jeri and lay her bare. "You did a great job calming that guy. It saved a police intervention that would've probably escalated things even more. Thank you. I'll catch you later." She'd exhausted her professional repertoire, and she'd vowed to stay away from Simone, so Jeri started toward the elevator.

"Jeri?" Simone called after her, knowing it was a bad idea but unwilling to stop herself. "Would you like to grab a coffee and talk?" Simone groaned inwardly. She sounded like such a therapist.

"Talk, huh?" Jeri grinned, probably thinking exactly what Simone hoped she wouldn't. "Nothing has changed. I'm still a mess, and you're still a shrink. And you're disregarding my very sound advice about keeping your distance."

Jeri was right. She should stay away, but the truth was she didn't want to. "I'd just like a cup of coffee and a few minutes to wind down. It was intense in there." She nudged Jeri with her elbow. "And I wouldn't mind some company." In addition to her strong attraction to Jeri, Simone felt compassion for her situation, so she should be able to support her as a friend. Her personal and professional boundaries were clear, and if she remembered her training, a casual friendship should be possible. Maybe she could even help Jeri tangentially.

"Okay to the coffee, but I'll pass on the talk, Doctor. I've had enough for one day."

They walked to Hot Shots, a twenty-four-hour coffee shop down the street from the Madison. The café provided a cozy oasis for the daily bustle that thrived on legal maneuvers and business deals, but after five, when the businessmen and lawyers departed downtown, the small establishment once again became a place of refuge for a quiet rendezvous.

Simone recognized the attendant from a couple of nocturnal visits when she couldn't sleep. The twentyish college student sported blond hair with orange highlights and a big smile that revealed a tongue stud to match the one protruding from the left side of her nose.

Simone and Jeri placed their orders and the young woman returned with their coffees and a big smile for Jeri. She set the cups in front of them, lit the candle in the center of their table, and winked. "Enjoy, Jeri. It's on the house."

"Thanks, Billie, but I'll pay when we leave." Jeri raised the steaming mug to her lips and blushed as she looked out the window.

"I think you'd be used to that." Simone nodded toward Billie.

"What?"

"You're an attractive woman, but you don't see it, do you?" She couldn't keep her mouth shut around Jeri, and the fact that she didn't see the effect she had on others made her even more charming. "Could be that cop thing that makes the girls gaga." She sipped her coffee and tried to think about something besides how vulnerable and adorable Jeri looked in her white shirt and fatigue jacket. "I shouldn't have said anything."

"You warned me you were blunt." The blush on Jeri's face deepened as she purposely avoided Simone's stare.

"It's good for business. Sorry if I was too personal. I meant it as an observation." The last thing Simone wanted was to make Jeri more uncomfortable or feel she was being analyzed.

"You're right. I don't see myself that way and I'm surprised when others do." Jeri rolled her coffee cup between her palms, still avoiding eye contact.

She hadn't anticipated Jeri's shyness, and the innocence of it tugged at her emotions. Simone felt her nurturing impulse rise to the surface along with something more primal.

"Thanks again for taking care of that guy tonight. You were awesome. I don't need to be in the spotlight any more right now. You're kind of my shero."

"My pleasure. So, would now be a good time to ask a favor?"

"Probably the best time. Don't want your shero cred to run out." Jeri gave her a broad smile, and Simone almost swooned.

She cleared her throat and refocused. "Some of the Fisher Park residents wanted me to ask if you'd support our request to form a Neighborhood Watch Association. They want to be more proactive."

Jeri stared at her coffee cup. "That's not really my—"

"Your area of expertise. I understand, but they consider you part of our community. You work the area and always stop to talk with folks or check things that seem out of the ordinary. They trust you, Jeri."

"Even now?"

Simone nodded. "They have questions but are willing to withhold judgment until the case is resolved."

"I can't make any official or public statement or even be too visible until I'm cleared."

"I understand. We're not asking you to wave the flag and lead the march, just recommend us if anyone asks. We're pretty much organized already."

Jeri studied Simone for several seconds. "Fisher Park is my area, and sooner or later I'll be patrolling it again. A little good will can only help in the future. Okay."

She raised her cup in a toast. "Thank you. We appreciate it." Simone finished her coffee, signaled for a refill, and waited until Billie left. "About dinner the other night. Do you mind if I say one more thing?"

Jeri grinned. "Can I stop you?"

"Probably, but I need to be clear." When Jeri nodded, Simone continued. "In Megan and Andy's defense, I believe they had good intentions." Jeri finally looked at her, and Simone saw her anger ignite and regretted bringing the subject up again.

"Maybe, but the way to help isn't through deception, well intentioned or otherwise."

"You made that clear to everyone, and I commend you for keeping your cool. I'm not sure I could have under the circumstances." Simone paused and stared at Jeri letting the statement register. She wanted Jeri to know she recognized her discomfort and honored her restraint.

"Thank you. That means a lot. And about earlier today, in your office. I appreciate what you did for me. I used to be able to control my emotions...until the shooting. Add Cleaves to the mix, trouble at home, and...other stuff and my boiling point is a lot lower. I apologize for involving you in my drama."

"No apology necessary." In professional mode, Simone would've asked about Jeri's lack of control—how she coped, if she was safe, responsible, and the other things complicating her life—but Jeri wasn't speaking to her as a client. And she'd already admitted to drinking and random sex as her new pastimes. "You needed a few minutes to decompress. I'm glad I was there, but I'm not sure I'll ever get the orange pimento cheese stain off my shoes." Some of the anger on Jeri's face faded and a smile tugged at the corners of her mouth. "Have you decided what you're going to do about Cleaves?"

"I'm stuck with him whether I like it or not. But I just don't understand how—" Jeri stopped abruptly like she'd almost revealed something significant. "I can't talk to you about this. You're in the same building, and as far as I know the two of you are close professional colleagues. For the record, I'll keep seeing him until I'm cleared for duty."

Torn between a desire to help Jeri cope with Cleaves and professional ethics preventing her intervention, Simone took a slow sip of coffee. "If things get too unbearable with Cleaves, please promise me you'll find someone else. You've been through enough already."

"Promise. Will you promise me something?"

Simone wanted to say anything but edited herself. "Probably."

"Be careful until this issue with the Madison is finalized. As you saw tonight, tempers flare quickly. The residents don't want their homes destroyed, the developer only sees profits, the city's pushing revitalization downtown, and POHL jumped on the bandwagon for the media exposure."

"I'll be careful. Believe it or not, Officer, I've had some experience with conflict."

Jeri smiled and her face glowed. Her demons were buried for the moment, but their talons lay dangerously close to the surface. Her emotional swings, self-critical comments, and references to risky behavior worried Simone.

She wanted to discuss Jeri's care with Cleaves, but it would be unethical, and he would not appreciate her input. All she could do was listen, keep Jeri's confidences, and support her as best she could. She was having enough difficulty maintaining a healthy distance until the shooting ordeal was over and Jeri was free again. Never in her life had she been so conflicted or so certain she needed to do more.

"Hello? You still here?" Jeri asked.

"Sorry." She quickly changed gears and returned to a question she'd let pass earlier. "When we came in, Billie said your coffee was on the house, but you insisted on paying. Why?"

Jeri shrugged. "I don't take gratuities."

"Not even a cup of coffee?" Simone was familiar with the general belief that cops accepted discounted or free items and services gladly and without question, almost as a right.

"Nope. Not a cup of coffee, meal, doughnut, or anything else. I've always worked for what I have and accepting gratuities feels wrong, especially for someone in a position of public trust."

Probably most officers on the force would disagree with Jeri and argue that a cup of coffee or a sandwich occasionally did no harm, but Simone respected Jeri's position and adored her even more for it. "Now, you're my shero."

Jeri nervously fiddled with the handle of her coffee cup. "Since we're being honest, and we both know this can't go anywhere, I'd like to tell you something."

Simone's stomach clenched the way it did when a client was about to tell her something important. "Okay."

"I liked you the moment we met. We had instant chemistry, but the other feelings I had surprised me. I'm sorry I didn't have a chance to learn more about you before everything turned upside down." Simone started to speak, but Jeri raised her hand. "Don't feel like you have to say anything. I just wanted you to know where my head was before it got scrambled."

Simone's pulse quickened and her defenses flared. In the carefully protected recesses of her heart, a glimmer of something familiar and essential threatened to expose itself. She warred between the desire to embrace Jeri and tell her how she felt and an urge to run away. She chose moderation and reached across the table, but Jeri's cell rang.

She looked at the number and said, "Excuse me. I have to take this."

Saved by the bell. She'd almost blindly followed her desire into a bottomless well. When Jeri walked away, Simone could hardly breathe but felt more alive than she had in years. When was the last time she'd been so emotionally present? Kay. Her body tingled with sensitivity so strong that it felt unfamiliar and frightening.

Denial was no longer an option. Jeri's admission scorched a path to her heart and unearthed the truth she'd tried to bury since they met. They had a connection, and they both felt it. *You can't do this, Simone.* Reason spoke sense. Her heart did not.

CHAPTER TWELVE

For the first time in almost three weeks, Jeri felt good about something she wanted to do—stay in this quiet, intimate coffee shop with Simone, continue their conversation, and find out if she shared her feelings—but her phone rang again. Megan. She offered Simone a weak smile, rose from the table, and hit the answer button. "Hello?"

"Did you forget I wanted to talk tonight?" Megan asked.

"I'm sorry. I'll be home in a few minutes."

She disconnected and walked up behind Simone at the counter where she was accepting change from Billie. Jeri inhaled the light scent of gardenia in Simone's hair and it reminded her of carefree summer days as a child at the lake with her parents. She reached around Simone, grazed the sleeve of her jacket, and placed her money on the counter. "Thanks, Billie."

Simone turned, and their bodies were inches apart. Heat swelled between them, and for several seconds neither moved. Jeri's mind snapped a burst of images. Simone's bright green eyes and the slow dilation of her pupils. Her full, inviting lips. The spatter of reddish-brown freckles across her slightly upturned nose. When Simone's face turned crimson and her breathing quickened, Jeri backed away. She'd seen the desire as plainly as if Simone had spoken it.

"I should...go. It's getting late." Simone looked toward the street and tugged nervously at her suit jacket.

"May I walk you home?"

"Thanks, but don't you have something to take care of?" She nodded toward the phone Jeri still held in her hand.

"Yeah, right. I'll see you at the next meeting. Thanks for listening. Who knew I actually wanted to talk?" Jeri winked and hurried home.

Before she reached the front door, it swung open and Megan stood with arms crossed over her chest and a scowl on her face.

"I told you we needed to talk, and you stay out half the night. What's up with that?"

"Again, I'm sorry. Can I change before we get into this?"

"No, I want to say this. Right now."

Jeri slumped into her leather recliner. She'd never seen Megan so determined and direct. "Go ahead."

"I'm moving out. Breaking up. I've had enough. You're never home, and when you are, we're always fighting. I didn't sign on for whatever's going on with you."

Megan stood in front of Jeri, her stare unwavering, with no tears or screaming, just simple facts. The words registered, but Jeri felt only a twinge of guilt. Totally opposite to the flood of emotions earlier with Simone. She waited for the sadness, but it didn't come. Her girlfriend was leaving, and she offered no argument or consoling words.

"Don't you have anything to say?" Megan dropped to the floor in front of Jeri's chair and grabbed her knees. She dug her fingernails into the sides of Jeri's legs and scratched at the cotton fabric of her slacks. "Can I get *some* kind of reaction please?"

"I…" Jeri struggled for something that wouldn't sound cruel, untrue, or patronizing and totally blanked.

"It's like you've sealed yourself off from your emotions. You never talk to me about anything—the shooting, our relationship, your parents' deaths, and not the other women—"

"Other women." At least it didn't come out as a question. They both knew she'd been screwing around.

"At least you don't deny it."

"I thought you understood we weren't exclusive. We talked about it."

"Seriously? You'll agree to anything when you start dating someone, but as time passes, you expect your girlfriend to stop fucking around and commit."

Jeri reached for Megan's hands, but she brushed her off and stood. "I'm sorry, Meg. You deserve better."

"Damn right I do."

"What about your stuff?" Jeri tried to show concern in the only way she could muster.

"That's so typical. Skip over emotions, straight to logistics. My *stuff* is gone. It's not like there was much anyway." Jeri rose from the recliner and started toward Megan, but she pressed her hand against Jeri's chest. "We both know it's for the best."

"Meg, I'm so sorry. I didn't mean to hurt you. I don't know what else to say."

"Take care of yourself, Jeri, and for God's sake get help before you self-destruct."

Megan was gone before her last statement registered. Two minutes ago, Jeri had a girlfriend. Yesterday, she'd thought she was a sensitive lover but learned she could enjoy and inflict pain during sex. Before the shooting, she had a career she loved. Now, her entire life was uncertain. Self-destruction certainly seemed her pattern at the moment.

She was exhausted but knew she wouldn't sleep. Her go-to was the bar, several drinks, and sex. Then she thought of Simone. Maybe something more tame tonight. She glanced out her bedroom window toward Mrs. Doyle's house. The light from a lamp beside her favorite recliner in the den still cast an orange glow through the curtains. A few minutes later, Jeri knocked lightly and heard Toto bark before Mrs. Doyle opened the door.

"Well, come inside, lass. I'm glad to see you."

She hugged Jeri against her petite frame in a familiar way that always made her want to laugh and cry at the same time. "Are you sure it's not too late?" She scooped Toto up in her arms and patted his head.

"Since neither of us is sleeping, I'd say it's the perfect time. How about a wee dram of Jameson's and a natter?"

"I'll take the whiskey but pass on the chat. I'm talked out tonight." Jeri plopped into one of the chairs at the two-seater kitchen table with Toto in her lap while Mrs. Doyle poured the drinks into shot glasses. She sported her signature blue cotton scrubs from her nursing days and brushed at white hair that rested against her head in tight, short curls.

"There we are, lass. Drink up."

She settled across from Jeri, sipped her whiskey, and waited. Mrs. Doyle was very good at waiting, and Jeri always crumbled under her patience. Maybe she did want to talk after all. Mrs. Doyle listened better than anyone she'd ever met—except possibly Simone, too soon to tell—and asked pointed questions without judging. "Megan's gone."

Mrs. Doyle nodded and after a few thoughtful seconds asked, "Was it your night terrors or…something else?"

Jeri glanced at her but couldn't hold her clear-eyed stare. "Probably both. I've been seeing other women, but she knew we weren't exclusive from the start."

"What a woman knows and what she really *knows* can be entirely different."

"Truth." Jeri gave Toto a final scratch behind the ears and placed him on the floor. "How did you know I was having nightmares?"

"Oh, lass, I may be old, but I'm neither deaf nor blind. These past weeks have changed you from the grounded, focused woman I met when you moved back here." She pointed to the windows that faced Jeri's house. "And my windows stay open year-round. Your screams are fierce."

"I'm sorry."

Mrs. Doyle patted her hand. "No need to be sorry. You're going through a rough patch. Screaming must be part of your healing process." Maybe it was the lilt of Mrs. Doyle's rich Irish accent that made everything she said sound comforting.

"You might be hearing a lot more of it. I used to think I managed life pretty well. My parents' deaths, finding a job, paying my own bills, dating, and finally saving enough to get my family home back." She downed the rest of the whiskey with one gulp and coughed. "Now, I'm sidelined at work, could lose my job entirely, possibly my freedom, and my chances of finding a woman to share my life seem less likely every day. And killing someone put a whole new spin on things. It's like a piece of my soul is missing. I can't imagine how his family must feel. How do I come back from that?"

"One second, minute, hour, and day at a time. It's a weighty burden you're carrying, lass. It'll take some doing, but you're up to the task. Do you think life is a bed of roses for me?" She chuckled and refilled their glasses without asking. "Look at me. I'm old, widowed, retired, overweight, gray-haired, and arthritic." She pointed to herself with each enumeration. "Any of that sound easy to you?" She broke out in a belly laugh, and Jeri joined in until her sides ached.

"Fair point. In other words, nix the self-pity?"

"My da used to say a person could get through anything with the right set of skills. It's not about using fists or angry words, but what's in here." She placed her wrinkled hand over her heart. "Inner strength comes from stepping up and standing up for what's right. And you know what's right about your situation."

"But I don't remember everything, Mrs. Doyle."

"Memory is a tricky thing. Sometimes it does us a favor by hiding things we're not ready to face. Other times, it masks the truth we're desperate to know and just torments us for sport. Don't try so hard, just live your best life every day. The memories will return. And in the meantime, don't stop looking for your life partner. She's out there, probably looking for you right now." She sipped her whiskey and winked before adding, "And always keep the four-leaf clover I gave you handy. A little luck of the Irish never hurt."

Jeri stifled a yawn and rose to leave. "I'm not sure how, but you always make me feel like I can do anything, Mrs. Doyle."

"'Cause you can, lass. You absolutely can. Sleep well." She followed Jeri to the door and gave her a hug. "Thanks for the visit."

Jeri wandered through her house peeling off clothes as she went. Nothing appeared disturbed. Megan was gone, but the house looked the same, almost as if she'd never been there at all. A few empty hangers and shelves in the bedroom and bathroom closets served as the only witnesses to her sporadic occupancy.

She conducted her nightly ritual of window and door checks before heading into her bedroom. She slid the Walther from her ankle holster and placed it beside the bed. Working in plain clothes on limited duty didn't require a weapon, but she felt naked without one and always carried off-duty, just in case. She stripped down to a T-shirt and boxers and paced aimlessly from room to room until she ached with exhaustion and fell across the queen-sized bed.

Her arms and legs were heavy. Thunder and lightning. She couldn't see or hear. Nausea churned her stomach, and she shivered from the cold. The strong stench of stale beer and urine assaulted and threatened to choke her. A figure lunged toward her, but fog clouded her vision. The piercing scream of a woman's voice. "He's got a knife."

"Stop!" Jeri jolted awake, tumbled off the side of the bed, and slammed her cheek against the hardwood floor. Her T-shirt and shorts were soaked with sweat. She lay still, her pulse hammering, and tried to separate truth from fantasy. Someone charged her…and a witness, the woman…or was it only a dream? It seemed familiar but not. She sighed in frustration.

Jeri turned on the bedside lamp and looked at her face in the mirror. Her cheek reddened and started to swell. She shuffled to the kitchen, wrapped ice in a dish towel, and pressed it against her face. The kitchen clock read six fifteen.

Unwilling to give up on sleep completely, she stretched across the sofa and closed her eyes. *Flap, flap, flap.* What was that noise? It sounded like a curtain blowing and slapping in a brisk wind. She'd checked all the windows and doors before bed. *Flap. Flap.* She crept through the darkness to the front window and peered out. A sea of posters and banners blanketed her front yard. *Stop police shootings. No justice, no peace.* The chief wouldn't have released her address in the news conference, but somebody certainly had.

Sleep wasn't happening again. She changed into sweats, packed work clothes in her backpack, slipped out the back door, and walked to a place she'd be safe from dreams and protestors.

Chapter Thirteen

Jeri left the main lights in the police gym off, preferring the shadows cast on the faded gray walls from the streetlights. The eerie shapes suited her mood and the current status of her life. She stepped on the treadmill and slowly increased the speed. One foot in front of the other. One second at a time, just like Mrs. Doyle said. Easy. Mechanical. She concentrated on the process and waited for the zone to blank everything but the burn in her body. Breathe and run. She settled into the rhythm and the euphoric runner's high. Finally, bliss.

"Yo, you spending nights here now, Wylder?"

Fluorescent lights flickered on overhead, and Jeri stumbled on the treadmill, grabbing the side rails to keep from face-planting. Damn. Her respite had been too brief and not nearly restorative enough. She stopped the machine, stepped off, and glared at Randy.

He filled the doorway with his six-foot-three frame and broad shoulders. "What?"

His white-toothed smile shone from a face with permanent five o'clock shadow, and his neatly trimmed dark hair and olive complexion reminded her of an Italian playboy. She never told him that because he'd wear it like a badge of honor.

"Fuck, who got hold of you?" Randy's upbringing hadn't included many niceties, and his New Jersey accent was thick and harsh. "That's a fucking shiner on your cheek there, partner. You ain't been that messed up since I whipped your ass in rookie school."

Jeri touched her swollen cheek. She'd completely forgotten about her little mishap. "You wish, but if you must know, I fell out of bed."

"More like hottie Megan kicked you out." Randy grinned wickedly.

"You're half right. She left."

"You mean she *left* left as in vamoosed for good?"

Jeri nodded.

"Now? When you're going through all this crap? Why?"

Jeri didn't want to talk about *all this crap* or Megan right now, but Randy was her zone partner, and they shared stuff. "Exactly that, I think. I've been a mess lately. Nightmares. Drinking too much. Screwing around. Never home. Can't really blame her."

Randy placed his mitt-sized hand on her shoulder and squeezed. "That sucks. Sorry, pal."

"Thanks. The workouts help after riding a desk all day. And I don't want to get flabby like you." She poked his stomach. Solid muscle.

"Don't hurt yourself." Randy laughed, pulled off his jacket, and started on a lat machine. "I hope you ain't sweating over these investigations. It was a righteous shoot." She raised her hand to stop him, but he said, "I know. We can't talk about it. I'm just saying, focus on your life, not this shit. It'll pass."

Hearing Randy say the shooting was justified made her breathe a little easier. "Where's your boyfriend?"

Randy glanced at the clock on the back wall. "Late, as usual."

She toweled the sweat from her face and headed toward the showers.

"You probably had no choice but to cap that fruit loop. I've seen guys through this before. It'll work out. Finish the mandatory psych stint, tell IA what they want to hear, and give yourself time."

Was Randy implying she *did* have a choice in the shooting? But he'd just said it was a righteous shoot. He'd been her assist that night, but was he actually there when it happened? She wanted to ask but couldn't. Maybe she was just paranoid.

"The shrink's doing you right, ain't he? 'Cause if he ain't, we'll have a word of prayer."

Jeri hesitated. She trusted Randy as much as anyone, but something held her back. As much as she hated the thought, she'd stick it out with Cleaves long enough to get cleared. She'd keep him on the shooting track, out of her personal life, and her temper under control.

Cops didn't trust easily, and criminals, lawyers, and shrinks were at the top of the list—an us-against-them mentality that seemed pervasive. She'd made headway with the first two, but shrinks were in a category all their own until she found one she believed in.

"That's right, you can't talk about it," Randy said. "The investigation's still going on. You never know what those IA fucks are going to say. Nobody can blame you for being paranoid. It's easy to Monday-morning quarterback from the comfort of your recliner the decision an officer makes in the field. Fuck that 'when-in-doubt-don't' bullshit they teach in rookie school. They weren't there. But don't worry. You'll come out of it just fine."

There it was again, the implication that she shouldn't have fired. "Maybe, but I'm totally in favor of not shooting anyone if I don't absolutely have to. Let internal affairs bring all the questions they want, and I'll stand by the truth...whenever I remember what it is. And if I was wrong, I'll own it. I just hate not knowing...and waiting."

Randy completed his reps on the lat machine and moved to the leg press. "Yeah, but you got that whole amnesia thing going on. They have to get the officer's statement. Forget about it. Let's talk about something more interesting."

"Have you had a chance to look for the woman who was there that night?"

Randy didn't look at her, and Jeri had a feeling it was intentional. "I can't get close to this thing, Jeri. If the detectives or IA find out I'm snooping around the case, I'll be on leave, and I can't afford that right now. My mom is in a bad way, and I'm working every hour of extra duty I can get to keep her round-the-clock care."

"Do you at least know if anyone's tried to find her?"

Randy shook his head. "Sorry, pal."

Thanks for nothing. "I need to shower." She grabbed her gym bag, bumped into Carl on his way in, and ducked into the adjoining women's locker room to shower and dress for work.

The personnel sergeant, a Barney Fife clone, stepped in front of each officer in the lineup formation with a sharp click of his heels. He performed daily inspections even though most of the officers wore plain clothes. When he reached Jeri, he stopped.

"Damn, you look like death riding a crippled spider. Bloodshot eyes, bruised cheek, and I bet not very well rested. You FFD?"

"Yes, sir. Fit for desk duty, just a little sleepy."

He lingered in front of Jeri, and she felt her anger rising. What the hell now? Could he tell how much she hated this assignment, how it drained her energy and self-respect? She understood the purpose of administrative duty and psych evaluations after a shooting and agreed with them in principle, but now it was personal and made her feel weak and fearful. The sergeant completed the inspection, and Jeri started to her desk.

"Wylder, with me." He motioned Jeri into his office and closed the door.

She held her breath and waited for the next round of fresh hell.

He hitched his belt up and looped his fingers over it. "Wylder, you didn't ask for this assignment like everybody else in the division, and you're probably going nuts as a desk jockey. How'd you like some fresh air occasionally?" Jeri's expression must've been comical because the sergeant laughed. "I take it that appeals to you?"

"Yes, sir, it does." Jeri felt the closest thing to joy she'd experienced in weeks.

"Good, now here's the deal. The rookie class is starting field exercises today at various locations throughout the city. You remember those don't you?"

"Yes, sir, mock crime scenes, vehicle stops, felony arrests, and firearms training." Jeri's attention didn't waiver as he continued.

"You'll ferry equipment back and forth as needed by the instructors. I'll give you a list each morning of supplies and locations. The time between deliveries is your own as long as you're available by radio and don't take any official action. Don't make me sorry for this."

"No, Sergeant." She grabbed his hand and pumped. "And thank you so much, sir. You have no idea how much I needed this." The bit of freedom felt like reclaiming part of her life.

He pulled his hand free and gave her a list of the day's activities. "Here are your car keys." He waved her toward the door. "Get busy." Jeri picked up the vehicle, collected the listed equipment from supply, and completed the delivery before noon. She couldn't believe her luck, the first she'd had in a while. The assignment was like permission to take charge of her life again. The missing pieces of the shooting puzzle were locked in a vacant house and inside her, and she needed to find them.

The abandoned house on Morehead Avenue looked the same, a run-down drug user's paradise. She parked in front, and several college-aged kids ran like cowards from the battlefield. A homeless man on the front porch chugged wine from a bottle hidden in a paper bag. She leaned across the steering wheel, and the Walther strapped to her ankle rubbed against the side of her leg, the rough handle comforting.

Jeri closed her eyes and focused on what she knew about the incident. The call, her route to the scene, arriving, and searching the house. A light. Urine and beer. A male and female subject. Cold. Moonlight. Her pulse quickened. Then what? Too many missing parts.

Flashes of her nightmares returned. Chilling wind, thunder and lightning. Foul odors. A figure charging her. Fog. And a woman screaming about a knife. Jeri shivered despite the close, heavy air inside the car. She rolled down the windows and inhaled deeply.

Jeri smelled the remnants of a wood fire nearby. Fire and smoke. She tensed and cold sweat bled through her Polo shirt. She willed herself to remember but only grew more anxious and unsure. She started the car to leave, but a gust of wind swept through the window bringing a stronger scent of burning. She opened the vehicle door and vomited her lunch on the pavement. The answers eluded her, but they were here, and she'd return until she ferreted them out.

The remainder of her day was a blur of comparisons between her nightmares and the images she'd flashed on at the scene. Today seemed like a breakthrough, but why? She hadn't gotten any definitive answers, but she knew she was on the right track.

After her shift, Jeri considered going home, but the empty, unwelcoming house held no appeal. She diverted to her other home, the Cop Out. She felt Casey watching her as she downed a second drink at her usual corner stool.

"All right, Jeri?"

"Sure."

"Sell that somewhere else. I'm not buying. You're headed down a one-way street without headlights. Let me get you some coffee. I've got something I'd like to run by you."

Jeri didn't look up from her drink. "You trying to handle me, Casey?"

"Busted. I'd just like to see you live a long and happy life. How about that coffee?"

"Fine." Jeri fidgeted with her keys, sipped Casey's strong coffee until her insides calmed, and scanned the bar customers. She recognized many of the women from various branches of the criminal justice system. They often socialized in the same circles, but recently Jeri chose to distance from the group because of the inevitable questions about the shooting.

Big plasma televisions mounted above opposite ends of the bar suddenly blared to life as one of the patrons jabbed the volume control. A scene that Jeri recognized all too well flashed across the screen, and the caption read, *Victim's Family Files Suit against Officer*.

The news anchor announced, "The Vanoy family filed a civil lawsuit against the Greensboro Police Department and Officer Jeri Wylder for the shooting death of Calvin Vanoy." The club quieted. "Mr. Vanoy was killed three weeks ago while spending time with his girlfriend inside an abandoned house. The suit claims Officer Jeri Wylder shot the unarmed man without provocation. The Greensboro Police chief said the incident is under investigation and the officer is on administrative leave pending the outcome."

Shouts of *bullshit* and *fuckers* echoed through the club. Several women Jeri recognized from the courthouse looked sympathetically in her direction and raised their glasses. She welcomed the support of peers who assumed the facts and imagined them encircling her like protective armor. The comfort of your clan. For a few seconds, she didn't feel so alone.

A woman next to Jeri at the counter turned to her and said, "Damn, wouldn't you hate to be that officer? As if criminal and internal investigations aren't bad enough, now he's got the pressure of a civil suit and all the press that goes with it."

"Shut the fuck up." Casey gave the woman a hard stare.

Jeri clenched her fists until the nails dug into her palms. Visions of lawyers placing liens against her family home she'd recently reclaimed and driving away in her car flashed before her eyes. They could levy civil penalties against her in the millions of dollars and garnish her wages for years, if she still had a job.

Her next thought brought another crush of emotion. What about Vanoy's family? Her potential losses were material, tangible, and couldn't hold a candle to the grief associated with the death of a loved one. Drink might temporarily dull the pain of ending a life, but it never completely washed it away.

She grabbed her car keys from the bar and hurried outside praying for relief from her rage and grief. Jeri pounded the steering wheel with her left hand, slammed the car into first gear, and peeled out of the parking lot, fishtailing across the center line. When a police cruiser pulled out behind her, Jeri choked with emotion.

Blue lights flashed in the rearview mirror, and Jeri cursed under her breath. Everybody in the Greensboro Police Department would know she'd been stopped after the officer called in her personalized tag. An arrest for DWI would officially end her downward-spiraling career in one swift motion. Maybe that would be best.

"Ma'am, would you step out of the vehicle please," the female voice requested.

Jeri recognized the officer as a recent academy graduate who still moved with the stiffness of a rookie uncomfortable with her authority. She'd also seen her a few times at the bar, always alone. Jeri rehearsed the series of sobriety tests that must inevitably follow. She glanced at the officer's name tag, Thompson, and stepped to the designated spot between the two vehicles. Jeri handed over her license and waited for the test instructions.

Officer Thompson took Jeri's license and compared it to the driver. A sudden look of recognition crossed her face. "Jeri Wylder…

aren't you..." An awkward silence fell between them. Protocol dictated that Thompson process the stop as if Jeri were any other citizen, but professional courtesy was learned in the early stages of training. If the situation wasn't serious or criminal and you could help a fellow officer, you did.

"Why don't you let me take you home? I'll pull your car back into Casey's lot and keep an eye on it." Thompson's expression showed no signs of judgment.

Jeri relaxed only slightly, afraid she'd sway, but inside she was shaking. "You should take the appropriate action, Officer. I don't want any special treatment."

"I don't have anything but an infraction for screeching tires, and I have discretion with those violations."

Thompson's tone remained professional, but Jeri felt her compassion. She swallowed hard and blinked back tears. "You know I just left the bar."

"All I smell on your breath is Casey's strong coffee." Thompson gave Jeri's license back and motioned toward the patrol car. "Let's get you home."

"Thank you, Officer Thompson. I really appreciate this." She shook the officer's hand. "I owe you one."

"You're welcome. With everything going on right now, you don't need any more trouble. Besides, you helped me during rookie school. I'll never forget the extra time you took after class to give me practical demonstrations of takedown techniques."

"Glad I could help." On the ride home, Jeri remembered Mrs. Doyle's advice and was pretty sure her behavior tonight didn't qualify as living her best life.

Chapter Fourteen

Simone punched the lobby button on the office elevator, the doors rattled shut, and she grabbed the metal rail, waiting for the jolting start. The old contraption had been an original feature of the building and was never upgraded. A smooth ride to the lobby was always a hit-or-miss proposition, but the car rasped to a halt, the door opened, and Robert Cleaves entered.

"Good evening, Robert."

"Sullivan."

He barely spoke to her since she'd bid against him for his coveted police contract, but she still made the effort to be congenial. "I hear your practice is going well." She fudged but it worked, and he finally looked at her and puffed out his chest. Appealing to his ego always elicited a response.

"Yes, business is very good. I'm even considering taking on a partner. The police department work is proving much more time consuming than I imagined and more lucrative as well." He grinned smugly, no doubt gloating about outbidding her for the contract.

Simone glanced at the floor indicator, praying the damn car would get to the lobby before she said something unfortunate. She shouldn't ask but had to know. "I imagine police officers can be challenging."

He tsked. "Of course, but nothing I can't handle. It's all about the approach."

And his approach with Jeri wasn't working. She wanted to ask him to be patient with her and build trust slowly, but medical professionals' egos were as deeply engrained as cops' and treading on them was fraught with danger. "Glad to hear things are going well for you."

He gave her another smug grin and said, "Who knows, Sullivan, if you play your cards right, I might even ask you to join my practice as a *junior* partner."

Simone met his gaze and started to fire back, but mercifully, the elevator door screeched open and Cleaves strutted off. "Pompous..." She struggled for the right word. "Pants-shitter." Jeri's description seemed perfect at the moment. She had no idea what kind of clinician Cleaves was but arrogance looked ugly on everyone.

She left the building and practically ran to Andrew's house, partially to expel some anger and partially because she hated being late. He was making dinner, his famous lasagna. She opened the front door, and the smell of baked deliciousness greeted her.

"Andy, if that's not done, I'm going to cry." She hugged him and looked around for his wife, Gwen.

"On a trip. The glamorous life of a flight attendant. I needed company, and no one's better than my baby sister. Sit." He nodded to the banquette overlooking the backyard. "You look like you could use a drink or three."

"You have no idea. I'll pour. You dish. And in honor of your luscious Italian concoction, I'll even drink red wine instead of whiskey."

"It is the perfect pairing."

She slid a glass from the wine rack, filled it, and took a gulp. "Great. Can I help?"

"Relax. I'm good."

She settled by the window while Andrew scooped lasagna, tonged salad, and plated them carefully like a *Top Chef* contestant. "You really love cooking, don't you?"

"If I wasn't a successful attorney, and if it didn't support Gwen in the manner to which she has become accustomed, I'd be a chef." He presented her with his creations.

"Beautiful. May I please eat now?"

"If you don't, I'll know something is seriously wrong with you." He slid in across from her and waited.

Simone took the first bite of lasagna and hummed. The perfect balance of pasta, cheese, and meat. Andrew grinned broadly, experiencing his food through watching others eat before tasting it himself. "This is beyond delicious. You definitely got all the cooking genes."

Seemingly pleased with her response, Andrew dug in. "Not bad." He clinked his glass against Simone's and switched topics, a talent he'd perfected as a teenager to throw their parents off the track of their sibling misadventures. "Remember Jeri, the cop, Megan's partner from dinner the other night?"

Simone almost choked on a bit of vinaigrette dressing. "Yeah, why?"

"Megan broke up with her. Jeri's in big trouble. She's having nightmares, drinking, and refusing to get serious help. Megan couldn't take it anymore."

"Is she terribly upset? How long were they together?"

"Actually, I think she's relieved. They'd only been dating a couple of months and never exclusively. Megan is a good person, but she's young and dreams big. A police officer never quite measured up to her image of a life partner, in my humble opinion."

"She told us about Jeri's problems before dinner, so what convinced her to leave now?"

"Jeri has apparently been sleeping around, something that happened before the shooting, just not as often."

Simone's gut knotted. She didn't like imagining Jeri having sex with strangers or anyone else. She flinched from the realization and reached for her wine. "But if they weren't exclusive…"

"Yeah, but you know how new couples always hope to change each other."

When had she become so possessive, or was it jealous, of Jeri? "That's unfortunate." What could she say without betraying Jeri's confidence?

"What was that?" Andrew studied her as only a parent, partner, or sibling could, intuiting things she tried to hide.

"What was what?" She took a big bite of lasagna and chewed slowly.

"You flinched the way you used to when Mom or Dad said something you didn't want to hear. What did I say?"

"I didn't flinch." But she couldn't meet his gaze.

"Look at me, Simone."

The silence grew and became awkward and telling. She swallowed hard and tried to steel herself against a stare that always pried the truth from her. When she made eye contact, Andy's expression was pure love and compassion. She fought back tears.

"You have feelings for Jeri." He reached across the table and cupped her hand. "Oh, my sweet sister."

She shook her head. "I didn't say that. I empathize with what she's going through. I met with a client just before coming here in the same situation, PTSD, family and relationship issues. It's just really fresh in my mind."

"But you've always compartmentalized work so it doesn't drive you crazy. Jeri means something to you. How did this happen? You've only met once, right?" His voice was soft as he gently stroked her hand. He would've been an excellent therapist too.

She blew out a long sigh and sipped her wine before answering. "You have to swear what I'm about to tell you will never cross your lips to another soul, even Gwen."

"I swear."

She told him the entire story—the chance meeting the night of the attempted arson, coffee at Green Bean, the community meeting, coffee afterward, and finally the run-in after Jeri's session with Cleaves. "The first two happened before I knew she was seeing Megan and certainly before the shooting. I clicked with her, and I'm certain it was mutual. Do you know how long it's been since I was seriously interested in anyone?"

"Kay in college. And we both know how that turned out."

"Yes, my parents and best friends conspired to banish her from my life." Most of the time, Simone was sure she'd dealt with her feelings, but occasionally, they reignited with a vengeance. "I'm sorry. That's not fair."

He gave her a sympathetic pat on the hand. "You're entitled. That whole situation sucked. I'm just sorry I wasn't around when it happened."

"Yeah, I'm blaming it on you because you were supposed to have my back." She refilled their glasses and smiled to reassure him that she was kidding. "Seriously, I should've stood up to them."

"I'd hate to see anyone try to bulldoze you now. What are you going to do? About Jeri?"

"I won't, can't, do anything. I feel like such a fraud. I have feelings for her. What they are, I'm not sure yet. The last thing she needs right now is more uncertainty and emotional upheaval in her life. And intellectually, I know she's unavailable in her current state. I want to help her but can't be anywhere near her case, except as a friend. It's a no-win situation for both of us."

"I wish I could help, sis."

"You have. Saying some of this aloud helps. I barely mentioned to Charlotte and Erica that I thought Jeri was cute and they went into super-sister protective mode."

"Got to love those Alpha Delta Pi girls." He ducked his head to make Simone look at him. "Have you forgiven them?"

Simone studied her wine glass. "Forgiven, yes. Forgotten, never. I know they've learned their lesson, and our friendship is strong, but I won't allow them to interfere again like they did with Kay."

"You're not that young, impressionable kid anymore. If I can do anything, I'm here."

"Just don't tell Megan about this conversation. She might get the wrong idea."

"I won't. It's too bad you can't help Jeri though," Andrew said, "but I understand conflict of interest and professional ethics."

Simone offered a weak smile. "I can't help everybody." At least she had somebody who understood and supported her. Did Jeri?

On the way home, Simone called the Fisher Park Community Watch group and found a willing partner for a late-night walk.

Their patrols didn't often go so late, but she wouldn't sleep if she went home, so might as well do some good. Bonnie, the schedule organizer and an empty-nest single mom, met her on the corner across from the Madison Building.

"Thanks for doing this, Bonnie. I'm a little keyed up and needed some air."

"I'm a night owl, so anytime."

They walked and talked sporadically about the zoning issue, next week's schedule, and Bonnie's children and grandchildren. The combination of fresh night air, exercise, and listening to someone's problems that she didn't have to solve helped Simone relax. Before she realized, a couple of hours had passed.

"Well, that's me done," Bonnie said as they approached her house. "You okay to get home from here?"

Simone grinned and pointed. "I'm right there. Don't worry."

"Oh, yeah. I forgot. Thanks for the walk."

Simone waited until Bonnie closed her front door before she crossed Fisher Avenue toward home. She passed the Leland cypress Jeri had jumped out of the night they met and smiled. If only the shooting hadn't happened, she and Jeri might be in a much different place. Simone thought she heard rustling in the nearby bushes and stopped. "Hello? Is anyone there?" What was she expecting, Jeri to pop out of the tree again?

She scoffed at her skittishness and started walking again, but someone grabbed her from behind. A man pinned her arms at her sides and placed a gloved hand over her mouth, stifling her scream.

"Shush," he whispered close to her ear. "Stop these fucking patrols and leave the Madison building, all of you, or you'll regret it." She squirmed, trying to get free or at least get a glimpse of his face, but he held her tightly against his broad chest. "Nod if you understand."

She struggled again, but his grip tightened and pressed. She grew lightheaded, saw spots, and felt herself losing consciousness.

"Do you fucking understand?" he growled.

She barely nodded before he shoved her to the ground. She went down in the grass on all fours, choking and pulling for air.

"I'm watching you."

When Simone caught her breath, she looked around for her assailant, but he was gone. No one had heard or come to her aid. He could've killed her in the front yard. She finally stood and ran to her building, checking behind her to ensure he wasn't following. She locked her door and collapsed on the sofa, her body shaking.

Simone dug her cell out of her pocket and scrolled to Jeri's number. She wanted desperately to call, to have Jeri beside her for security and comfort. Her finger hovered over the number, but she couldn't do it. Jeri had enough on her plate right now, and Simone refused to add to her load. She'd just file a report, for all the good it would do, add another statistic to the crime rate, and try to forget.

CHAPTER FIFTEEN

Jeri rolled over in bed and buried her head under the pillow. Was someone yelling in front of her house? Probably another dream. She checked the time—seven in the morning—and snuggled back under the covers and closed her eyes.

"No justice, no peace. No justice, no peace."

Damn. Protestors. Too close. After Officer Thompson brought Jeri home last night, they'd shared a plate of Mrs. Doyle's bangers and mash with mushy peas before stuffing the posters and banners from her front yard into the trash. She thought that was the end of it, but the protestors were committed.

She crawled out of her warm bed and peered between the slats of the shutters. At least twenty people marched back and forth on the sidewalk waving signs and chanting. A couple of officers stood to the side monitoring but not interfering. Her neighbors stared and kept a safe distance. She couldn't blame them.

Yesterday had been a day from hell. Her name released to the press, and her address leaked by someone. Megan left. Her nightmares worsened. She was being sued for something she couldn't remember, and she'd been stopped by a rookie for acting like an adolescent. Add all that to her other problems and she was doing just great. She had to get out of this house for a while because being cooped up just led to circular thinking with no good end. And she needed to be clear-headed before the community meeting tonight.

She dialed Randy's cell and paced restlessly until he answered. "What's up?"

"I need an extraction. Two dozen yahoos are protesting in front of my house, and my car is at the Cop Out. Can you give me a lift?"

"Heard a rookie stopped you last night. Lucky she didn't haul your ass in for drunk driving. You were drunk, right?"

"Randy."

"Too soon?"

"Are you going to help me or not?"

"Be there in fifteen. I'll park on the street behind your house."

"Roger that." Jeri took a quick shower, dressed, and sprinted across her backyard to meet him. "Thanks for this. I'm sure you've got better things to do."

"No problem. I was on the way to the drug store anyway. Took Mom to the doctor again yesterday, and he upped her meds. I'm thinking about moving her in with me, but she wants to stay in her own place. Plus, my apartment is upstairs. Not good for someone with COPD."

"Sorry, pal." He was quiet for several seconds and stared straight ahead. When she looked over, his Adam's apple worked up and down as he fought back tears. "I'm here if you need *anything*."

"Thanks, Jeri. The doctor says she's going to need more help as her breathing worsens and her organs shut down. That kind of care ain't cheap."

"We'll figure something out even if I give you all my savings." She punched him lightly on the shoulder and added, "There's always a GoFundMe page."

"Yeah, right, like I'd take charity. I'm Italian. We're resourceful." When they rounded the corner close to Jeri's house, Randy gave the protestors a disdainful glare.

"Don't say whatever you're thinking. They believe in their cause as strongly as we believe in ours, and they have a right to be here. We fight for that every day."

"Yeah, but I'd like to see one of them make a split-second decision whether to shoot or be shot."

"They didn't choose our profession. We did." Sometimes Randy's comments rubbed her the wrong way. Often, she challenged him. Sometimes she let it slide and felt worse afterward. When Carl joined the force, she'd considered letting the two of them team up since they were so close. They'd be perfect together, or they'd be a nightmare. Maybe after she was cleared, she'd finally do it. "You can just drop me in front of Cop Out. My car's in the back."

"Any word on the investigations yet?"

"Nope."

"And you really can't remember anything?"

"Once I get to that last room, it's a complete blank. It's frustrating as hell."

Randy glanced at her. "How much longer do you think they'll let this go on? Won't they have to clear or charge you eventually?"

Jeri's breath caught in her throat. "What do you mean charge me?"

Randy parked in front of the club and turned to her. "Look, partner, I'm not trying to scare you, but the mayor and the chief have reporters on their asses daily. Politicians crack under public pressure like rotten eggs. The district attorney could file criminal charges now, make you defend yourself, and toss it to a jury. And then there's the civil case. You need to make some kind of statement soon and stick with it."

"I can't do that until I know for sure what happened." She was having trouble keeping up with Randy's well-meaning advice lately. One minute he sounded supportive, and the next, she wasn't so sure. She wanted to ask him what he remembered, what his body camera showed, but was forbidden from talking about the specifics of the case with anyone except the investigators and Cleaves. She wasn't allowed to view her own camera footage until the internal investigation concluded, nor inquire about the ongoing criminal investigation or any of the physical evidence since she was the subject of both inquiries.

"Whatever you say. By the way, did you hear about your girl getting clocked last night?"

"Megan?"

"No, your other girl. That doctor at the Madison. Saw it in the daily briefing."

Jeri tensed, tried to act cool, and failed. "First, she's not my girl. What the hell happened? Was she hurt? Did we catch anyone?"

Randy raised his hands. "Don't shoot the messenger. She was walking home, and some schmuck grabbed her and told her to leave the Madison. He scared her pretty good but no serious injury. She didn't get a look at the guy, so no arrest."

She reached for the doorknob, eager to leave before Randy saw the panic she was trying to hide. "Thanks for the ride."

"Watch your six and let me know if you need another extraction."

The entire day was a blur of supply runs, endless paperwork, and checking the clock too often to concentrate. She considered texting to check on Simone but had to see for herself that she was unharmed. Why would anyone attack her, and what were the threats about? Was it random like the unexplained crime spree in the area or something more focused?

At four forty-five, she bolted to the meeting. The small community room of the Madison was filled to capacity again. Jeri searched the crowd for Simone but didn't see her and took a seat at the back. She replayed both of Randy's bombshells and grew more anxious and uncertain. Had he actually suggested she make up a version of events to satisfy detectives and IA and conclude the investigations? She wouldn't do it, no matter how long it took to get her memory back.

And where was Simone? Had she been more seriously injured? Jeri sat through the meeting, half-listening and waiting for Simone. As the final speaker rose to the podium, Simone entered through a side door. She looked gorgeous in skinny jeans and a silk blouse a shade darker than her strawberry-blond hair, but her lips were tight, her jaw clenched. Jeri could almost feel the tension in her body.

The POHL rep concluded, "High-rise condos and history don't mix."

"This building is not historical." Mr. Finelli's voice carried an Italian-born accent tempered by years of Americanization. "There is no such evidence. We need this project downtown. It will provide retail and residential opportunities. This helps all of us."

Mr. Caswell rose from his seat and yelled at Finelli. "But money shouldn't always take precedence over the welfare of residents and the community. What about the older citizens who live in the Madison Building? Are you going to pay to relocate them to other affordable housing?"

"I'm sure the building owner will make some sort of arrangements," Finelli countered with a dismissive wave of his hands.

Caswell's face glowed red as he pumped his fist in the air. "Of course, you don't care. As long as the project goes ahead, you make money."

Simone stood and moved to Caswell's side. "We're all concerned about our homes. I have someone researching the historic angle, and nothing will be decided until I receive that report. I have the city manager's word. In the meantime, my attorney is working with the building inspectors to confirm that the Madison is safe and in no way hazardous to our residents. Any statements to the contrary are totally false and unfounded. If I won't sell, the city can't condemn my property merely because a company wants the land for development. That's not how this country works."

Caswell scoffed. "You'd probably get a kickback from the developer to sell us out." Caswell moved closer to Simone. "Watch yourself."

Jeri's muscles tightened at the implied threat. Was he the one who had assaulted Simone last night or paid someone to do it? If so, why would a resident threaten the landlord who was trying to help him? She started to get up.

"I'm sorry you feel that way, Mr. Caswell," Simone said. "I take great pride in my property and its upkeep and have no intention of selling, but I'd gladly relinquish the dubious honor of representing our residents to anyone who'd like to take it on. You perhaps?"

The committee chairman motioned for silence and wiped sweat from his forehead with a shaking hand. "Calm down. I think everybody recognizes the various issues involved here. Please take a copy of the survey before you leave. Fill it out and return it to the planning office before our next meeting. Thank you all for coming. We're adjourned."

The attendees collected surveys and then filed out more slowly than usual. Finally, Simone emerged at the rear of the procession, stared straight ahead, and passed Jeri without acknowledging her. Maybe she was preoccupied about the meeting or about her assault. Jeri debated letting her leave. She'd told Simone to stay away, and violated her own rule once, but had to know if she was okay.

"Simone?" Jeri called.

Simone kept walking.

"Wait up." Jeri ran alongside. "Didn't you hear me calling?"

Simone finally looked at her. "Oh my God. What happened to your face?" She almost brushed Jeri's cheek but drew back before making contact. "You and Megan didn't—"

"God no. A stupid accident." Jeri wiped absently at her swollen cheek. "Are you okay? I heard about the assault last night."

"I'm fine. More shaken than hurt and obviously distracted. I'd just left Bonnie across the street, and he came out of nowhere and grabbed me from behind."

"Just thinking about someone manhandling you makes me feel sick. I'll find out who did this. I promise." She studied the smooth skin of Simone's face and neck for bruises. "Are you sure you're okay? I heard he got rough with you."

"Jeri, I wasn't hurt. Really. I'm more concerned about the recent increase in crime and false reports to code enforcement. Someone is trying to make me sell the Madison to clear the way for this lucrative high-rise. The developer is probably involved, but I don't know who the muscle is behind the intimidation."

"We'll get to the bottom of it. Trust me." Jeri stepped closer, hesitated, and then reached out. "May I hug you?"

Simone smiled and nodded. "Is it for me or you?"

"I'm guessing both." Jeri drew Simone into her arms for the first time and almost groaned at how right they felt together. Simone was soft where Jeri was hard, rounded where Jeri was flat, and petite against Jeri's broad frame. Perfect. She'd wanted to hold Simone since the day they met, but the timing had never been right. And it definitely wasn't now, standing in a public place surrounded by strangers. Her life was still a chaotic mess of past, present, and future problems all related to the shooting. She memorized the press of Simone's body and the mixture of peace and arousal she felt. "Thank you." She hoped Simone couldn't see how much she wanted and needed her.

CHAPTER SIXTEEN

The moment they touched, Simone realized she shouldn't have hugged Jeri. They joined so perfectly that no space existed between them. Jeri's full, moist lips were inches from hers, and Simone saw the hungry look in her eyes and the nervous flutter of her eyelashes. Her gaze exhumed desires Simone shouldn't be having and made her want more.

She forced herself to release Jeri, stepped back, and scanned her faded jeans, plaid flannel shirt, and old Army jacket. More rebel than cop, but the vulnerable look on her face melted Simone. Who wouldn't be attracted to her? It was perfectly natural and perfectly innocent. "Thanks for your concern...and the hug."

"Okay. I mean, thank you too." Jeri shuffled her feet nervously. "Guess I'll go. You'd probably like to be alone...without me hovering."

The perfect out. Simone should take it. She'd resolved to keep her distance from Jeri until the redevelopment meetings were over and then there would be no reason for them to see each other again until...until what? The shooting case was over? Jeri wanted to see her socially? She tried not to look at Jeri, but she was weak. She blurted, "Not really."

Jeri grinned. "How about a walk? Sometimes the empty streets help clear the mind."

Simone was exhausted, but Jeri looked like she needed to talk. "A stroll would be nice."

They fell into a slow, relaxed cadence along Elm Street through the center of town, stopping to window shop at things neither was interested in.

"This is my zone, when I'm working. I used to get out and walk until I got a call," Jeri said wistfully. She surveyed the street ahead of them, her eyes constantly in motion.

"You don't do it anymore?" The question caused the slightest hesitation in Jeri's step. "I'm sorry. You don't have to answer that if you don't want to."

Jeri cocked her head to one side and gave Simone a sideways glance. "How *do* you do that?"

"Do what?" Simone stopped.

"Tell so much about a person from the simplest thing? You did it with the guy at the first meeting and then again just now with me. You detect emotions from the slightest facial tic or body movement. It's feels, I don't know, intimate somehow."

Practicing her craft was intimate, which was one of the reasons she loved it. Psychology gave her permission to delve into and examine emotions without experiencing them herself. It was safe and immensely rewarding. "Years of practice I guess. It's part of the job, like yours."

Jeri nodded. "And you're right. I don't walk here anymore. It's too quiet, which reminds me I can't remember. Enough about me. Why were you late tonight, if you can say?"

Simone accepted Jeri's need to redirect the conversation. "I'm concerned about a young man recently home from active military duty who's suffering with PTSD. He has all the classic symptoms, and his family is very worried. We've done some work together, but he's regressing. I'm really afraid for him." Jeri pushed her hands into her coat pockets, and Simone feared the topic was too close to the bone. They walked in silence for several minutes.

"What kind of PTSD symptoms?"

"Insomnia, nightmares, restlessness, excessive drinking, and hypervigilance. Generally reckless behavior."

Jeri's pace slowed, and Simone adjusted to stay in step.

"Are those pretty common symptoms? I mean are they the same for everyone?"

Simone deliberately kept her answers generic, hoping Jeri would find something useful. "Symptoms vary. A person could also suffer fatigue, headaches, short temper, anxiety or panic attacks, depression, lowered sex drive or promiscuity, guilt, fear, anger, denial. The list goes on."

"Are all those reactions considered normal?" Jeri kept looking straight ahead.

"They're not unusual. The trauma is often so overwhelming to the senses that the mind and body find manageable ways to deal with it or avoid it."

Jeri stopped in front of a small art gallery and stared at the display. Simone sensed her emotional turmoil and respected her need for silence. When Jeri wiped a tear from the corner of her eye, Simone wanted to reach out so badly she ached, but instead pretended she hadn't seen the reflection in the shop glass.

After a few seconds, Jeri started walking again at a more leisurely pace. "Are these people totally broken?"

The agony in Jeri's voice caught her off guard. Jeri seemed to search Simone's face for answers she could understand and apply to herself, but she wasn't ready for the entire truth. Simone reached for something nonthreatening to relieve her discomfort.

"They're not broken at all, just in need of a little assistance." She slid her arm through Jeri's as they walked, inched closer, and lowered her voice as if the decreased volume would soften her words. "Once they acknowledge they need help, they're halfway home."

"You must be an excellent therapist because I feel your compassion, but I'd never want that particular look directed at me."

"Which look?"

"Pity. It would destroy me if someone I loved looked at me that way. I had enough pity after my parents…I wondered if anyone would ever see me as whole again."

"Sometimes looks don't accurately portray what the sender intended. Besides, I find it hard to believe anyone would pity you, Jeri Wylder. You're a strong, independent woman, and the mind is amazingly resilient."

Jeri's blue eyes sparkled, and she flashed a brilliant smile that Simone knew she'd replay often. "That's good—for them, I mean." "Yes, it is." She waited a beat before circling back to the thought Jeri purposely didn't finish. "You mentioned your parents." "They died in a plane crash my last year of college. I never bring up the subject because it's taken too long to say that sentence without breaking down, but the way you look at me makes me actually *want* to share. Must be that shrink thing."

"I'm so sorry for your loss, Jeri." Simone squeezed Jeri's arm and paused a second before continuing. "I can't imagine how difficult that must've been for you at such a young age."

"It was a challenge, but I managed." She stared straight ahead.

"Do you want to talk about it?"

"My father dreamed of becoming a pilot all his life. When he finally got his license, he couldn't wait to take my mother up. I would've been with them that day but was cramming for midterms. Dad lost his bearings in a sudden thunderstorm while trying to land at a private airstrip in Guilford County. They died instantly."

"Oh, Jeri."

Their arms were still joined, and Jeri tightened her grip. "If that wasn't bad enough, the owner of the plane sued my parents' estate. He took our family home and cleaned out their bank accounts, all for one crappy airplane and what he called future loss of business."

"Adversity can bring out the best or worst in people. Was there no other family to help out after your parents passed?"

"Not really, at least none that came forward after the accident or…funeral."

"How did you manage? You were so young." Simone's gaze met Jeri's and held. She genuinely wanted to know.

"Fortunately, I was in my senior year, so I worked to pay for the last semester and then got a full-time job as a club bouncer. A friend of mine, Casey, owns the Cop Out downtown and had a small apartment over the bar I rented for next to nothing. I finally bought the family home back a few years ago. Anyway, Casey's retired NYPD and encouraged me to give Greensboro Police a chance. And here I am."

"You've done well for yourself. You should be proud. I'm sure your parents would be."

"I like to think so."

"Did you talk to someone after your parents died, a therapist, to help with the grief?"

Jeri hung her head and slowly pulled away from Simone. "Yes and no. I was raised to believe asking for help was a weakness, so I resisted for months and tried to work through the grief on my own. When I finally did go see someone, I couldn't open up. I kept hearing my father's voice and feeling like I was betraying everything he'd taught me. And I couldn't really afford the rates, so I stopped."

Simone wanted to hug Jeri, console and protect her, but sensed Jeri couldn't take her kindness at the moment. Her history certainly explained why Jeri wasn't comfortable asking for help. She hadn't had the skills or trust to do the work when she was young so therapy had failed her when she needed it most. Simone stopped walking and took Jeri's hands. "I'm so sorry all of that happened to you."

Jeri stared over Simone's shoulder as if gazing into the past. She waited to see if Jeri would offer anything further, but when it became obvious the time for revelation had passed, she reluctantly withdrew her hands from Jeri's and waved toward her building. "This is my stop."

"I had no idea we'd walked so far." Jeri glanced longingly from Simone to the building and back. "Can I—?"

"Can you what?" Simone's heart rate quickened with the possibility of what Jeri was about to ask and the fear of her answer.

"Never mind, it's late. Thanks for the walk. Sleep well."

Only when Jeri disappeared around the corner did Simone's urge to call after her also vanish. Jeri's deep, almost chronic suffering wrenched at Simone's need to help and at her heartstrings. It was her personal weakness and her greatest source of professional accomplishment but combining the two was asking for disaster for both of them. She had to keep their relationship on a strictly friendship level.

In the safety of her condo, she pushed her emotions aside and reviewed Jeri's story from a more analytical perspective.

Orphaned in her early twenties, Jeri lived on her own without the help and support of family. Some young folks would've developed a rebellious attitude and sizeable chip on their shoulders, but not Jeri. Stripped of her family and finances, she found respectable employment, eventually regained her family home, and made a new life for herself. Remarkable woman.

She crawled in bed and hugged a pillow to her chest. Jeri's touch stirred more than physical need. She'd ignited a hunger for intimacy that Simone hadn't wanted since Kay. The pain of really loving someone had been too devastating once. Could she open up again? Did she want to? She closed her eyes and willed the memories and feelings of the past into the present. But when she fantasized of deep kisses, intimate touches, and desire, this time she wasn't with Kay. Jeri inhabited her thoughts and dreams, mined her passion, and freed her body and spirit.

Simone jerked awake, rolled onto her back, and ran her hands across the cool bedsheets. Only a dream. Triggered by Jeri's touch. The psychological significance was clear—a reminder of what she'd been missing, or avoiding, all these years.

And a simple hug catapulted Simone into an emotional dilemma of epic proportions. Why now? Why Jeri Wylder? An old proverb her mother used to recite came to mind: What I'm afraid to hear I better say first myself.

CHAPTER SEVENTEEN

Coward. Jeri left Simone standing in the street last night, unable to ask for what she wanted—to go upstairs and continue their conversation. Had it been Simone's comments about PTSD that made her seem not so crazy, her own admission about failing at therapy, or Simone herself that accounted for Jeri's calm and peaceful feeling? But calm and peace eventually vanished, and anxiety and turmoil took over. The inventory of reasons she shouldn't get involved with Simone scrolled through Jeri's mind again as she drove back to the office after her final pickup that afternoon. She was almost at the station when the call was dispatched.

"Car Eleven-fourteen, respond to the Madison Building at Elm and Fisher, reference possible shots fired on the fourth floor. Male complainant in 4A."

Randy acknowledged the call, and Jeri executed a U-turn in the middle of the street. If Simone was in trouble, Jeri was going. Regulations be damned. She'd check things out and be gone before Randy arrived. If not, he wouldn't report her.

She clutched the steering wheel and skidded to a stop in front of the building. The windshield of Simone's vintage Mustang parked in the lot shimmered with wet graffiti. Vandals, hopefully nothing more. She bolted up four flights of stairs, noting firecracker residue near each exit door. On the top landing, Jeri took a deep breath and looked through the glass window into the hallway. The door to 4A was farther down to her right and slightly ajar.

Jeri unholstered the off-duty weapon from her ankle, eased open the stairwell door, and slipped into the hall. Doors on either side. Her breathing quickened. She listened and then edged forward, shivering as cold sweat prickled her skin. With her free hand, she nudged Simone's door wider. "Greensboro Police, is anyone home?" No response.

She stepped inside, pointed her weapon, and scanned the large open living space. Her hand shook and her pulse pounded in her ears. *She couldn't hear.* No. That was before. Crouching behind the kitchen counter, she listened for voices or movement. She wiped sweat from her eyes and willed her hand to steady. *Wait for backup.*

What if she had to fire her weapon? Could she do it again? Could she shoot another person if faced with the same situation again? Would she freeze or simply give up? She shouldn't be here, but Simone could be in trouble. She peered around the counter and spotted a glass block wall at her eleven o'clock.

A shadow crossed behind the enclosure. Had she imagined it? Jeri partially stood, her legs wobbly, and edged closer. Another flash of movement. She flattened against the partition and slid around the corner into a bedroom. Clear. Ahead, another damn door.

The last door. *Why can't I remember what's behind the last door?* "Stop it. Focus on now," she muttered under her breath. The next few feet toward the door stretched like miles in a minefield. When she was within striking distance, she leveled her gun and raised her leg to deliver a kick.

The bathroom door suddenly opened, and Simone stared down the barrel of Jeri's Walther .380.

"Oh my God!" Simone raised her hands, her face ashen.

Jeri collapsed against the glass wall and slid to the floor. "Oh fuck, fuck, fuck." She dropped her weapon in her lap and buried her face in her hands. "I almost killed you."

Simone stooped beside her and lightly touched her shoulder. "I don't know about that, but you sure gave me a fright. Are you okay? You're shaking."

"I saw…that night…damn. I shouldn't be here." She tried to get up, but her legs wouldn't hold her. She slumped again. "I'm sorry."

"Shush." Simone cupped Jeri's chin and searched her face. "Your pupils are dilated and your pulse is racing. Concentrate on my voice and try to steady your breathing."

"Wh—what's wrong with me?" Jeri pulled for breath.

"Possibly a panic attack or anxiety from the memories. Just breathe."

Simone's soothing voice and the motion of her hand working small circles on Jeri's back slowly calmed her. "I need to get out of here before another officer arrives. I'm not supposed to take any law enforcement action while I'm on limited duty."

Simone stood, held out her hands, and pulled Jeri to her feet. "Then why are you here?"

"I heard the call of shots fired and had to see if you were okay." She motioned toward the front door. "I announced myself, and when you didn't answer, I came in." For the first time, Jeri really saw Simone. Her white tank top and cut-off jean shorts covered little. "You're..." she waved her hand absently.

"Yeah. I was about to shower and go out for dinner." She pointed back toward the bathroom. "Did the call come from here?" Simone glanced around the flat nervously as if the situation suddenly registered. She'd been busy taking care of Jeri.

"Yeah. Male caller, and your front door was open when I arrived."

"I'm certain I locked it when I came home. If someone called from here, they broke in."

"We'll file a report." Jeri turned to leave. "I really need to go."

"Greensboro Police officer. Anyone home?"

"Damn."

Simone grabbed her arm and led her toward the front door. "We can say you're visiting, if you'd like. I don't want you to get in trouble."

When Randy entered the apartment, his gaze went first to Simone's scantily-clad body, and a grin formed at the corners of his mouth. Then he did a double-take at Jeri. "What's up, partner? What're you doing here?" The glimmer in his eyes told her that Randy had jumped to a very wrong conclusion. "Uh...never mind. I see."

Jeri rolled her eyes and eased Randy back toward the hallway, closing the door behind them. "No, actually, you don't. Let's talk out here." She appreciated Simone's offer to cover for her, but she wasn't going to lie.

Before she could clarify the situation, Randy said, "So, this is why Megan broke up with you? If you ask me, it's an improvement. That broad is hot."

"Stop thinking with your dick for a minute. She's Dr. Simone Sullivan. We're on the downtown redevelopment committee, and nothing's going on but that. Got it?"

"I'm right, and you're in denial. It's a tough time to be thinking about love when the rest of your life is in the crapper." Randy meant well, and his amateur psychology was frighteningly accurate, but she wasn't about to admit it. "Whatever you say, Jeri. So, why *are* you here? I didn't see a meeting going on." His eyebrows arched in that annoying fashion that told Jeri he wasn't buying a word she said.

"I was on my way back to the station from my delivery run for the recruit class and heard the call. Tempers have been pretty high about demolishing this building to make way for condos, and Simone was assaulted the other night, so I wanted to check it out." Randy's expression didn't change. "I was practically in front of the place. Give me a break, will you?"

"All right. I won't report you if you promise to give me all the juicy details when you nail this one." He grinned and clapped his hands together. The muffled slap of leather echoed down the empty hall.

"Shut up, Randy, and get to work." She wasn't sure why his snide remarks bothered her because they shared most of their conquest stories, but the way he'd looked at Simone earlier made her want to throttle him. "She'll need a burglary report, not just vandalism to her car, and a CSI. Somebody was actually inside her place and used the phone." She opened the door and motioned Randy back inside. "I saw firecracker residue in the stairwell as I came up, probably the shots fired part of the call."

"Okay, we'll handle it from here if you want to take off."

"I'll stay until you finish."

"Whatever."

Randy completed the case report, and a lab technician processed the scene. When he returned to give Simone the incident number, he said, "Let me know if you have any more problems, Ms. Sullivan. I'll be on duty all night." He handed her his card, winked at Jeri, and left.

"Friend of yours?" Simone asked, closing the door.

"Randy and I go way back. He won't be a problem."

"Then what was that little tête-à-tête in the hallway when he arrived?"

"I couldn't lie to him." She blushed and hoped Simone didn't notice. "My partner has an overactive imagination where women are concerned, so I needed to set him straight about why I was here. He thought you were the reason Megan left me."

"I see." Simone kept her tone and expression neutral, careful not to let on that she knew about the breakup from Andrew. Had Jeri said something to Megan about the attraction between her and Jeri, or had Megan just sensed it? Were they that obvious? Was Jeri really *that* interested in her? "And did you...set him straight?"

"Yeah. Megan and I had problems before you and I met. She left because I've basically been a dick since the shooting...and because I apparently wasn't clear about our relationship."

"In what way were you unclear?" She'd watched Jeri conduct her focused sweep through the loft and had engaged in several candid discussions with her and couldn't imagine her actions, professional or otherwise, being unclear. She moved with the assurance of years of training and experience, but she also consumed risk like fuel. The thought gave Simone chills.

"I told her at the beginning we weren't exclusive. She thought I'd change."

"I see."

"Careful, Dr. Sullivan, you sound like a therapist. You must be over the shock of someone invading your home."

"I'm not sure about that. And the thought that someone has a key to my place is chilling."

"You should definitely get the locks changed ASAP." Jeri stuffed her hands in her pockets and rocked back and forth.

Simone recognized Jeri's nervousness and wanted to help her relax and maybe talk about her earlier incident. "Can I get you anything, a glass of water, a drink? I could use a stiff shot of whiskey."

"If you have a Coke, that would be great. I'm still in the city vehicle."

While Simone fixed drinks, she watched Jeri taking in the loft, looking at pictures and picking up knickknacks. *Her* personal items. This was the first time they'd been alone and not in a professional setting. Simone's stomach fluttered. She liked seeing Jeri here and imagining them together lounging on the sofa, preparing a meal together, and then…She stopped before they made it to the bedroom.

"I love your place. It's light, airy, and not too cluttered," Jeri said. "Sort of my style."

Simone handed Jeri her Coke. "Thanks. Have a seat." Jeri settled at one end of the small sofa, and Simone took the other. "I can't thank you enough for checking on me. After the assault the other night, I've been a little jittery."

Jeri placed her glass on the side table, wiped her hands on her jeans, and stared off in the distance for several seconds before speaking. "I'm sorry about my behavior earlier…when I came in. I think I had a partial flashback, if that's even possible. If you'd been an armed suspect, I'd probably be dead. I froze."

Simone set her drink down and edged closer. "But you rebounded quickly. You were alert at all times, heard and responded to my voice, and recovered. That shows strength and courage."

"Maybe. It's hard to face people these days and even harder to figure out what they're thinking. Friends look at me differently. My peers think I'm weak and are afraid they'll be me one day. Or maybe I'm imagining all of it, being paranoid."

"You'll get through this, Jeri. Trust me."

Jeri glanced over, her gaze settling on Simone's lips. "You probably won't believe this, but I actually do trust you, at least more than anyone else in my life right now. Sometimes I'm not sure what is real, but you're consistently honest and uncomplicated."

"I wish." Simone said the words without thinking. She was anything but honest or uncomplicated when it came to Jeri. Her feelings were scattered and conflicted, and when they were close, she had to force herself not to touch Jeri.

Jeri grinned. "What does that mean, Doctor?"

She gulped the whiskey and welcomed the heat. "You know exactly what I mean."

"Tell me. Please? I need to know my instincts about at least one thing in my life are real."

Jeri stared at her with those blue-gray eyes, and Simone was lost. Her brain yelled *run*, but her heart cried *tell her*. "I'm attracted to you, Jeri. I want to touch you so much it hurts, but I can't. We've agreed to keep our distance. You're in trouble, and I can't help. And even if I could—"

"I don't want you like a shrink." Jeri scooted closer on the sofa until their legs pressed together. "I want to kiss you, hold you, and make love to you."

Jeri trailed her fingers up Simone's arm and over the naked patch of skin between her tank top and cut-offs, sending shivers through her. "Jeri, please." Her chest ached and she pulled for breath. She wanted the same things, but the timing was wrong.

Jeri leaned closer and kissed Simone's ear. "Let me."

Her tenderness called to Simone, urging her to give in. And then her mind kicked in. "We shouldn't do—"

"Don't talk."

Without warning, Jeri kissed her, and Simone responded hungrily. She fumbled to set her glass back on the table and entangled her fingers in Jeri's hair. Her skin burned, nipples hardened, and her sex throbbed. She wanted this so much, needed it, but not now. *Think, Simone.* Jeri wasn't ready, and if Jeri wasn't, she couldn't be either. "I can't."

"You can." Jeri pulled Simone onto her lap and buried her face in Simone's breasts. "I need you so damn much right now." She grabbed Simone's ass with both hands and tugged her closer. "You want this too. I feel it every time we're together. Be honest."

The intensity and urgency of Jeri's actions stunned Simone, and she pushed away from her. "Stop. I said no."

Jeri tensed, gasped for breath, and pulled back.

Simone sensed the dark, lost side of her trying to take control. This was another Jeri, not the one she'd first met, not the one who'd kissed her so tenderly just seconds ago.

"I'm really sorry. I got carried away. Forgive me?" She scanned Simone's body as if checking for signs of physical injury. "Did I hurt you?"

Simone cupped Jeri's face. "No." She waited until Jeri made eye contact. "This, whatever just happened, is not okay. I asked you to stop."

Jeri stood and stared at the floor. "I'm so sorry. I have no excuse. I'd never do anything without your consent."

"I want to believe that because you're going through a lot right now, but we need to talk about—"

"Hey, open up. We're starving out here." Erica's voice sounded outside the door along with insistent pounding.

"Damn," Simone muttered. "I forgot about dinner."

"I should go." Jeri hurried to the door, opened it, and waved Charlotte and Erica inside.

"Well, hello, tall, dark, and butch," Charlotte said. "Are you joining us for dinner?"

"No," Jeri said, trying to get around them in the doorway.

Erica blocked Jeri's path and studied her before giving Simone the once-over. Simone knew exactly what she was thinking and prayed she wouldn't say it. "Booty call?"

"Seriously, Erica? My place was burglarized, and Jeri came to check on me."

"Oh, my God." Charlotte hugged Simone. "Are you okay?"

"Fine. Just a bit of drama and inconvenience." She waved toward the black fingerprint dust on everything. "Jeri and I are on the redevelopment committee."

"Maybe you should invite her to the Guilford Green gala fundraiser," Erica said, "as a reward for taking such good care of you. She wouldn't have to donate. We should appreciate our public *servants*."

Simone cringed at Erica's emphasis, and her emotions of the afternoon bubbled over. "Shut the hell up, Erica." She turned to Jeri. "I'm really sor—"

"I'm the one who's sorry. Enjoy your dinner." She shouldered past Erica out the door.

Simone couldn't be in the same room with Erica right now or she'd say something else she'd regret. "I'll be ready shortly. Help yourself to drinks." She hurried to her bedroom, desperate for a few minutes alone to think.

She'd crossed a line with Jeri. The passion of their initial kiss burned a hole through Simone's defenses. Pretending her feelings were friendship didn't hold up any longer. She'd seen a glimpse of Jeri's tenderness, strength, and dominance, and it piqued her desire.

CHAPTER EIGHTEEN

The following afternoon, Simone locked her office door after the last client left, kicked off her shoes, and propped her feet on the desk to return calls. She scrolled past Erica's three messages. Even two free Bushmills last night with dinner hadn't softened her after Erica's callous remarks about Jeri, and she wasn't in a forgiving mood today either.

She searched her phone again, hoping for a call or message from Jeri to explain what had happened to her last night or at least an invitation to talk about it. Wishful thinking. She started to call her but hit redial for the librarian who was researching the historic status of the Madison instead and turned toward the window.

"Hello, Simone."

"Thanks for calling. Do you have good news?"

"I think you'll be pleased. I've found newspaper articles in the archives about the Madison Building, and I've spoken to locals, great-grandchildren of original residents." The woman paused and shuffled some papers on her end.

"Please, don't keep me hanging."

"The Madison Building served as housing for Vicks executives and staff dating back to 1919. Some of the most popular Vicks products were conceived and perfected by people living in that building. Two of the National Registry of Historic Places criteria are that the property be associated with events that have made significant contributions to our history or that are associated with the lives of persons significant in our past. I'd say you have enough to apply."

Simone let out a slow breath of relief. "Thank you. This changes everything. Will you fax me copies of those articles and the statements?"

"Of course. I'm glad I could help."

This news wouldn't make Capstone Development happy, but she didn't care. She and her residents would be safer if she could get the historic designation. As long as she filed the paperwork, the property would be untouchable until a final ruling came down. Finally, a bright spot. She checked her next voice mail message as she slid on her shoes.

"Dr. Sullivan, Randy Mardis, Jeri's zone partner. Would you give me a call at your convenience? I'd really like to talk to you."

Why was Randy calling her? Cleaves handled the police department's therapy business. She dialed back. "Randy, this is Dr. Sullivan."

"Oh, hey, Doc. Thanks for calling. You available for a cup of coffee?"

The invitation surprised her. "Is this about the break-in at my place?" He knew she was a lesbian because he'd kidded Jeri about being attracted to her, so what else could he want?

"No."

"If it's a therapy question, Dr. Cleaves—"

"It's not really. I actually need your advice on a couple of personal matters, my mother and Jeri. She speaks highly of you, and cops never say anything nice about shrinks, so you must be okay. I promise it won't take long. I'll even pay for your time."

"That won't be necessary. Where would you like to meet?"

"Hot Shots in fifteen?"

"See you there." Simone packed her bag, still unsure what Randy really wanted. Something about the invitation felt off. Maybe the mention of Jeri made her too sensitive or too curious to refuse. She'd been edgy since their kiss, unable to face talking to Jeri about it, and unable to forget it.

When she opened the café door, Randy waved her to a booth in the back. "Thanks for doing this."

"You might want to wait on the appreciation. I'm not sure what I'm doing yet."

"Fair enough." He helped her off with her coat, folded it, and placed it on the seat beside her. "What would you like to drink? On me."

"Decaf mocha latte, please." She watched Randy at the counter placing their orders and flirting with Billie. He was attractive in a rugged sort of way and seemed like a nice guy, but his macho vibe was strong. If Jeri liked him, there had to be more under all the bravado.

"Here you go." He placed their coffees on the table and sat across from her again. "Okay. I won't waste your time. I'm in a difficult situation. My mother is in the late stages of COPD and heart and kidney failure."

"I'm so sorry, Randy. I didn't know."

"It's been a long and expensive road so far, but she refuses to go into managed care."

Simone's heart ached for anyone dealing with hospice care for a loved one. "How can I help?"

"The financial part is a daily struggle. I do extra duty every hour I'm not on the job, which is a lot of added stress."

"As if your work isn't stressful enough."

"Right? So, I was wondering if you had any tips about how to deal with the stress?"

The question sounded too simple, more like a prelude to the real issue, but either way, it was definitely why Cleaves got paid the city dollars. "I'm sorry for your difficulty, Randy. There are lots of ways to reduce stress, but shouldn't you be talking with Robert Cleaves about this? He is the department's psychologist."

Randy shook his head. "No can do, Doc. I can't have a psych visit on my record. And if he thought I wasn't FFD for some lame-ass reason, I'd be out of work, without my off-duty jobs, and in deep shit." He laced his gloved fingers together and squeezed.

Wound tight definitely described Randy Mardis right now. His muscular body practically vibrated with suppressed energy. She could almost be convinced he was on something or at least very nervous about this meeting. "I see."

"Do you?"

"It's understandable with everything you've got going on that you'd be stressed. All the worry and added responsibility of your mother's illness, combined with your regular job can certainly take a toll. As far as stress management, keeping a positive attitude is a must and accepting that there are things you can't control. Sharing your concerns about your mother's condition and care with her might help both of you." Simone paused to make sure Randy was listening. "Is this making sense? Do you want me to continue?"

"Yes, please."

"I'd also recommend you practice some relaxation techniques like meditation, yoga, or tai chi." She expected to see Randy roll his eyes, but he was very serious and focused. "Exercise regularly, which it looks like you do anyway, and eat healthy meals. If you can, find a hobby that takes your mind off of work and being a caregiver. Try to get enough sleep and talk to friends. Venting helps. And don't rely on drugs, alcohol, or other risky behavior to manage your stress."

He raised his hands palms up. "For sure. I don't want to end up like Jeri."

"Randy, I can't talk about Jeri." She wanted him to stop but also wanted to know if something else had happened.

"She's just something else I deal with every day. Work, my mother, and a friend who's off the rails. I was taking care of Mom last night when Casey called from the Cop Out. She said if I didn't come get Jeri, she'd have to call it in. By the time I got there, she was arguing with another woman, and they were close to blows. She'd apparently made a pass at this woman's girlfriend on the dance floor."

After I turned her away. Damn the timing of that whole evening. Jeri's flashback, Randy showing up, and the kiss topped off by Charlotte and Erica's arrival. She needed to talk to Jeri, not Randy. "I should really be going. If nothing I've said helps with the stress, I suggest you seek professional help. That kind of anxiety can have a detrimental effect on your psyche and body. And of course, the sessions are completely confidential and won't impact your job."

"Thanks." She started to get up, but he caught her hand and made eye contact. "Please, just one more question before you go?" Simone nodded, and he continued, "Has Jeri said anything about the shooting? Is she remembering yet? I'm really worried about her."

Simone's therapeutic alarm bells sounded. *This* felt like the real reason she was here. Like so many reluctant clients, Randy had buried the lede. "We haven't talked about that, and even if we did—"

"I know. You couldn't tell me. I just thought if she remembered something and it wasn't exactly right, I could steer her in another direction. Are you sure?"

"Why don't you just ask her?"

"The officers involved aren't allowed to talk about it to each other while the investigation is ongoing."

So, why was Randy so insistent on finding out what Jeri remembered? If he'd been there, didn't he know what happened? She suddenly felt very uncomfortable and rose to leave. "I can't help you, Randy."

He stood, helped her into her coat, leaned close, and whispered, "I can see why Jeri likes you, Simone."

She sucked in a breath. His whispery tone reminded Simone of her attacker, at least what she remembered about the voice during her highly fearful state. Nothing that would hold up under scrutiny. Randy took care of his sick mother and worked multiple jobs to do it. He wasn't assaulting people on the street. She shook off the troubling memory, smiled, and said, "Thank you for the coffee, but I really should go. It's been a long day."

CHAPTER NINETEEN

Between her supply runs the next day, Jeri went by the Morehead house again, but another walk-through didn't jog any other details from her memory. She showed the picture of Melony Wright around the UNC-G campus and searched for her on the street, but her focus constantly returned to her double meltdowns with Simone yesterday and the near-fight at the club last night.

Jeri had flaked out on the call at Simone's and afterward, misread the signals between them and kissed her. For a few blissful seconds, their kiss had been perfect—tender, real, meaningful—until Simone stopped her. Hyped on adrenaline and still wound up about the flashback, Jeri had been too aggressive, too demanding. Damn it. The way Simone kissed her in the beginning felt like she cared, but her rejection stung. Jeri had tried for too much too soon instead of the slow, gentle wooing Simone deserved. Maybe Simone's response wasn't really rejection, just a not-now intermission.

She parked in front of the office building that housed one person she didn't trust, Robert Cleaves, and one she—what? How *did* she feel about Simone? Before their kiss, she thought they were becoming more than friends, but now she had no idea and couldn't think about it any longer. She needed her strength and defenses to deal with Cleaves.

"I wasn't sure you'd show today...after our last session." Cleaves's voice held a hint of genuine surprise, and Jeri found it satisfying that he found her unpredictable.

She claimed her usual place in the leather recliner without responding. *Just get through this hour without losing your cool.* Simone was only two floors above them, and she'd once told Jeri she could do anything. She drew courage from the words and their brief kiss.

"Yeah, sorry about that, Doc. I'm just frustrated with this whole thing."

Cleaves opened his notebook and scribbled. "Well, that's certainly understandable. It's a traumatic incident under the best of circumstances, and yours are anything but ideal. Have you had any further memories of that night?"

"Not really." Jeri purposely lapsed into long silences during their sessions and feigned deep thought, determined to control how much information Cleaves got and to use as much time as possible in the process. Cleaves seemed to accept her silences as signs of introspection.

"I have the same dream. A closed door I can't open, two voices, smoke or fog, a shiny object, possibly a weapon, and cold air. And the smell of stale beer and urine—that's the only thing I'm sure *is* real." She'd repeated the same details so many times she wondered if they were accurate or just bits of meaningless detritus.

Jeri guarded the fact she'd visited the scene almost every day recently. Neither Cleaves nor the department would think her visits were okay. Each session, she gave him just enough information to show she was trying to remember and to hopefully get her released as soon as possible.

Cleaves shifted in his seat and scooted closer to Jeri. "Have you been able to talk to anyone else about your situation? A friend, confidante?"

"A little." She thought of Simone but didn't dare reveal her name. "No great revelations, just a bit more insight into why I don't do well with therapy."

That seemed to please Cleaves greatly. He smiled for the first time since she'd been seeing him and settled back in his chair. "If you're comfortable, I'd like for you to share that with me. It might help us going forward."

She wasn't comfortable but realized it might actually do her good to be more open. Keeping quiet and thinking she could handle everything hadn't worked, so if revealing her past helped clear her for duty faster, she could do it. "Let's just say I had an unfulfilling experience with a therapist when I was much younger."

"Unfulfilling how?"

She filled him in on her parents' death, her resistance and fear of disappointing her parents by asking for help, and subsequent lack of funds to continue the costly process. Once she started talking, she found it hard to stop. One revelation led to another and to more explanations. Maybe telling Simone all this had been cathartic and made the repeating less traumatic and difficult. When she finally stopped, Cleaves nodded and offered a subdued smile. "What?"

"I'm proud of you, Jeri. That's very good work indeed."

For the first time since she'd been seeing Cleaves, she felt they'd had an honest exchange. She opened up a bit, and he recognized and appreciated it. Maybe she could do this after all. Simone and Mrs. Doyle believed in her. Then another feeling floated to the surface, just as vehement and eager to be released as her past pain.

"And another thing."

Cleaves rolled his hand. "Yes, please, continue."

"I'm so pissed off I can barely control it. I feel the anger bubbling up just sitting here. Wouldn't you be angry if your whole life was on the verge of collapse and there was nothing you could do to stop it? I can't go out my front door because of protestors. The job I love is now limited to shuffling papers. My name is splashed across the newspapers and internet almost daily, and detectives in two divisions are trying to decide if I'm guilty of criminal or procedural violations. I apparently killed a man and can't remember it, much less tell his family that I'm beyond sorry. And then there's you. I *really* hate that you get to sit in judgment of whether or not I'm fit for duty, whether I'm too damaged or weak to do my job. Sometimes it feels like I'm the only one who isn't controlling my life." She was surprised that her voice sounded calm, matter-of-fact, and honest.

"And that is a very normal reaction to what you're going through. What becomes troublesome is when that anger is acted out in destructive ways."

"If you're talking about drinking, yes, I drink, but no more than any other cop." Her words sounded hollow, especially after what had happened at the bar last night. She'd just revealed a very painful part of her past, so why was this so hard to admit? "You've warned me about that before." Cleaves loved having his words parroted and being proven right.

"So, drinking is not problematic for you?"

The hairs on the back of Jeri's neck bristled. She glanced at the clock. Only five more minutes. She could do this, but then she saw Simone's face, heard her encouragement, and wanted so desperately to be herself again. "If I'm totally honest, yes, it has been a problem, but I'm starting to deal with it."

"That's very good news, Jeri." He waited, giving her an opportunity to say more.

Sporadic sexual liaisons with Tom. Red, angry bite marks. Pain mixed with pleasure. Rough sex without tenderness. And last night, manhandling Simone, and a shouting match over another woman's girlfriend that Jeri made a pass at on the dance floor. She stared at Cleaves. Maybe he did make some sort of sense. Maybe drinking and random sex helped her cope with the anger, fear, and pain. Simone had said they were possible symptoms of PTSD, but she didn't need to admit that. "I'm making progress."

"Excellent." He glanced at the clock. "Looks like our time is up. You've done very well today, Jeri. Thank you for sharing with me."

Jeri walked slowly to her car wondering if she and Cleaves had turned a corner. He'd listened without interrupting when she opened up, been encouraging, and made no judgments about anything she said. For the first time, Jeri believed she could handle therapy and eventually remember the shooting. She deserved a celebratory drink, but after her session, she diverted to Hot Shots instead for a coffee. Maybe she'd share the news with Simone later if she wasn't busy.

Jeri parked beside Billie's rusted out VW Bug and walked around the corner to the coffee house. She stopped in front of the plate glass windows and stared at the attractive woman seated in a back booth. Simone. Her first impulse was to go in immediately and tell Simone about her breakthrough with Cleaves. The next thought was how truly beautiful Simone was in the soft light of the café. She stood in the dark and just stared.

Simone's wavy reddish hair hung loosely across her shoulders. The flicker of a candle on the table danced over her creamy beige skin and highlighted the sparkle of her eyes and plump lips. Jeri wanted to claim those lips and the woman she believed in her heart was meant for her. But Simone had spurned her last night, and the rejection still stung.

When had she become so invested in Simone, so attracted to her? Jeri's body answered with desire that burned and settled deep in her core. The first time they met, purely by chance, Simone's compassion and nurturing had soothed and drawn her in, and Jeri's feelings had grown every day since.

But Simone was *here* with someone else, in a place Jeri thought was special to them. Was this a date? It certainly could be. They'd agreed nothing could happen between them. The desire that flared inside twisted like a dagger and brought pain. She wanted to be the one sitting across from Simone, the object of her attention. No one else. Ever.

She stretched to get a better view but was unable to see Simone's companion. What she did see was someone's gloved hand holding Simone's and the two of them playing a game of hand over hand. A knot twisted in Jeri's stomach. She remembered the touch of Simone's hands, the softness of her lips, and jealousy blazed through her until all she saw was red. She had to know who Simone's friend was, the person causing such turmoil.

Jeri gathered the courage to enter the coffee shop, waved a casual greeting to Billie, and glanced around. When her gaze settled on the other person at Simone's table, she froze.

Sitting across from Simone, his hand still holding hers, was Randy Mardis. She should've known. Those black Italian leather gloves were his signature. The three of them stared at each other, and no one spoke while Jeri focused on their joined hands in the center of the table.

❖

Simone followed the direction of Jeri's gaze and withdrew her hand from Randy's. Jeri's eyes darkened and color drained from her face. Her trust was already fragile after their kiss yesterday and seeing her with Randy wouldn't help. She'd misinterpreted the situation badly and immediately gone to a dark place. Simone ached from the pain she saw on Jeri's face and with the knowledge she'd contributed to it.

"Hey, partner, you going to stand there all night or join us for a cup o' joe?" Randy scooted over on the bench seat and patted the space beside him.

"Yes, please join us." Simone kept her tone calm though her insides were roiling. Jeri looked at them like she couldn't imagine anything more distasteful.

"I've got to go. Carry on with *whatever* you're doing." She turned and rushed to the exit.

Simone reached for her coat, but Randy grabbed it, helped her into it, and said, "Let me go. We've known each other a long time. I'll straighten this out."

"Actually, Randy, I should go. I'm trained to deal with emotional situations." She gave him a quick handshake. "Thank you for the coffee. Sorry I couldn't be of more help."

"No problem. You two behave. I'm watching you."

Simone shivered at the familiar phrase. Her attacker had said the same thing. Probably coincidence. He certainly wasn't the only person who used those three words together. She stared at him for several seconds before running out. "Jeri."

Jeri was about to close her car door when Simone reached her. "I have to go."

Simone wedged herself between the door and Jeri. "Would you please let me explain?"

Jeri tugged the door, trying to close it. "Can't you take no for an answer?"

"Not when a quick explanation would solve a terrible misunderstanding."

Jeri glared at her. "Misunderstanding? Weren't you just holding hands with my partner? Not that who you date or sleep with is any of my business, but *one* of you could've told me."

"Jeri, nothing is going on between Randy and me. Surely you know that after our conversations. He called and wanted to talk about his mother...and you. And I admit, I was curious and worried that something might've happened to you. If you needed anything, I doubt you'd ask me for help."

Jeri looked at her suspiciously. "Did he tell you about last night, at the bar?"

Simone didn't want to answer because that really sounded like they were gossiping, but her silence was an answer. "Jeri—"

"Great. Nothing fills me with more trust than the two of you talking about me behind my back." She tugged on the door again, but Simone held firm.

"He wanted to know if you'd remembered anything else about the shooting, but I didn't take the bait. I didn't know anything and wouldn't tell him if I did." Simone squatted beside the car and looked up at Jeri. "Haven't you learned anything at all about me?" She reached for Jeri's hand, but she pulled away. "I didn't participate in Megan's ambush at dinner, and I didn't discuss you with Randy. It's not how I operate."

Jeri stared off in the distance, her jaw tight. "Why would he ask you about the shooting?"

"I have no idea, Jeri, but he was pretty insistent. And he asked for advice about dealing with stress over his mother's illness, nothing else. If you'd looked more closely, you'd have seen the hand holding was actually me pulling out of his grasp."

Jeri cleared her throat and finally looked at Simone. "Really?"

"Yes. What you saw probably felt like betrayal by me and the person you trust most in your life right now, but I promise, Jeri, it wasn't." Simone stroked the side of Jeri's face, and she leaned into the touch.

"I really want to believe you, to trust you, but it's hard. Something good happened today, and you're the person I wanted to share it with, until I saw you with Randy. This is the place we first talked openly about our feelings."

"Oh, Jeri, I remember, and it's special to me too. I wasn't *with* Randy and I didn't betray your confidence. Please believe me." Jeri put the keys in the ignition and tugged on the door, and this time Simone didn't try to stop her.

"I'm emotionally drained. My flashback yesterday, that kiss, today with Cleaves, and now this. I just need time to think."

Simone winced at the resignation in Jeri's voice. This conversation wasn't getting better. She steadied herself against the door and stood. "I would never betray your trust, but until you believe me, it doesn't matter what I say. If you want to talk, call me. Good night, Jeri."

Chapter Twenty

The community meeting two days later arrived too quickly for Jeri. She'd been twisted in knots since seeing Simone and Randy in the coffee shop. Should she believe her eyes or Simone's words? Maybe her skepticism was tied to the past and her determination to do everything on her own. She wanted to believe, but her guidance system was so skewed she couldn't trust herself much less anyone else.

The meeting room was lit by emergency exit lights when Jeri arrived, and the chairman flashed a PowerPoint presentation on a bare wall. The slides represented crime statistics in the area of the Madison Building over the last three years compared to the months since the announcement of the downtown revitalization efforts.

"And the latest incident at Dr. Sullivan's loft in the Madison Building brings to twenty-five the number of reported cases of burglary, theft, or vandalism in this area recently. Maybe Officer Wylder can help us understand the numbers." He turned on the lights and looked around the room. "Officer Wylder, are you here?"

Everyone stared at her, but the only one who mattered was Simone. The welcome in her eyes stole Jeri's breath. How could Simone look at her with such openness and joy after their last meeting? *Because she was telling the truth.* Her heart knew, even if her screwed-up mind didn't. Jeri forced her attention to the chairman.

She rose slowly, grappling for something relevant to say. "I'm afraid I can't be of much help. I haven't seen these figures until now, but the spike does seem unusual for this neighborhood."

Anton Finelli, project manager for Capstone, stood and waved his hands. "It doesn't take a brain surgeon or a cop to figure out what's going on. This area is not safe. Maybe now is the time to sell for everyone's sake before it gets worse."

Jeri made a note to check on arrests associated with the recent incidents and to talk with the arsonist she'd charged. If someone was funding a crime spree to drive down property values and scare residents away, a guy facing jail time might be willing to make a deal.

Simone stood and raised her hand to be recognized. She was beautiful in a black suit and white blouse that hugged her body the way Jeri wanted to. Simone said, "I have information that will affect this project going forward. Today I filed paperwork to have the Madison Building declared a historic place on the National Registry. Nothing can be done until we have a ruling on the application."

"You *what?*" Tim Adams of Capstone Development glared at Simone. "There's no evidence of historic significance or the city planners would've mentioned it."

"City personnel weren't aware of information contained in the archives. I assure you, Mr. Adams, the proof is pretty compelling. In addition, my attorney and city inspectors have confirmed that the Madison is safe, and the claims of code violations are entirely false. I'm afraid you'll have to find another piece of land for your high-rise condos."

The chairman approached the podium, his cheeks flushed, obviously rattled by this latest news. "Thank you, Dr. Sullivan. Since further action depends on the outcome of this latest development, we're adjourned."

The room erupted in cheers and clapping, and the Preserve Our Historic Landmark group waved banners at the back of the room. Jeri used the ruckus to head for the door. She didn't want to risk an encounter with Simone, but the line of people also exiting the single door created a logjam, and she swore under her breath.

"I've heard that really doesn't help."

Simone's low sexy voice sounded from behind and sent a quiver down Jeri's spine. She took a deep breath and vowed not to look into her eyes because Simone would see into her soul. "I need to get out."

Simone cupped Jeri's elbow and leaned closer. "Do you have a few minutes?" She raised her hand. "I know I told you to call, but it's important or I wouldn't ask."

"As long as it's work related." Not at all what she wanted to say, or what she felt, but Simone had dismissed her last night for not believing her. And now, Jeri knew better, felt the truth deep inside. Time to face her mistakes like she'd done with Cleaves. "Okay. Let's talk."

"Thank God." Simone released a huge sigh. "Where shall we go?"

"Cop Out?"

"The bar down the street? Can we even hear ourselves there?"

Jeri nodded. Why had she suggested that of all places? She didn't want to risk running into Tom and exposing the shadow side of her life to Simone, but people pretty much ignored you there. "Casey has an upstairs loft that's usually cordoned off for special occasions. It's relatively private." She glanced around the parking lot and reconsidered just talking here, but too many people were still lingering. "See you there in ten minutes."

"Thank you."

Simone was suddenly shoved up against Jeri in the throng of people surrounding them, and the suppleness of her body and the flowery fragrance of her perfume made Jeri ache. She wanted to hold Simone, kiss her, and finally know the pleasure of being with her. When she reached the door, Jeri charged into the frigid night air and ran to the club, as much to escape her feelings as Simone.

"The usual, Casey," Jeri said as she stopped at the bar. "Would it be all right if I took a friend to the loft? We need to talk undisturbed."

"Sure, but we need to get something straight." She eyed Jeri hard. "That shit you pulled last night can't happen again. I almost called it in. You don't need the trouble, and I don't need a strike against my bar."

"Understood. It won't happen again. I'm getting my shit together. Really."

"Good, because you're a friend, not to mention one of my best customers, and I'd hate to lose you." She started mixing her drink but turned back. "FYI, Tom is asking about you." She nodded toward the pool tables.

"Thanks." When Casey brought her drink, Jeri added, "A gorgeous strawberry-blonde will be here in a few minutes. She'll have a Bushmills. Take care of her, put it on my tab, and send her up."

A few minutes later, Simone slid in across from Jeri with a lowball glass filled with whiskey and one ice cube. "The bartender doesn't seem happy. She's throwing eye daggers your way."

"That's Casey. She gave me my first job after college, rented me the apartment upstairs, and recommended me to the department. Sometimes I do stupid stuff and she reminds me I'm better than that. I caused a scene last night, and she almost called in on me."

"So, she's like your mentor. Nice to have someone in your corner you can trust." Simone took a sip of whiskey, closed her eyes, rolled the flavor around in her mouth, and slowly swallowed. Her cheeks turned pink, and when she opened her eyes, they shimmered. "Ahhh, burns so good. I needed that."

Jeri laughed. "Your expression looks more like torture."

"Sometimes pleasure is painful," Simone said before taking another sip.

Pleasure and pain, exactly what Jeri did not want to think about in this place. She checked the club for Tom, avoiding Simone's gaze. "You said it was important?"

Simone placed her glass on the table between them and cleared her throat. "First, I did not betray you with Randy. Believe what you want, but that is the truth. I swear it."

Simone's unwavering gaze and sincere smile, along with her earlier revelation, erased Jeri's uncertainty. And just like that, she believed her. Maybe because she wanted to, maybe because something inside told her she could. The realization brought another—she cared deeply for Simone. "I owe you a couple of apologies. First, about that kiss. I'm really sorry. Manhandling a woman is never okay, and I'd never hurt you or anyone else intentionally." She thought about Tom. "Without permission. Ever since the shooting, I've felt like something is trying to claw its way out of me. I don't know if it's anger, the amnesia, or fear of not knowing what's going to happen to me and when."

"Thanks for the apology. I wasn't hurt, more surprised at how quickly you shifted from gentle to demanding and then forceful."

"I guess that's why I come here, to exorcise my demons." Jeri's cheeks heated, and she stared into her drink glass. "I met a woman here. We share a sort of trauma bond. She likes rough play, and we help each other sort of purge the anger and pain. Does that make sense, Doctor?"

"It does. Do you find it helps?"

Jeri shrugged. "I forget for a few seconds, but usually feel worse afterward."

"I'm sorry, Jeri."

"Now you know why I told you to stay away from me." She rolled her glass between her palms. "And I'm sorry about last night, with you and Randy. I might've overreacted. Strike that, I did overreact. I trust you and Randy more than anyone else in my life. If I don't believe that, I'm more lost than I thought."

"Thanks, really." Simone's gaze darted around the club before finally resting on Jeri again. "I have something I'd like to share with you. I wanted to the night you told me about your parents, but that was a pretty emotional time, and we were both exhausted."

"Okay." Jeri took Simone's hand and kissed it. Whatever she had to say was going to be painful because she'd never seen her so uncomfortable. "I'm listening."

"It's not really a natural state for me to trust people either." She clasped her hands and took a deep breath before continuing. "I fell in love with my college roommate, and we had a short relationship. I'd never felt the things I did with Kay. She was my entire life. We shared everything. Six months after we became lovers, I woke up one morning, and she was gone. No note, call, or text. I had no idea what had happened to her."

Tight lines around Simone's mouth and tears pooled in her eyes broadcast her pain. "I'm so sorry," Jeri said. "Did you ever find out what happened?"

"Later, I learned my parents paid Kay to disappear because they thought she was *unsuitable* for their socialite daughter. Charlotte and Erica knew about the payoff but didn't tell me right away."

Jeri stared at her and shook her head. "You've got to be kidding?"

"I wish."

Tears burned Jeri's eyes as Simone brushed hers away. "Oh, my God. How horrible."

"It was a long time ago, but as we say in my profession, it affected the way I view love, trust, and relationships. It's natural that we're molded by our pasts." Simone was trying to be strong, trying to make a point about Jeri's life and the choices she'd made. "So, you see, you're like the rest of us, perfectly flawed, yet perfect, just the way you are."

Jeri had never loved anyone as much as she loved Simone at this moment. "You always know exactly what to say. Thank you for telling me about Kay." She cupped Simone's hands where they rested around her glass. "I know it wasn't easy." She studied Simone for several seconds, unsure if she wanted to delve further.

"What is it? You have a question. Might as well ask. You know all my secrets now."

Jeri chuckled. "I actually love and hate that you read me so well. I was just wondering how you forgave your parents and best friends after what they did."

"It was a process. Erica and Charlotte, mostly Erica, fueled my parents' dislike of Kay by feeding them stories about her and magnifying our problems. When my parents paid Kay to leave, Erica delivered the message and the money. When Charlotte and Erica finally told me about the payoff a year later, Kay was long gone. I spent months trying to find her, but she didn't leave a message and never contacted me. She talked about becoming a chef in Italy, so maybe she did. As far as the forgiveness part, I eventually decided it was easier than holding the anger. I only had to forgive once but being angry all the time required a daily commitment. I got tired... and I missed my parents and my closest friends."

"And you trust them now?"

"That's been a process too. I've established very clear boundaries, especially as it pertains to women I date. So far, it's worked, though Erica can be particularly abrasive, as you've seen firsthand."

"Seriously." Jeri grinned. "And I thought I had problems. Maybe you need to see a shrink. I can refer you to a very qualified woman."

"Can you now, Wylder." Simone reached across the table and took Jeri's hand.

Her simple touch warmed and aroused Jeri deeper than drink or sex ever had. She felt her life starting to open up again. Maybe her memories would be next. Simone was her safe place. She'd be there no matter what.

"Well, well, what do we have here?"

Simone jerked her hand from Jeri's and her eyes widened. Her rich friends from the condo, too fancily dressed for Cop Out regulars, stood beside the booth staring at them.

"Erica. Charlotte. What are you doing here?" Simone's voice was tight and sharp.

"Heard this was a great bar," Charlotte said. "You?"

"Checking out the local fare?" Erica asked. She pointed at Jeri. "We've seen you before. Simone's place the day of the break-in? I didn't know you and our girl were so close."

When Simone glanced at Jeri, something resembling fear or possibly embarrassment flashed in her eyes. Either way, she was struggling for words, unusual for her. Jeri should let her flounder but extended her hand to Erica. "I'm Officer Jeri Wylder. Dr. Sullivan and I are on the Fisher Park redevelopment committee."

"Work, of course," Erica responded.

"I hope you're Simone's date for the gala, because I'd love to dance with you." Charlotte smiled until Erica elbowed her in the ribs. "Well, I would. You can be an asshole, but she's hot."

Their privilege and condescension felt smothering and settled over Jeri like a thick fog. *Or smoke.* She suddenly felt fearful, like these women could dramatically change her life as they'd done Simone's all those years ago. Jeri's ears rang from the loud music, and her pulse quickened. The women in front of her faded, and she was standing at that last door again, unable to open it, afraid of what lay beyond. She glanced at Simone who was distracted by something Erica said. Jeri couldn't let her see what was happening.

"Excuse me." She bolted toward the restroom without waiting for a response. By the time she made her way across the dance floor and closed the door, her shirt was damp and sticky. She grabbed the cool porcelain sink to keep from falling. The overhead fluorescent light sputtered, casting her in flickering dark and light, and cold air whipped in through the open window. She swayed sideways, lightheaded and disoriented. That room. The last room. She reached for the final door handle.

Her reflection in the mirror was a terrified stranger—eyes wide, nostrils flared, and gasping for breath—but she pushed the door open in her mind. A male and female on a stained mattress in the corner. The woman held a cylindrical object. Flashbang. The man clutched a beer can. And? And then what? Jeri closed her eyes, desperate to recall, but her chest ached, and she shook violently. *Think. Stay with it.* Another gust of wind stirred the bitter smell of unclean bodies mingled with disinfectant, and she opened her eyes.

The man reached behind him and pulled out…something long and shiny. The woman screamed. *Knife.* He lunged toward Jeri. An explosion followed by blinding light. And Jeri shot him. That didn't feel right. He hit her. No, she fell. Damn it.

She splashed her face with cold water, backed against the wall, and concentrated on the quivering bulb overhead. "One one-thousand, two one-thousand, three one-thousand." She counted each inhale and exhale. "Did I shoot him?"

"Hey, babe. What's wrong?"

A figure moved toward her. Was he armed? Jeri searched for an escape route. The window. "Stop. I'll shoot."

"Jeri, it's Tom. You're safe."

"Tom? Really?" She blinked to clear her vision and saw a stranger's face with the eyes of a friend.

"Yeah. I'm here. You're going to be okay." Tom encircled Jeri's waist and guided her backward to a small stool under the window. "Sit."

"I'm o—kay." She gasped.

"Like hell you are. I was in Iraq and know what a panic attack looks like. Focus on me." Tom knelt between Jeri's legs, partially unbuttoned her shirt, and reached for her belt.

"Can't do that...now."

"Relax, Jeri. Let me help you."

"Need Simon—" She didn't want Simone to see her like this but desperately needed her. It had to be Simone.

"I don't know Simon, but I can help, babe. Relax."

"Simone!" Jeri yelled.

CHAPTER TWENTY-ONE

Simone stood to follow Jeri to the restroom, but Erica grabbed her arm. "What's going on with you?"

"I can't talk right now. Jeri is in trouble."

"So are you if you're chasing after her like a lovesick puppy."

Simone jerked her arm loose and glared. "Don't do this, Erica. We've been here before, and it won't end as well for you this time. I let your snide remarks about Jeri pass once but not again. I'll assume your concern is for my well-being and happiness and not some misguided jealousy. You have no idea what's going on and wouldn't understand if you did."

"Tell us," Charlotte said, her voice laced with genuine concern. "I'm worried about you."

"Worried? Why?" Simone looked from one to the other, but neither spoke. "Never mind. I don't really care. Just leave." She elbowed her way through the bar to find Jeri.

When she opened the restroom door, Jeri was seated on a stool by the window with a woman kneeling between her legs. Jeri's shirt was unbuttoned halfway, and the woman tugged at her jeans. "Get away from her."

The woman looked over her shoulder. "She's having a panic attack."

"I'm aware. Step aside." When the woman didn't move fast enough, Simone grabbed the waistband of her jeans and tugged her backward. "Wait outside and don't let anyone else in."

"Simone?" When Simone nodded, the woman said, "She asked for you. I'm Tom. I loosened her clothes so she could breathe easier."

"Thanks. I've got her now." Simone waited until Tom was gone and took her place between Jeri's legs. "I'm here, Jeri. Can you hear me?"

Jeri nodded.

"We need to slow your breathing." How could she distract Jeri without asking about work or Tom, who seemed way too familiar? "Tell me about Vita's Boston terriers."

Jeri glanced at her through wide, bloodshot eyes. "Black… and…white units. Four-legged…pandas. Put a blue light…on them and…" Her gasps came more slowly. "Call them police dogs."

"That's good, Jeri." Simone stretched over the sink, pulled a paper towel from the holder, and ran cold water over it. "Is it okay if I cool you off with this?"

Jeri nodded again.

Simone wiped Jeri's forehead with the wet towel, folded her shirt open wider, and patted her naked chest. "How does that feel?"

"Good. Really good."

Jeri's pupils constricted, and her carotid pulse slowed as she recovered from the fugue state. Simone breathed a sigh of relief and momentarily shifted from psychologist to a woman with feelings. "You're back with me."

"Sorry I freaked out." Jeri sat up straighter. "Was I rude to your friends? I felt, I don't know, like I was smothering around them. And then I went into a full-on flashback." She looked down at her clothes. "Were you trying to take advantage of me, Doctor?"

Joking was good. "Your friend Tom beat me to it." Simone stood and took Jeri's hands to help her up.

"Tom?" Jeri looked on the verge of panic again. "What? Were we—?"

"Calm down. She was trying to help when I got here. I gave her guard duty." She nodded toward the door. "If you're up to it, we should probably get you home."

"I parked in back and walked to the meeting." Jeri captured Simone's hand as she turned to leave. "Thank you for helping me. I'm sorry if I caused problems with your friends."

The look in Jeri's eyes was pleading, hypnotic. Simone wanted to comfort her, and so much more, but another time, in another place. How often had she said those words recently? Would she and Jeri ever have a right time? "My friends will understand, or they won't."

"Simone, I remembered. Almost everything. I think," Jeri said. "Would you help me with the rest, while it's still fresh?"

Her first instinct was to say yes, but she shouldn't. "Wouldn't you prefer to call Cleaves?"

"I think I should stay with the memories, but if it's a conflict for you, don't worry. I'll do the best I can tonight and call him tomorrow."

The desperation in Jeri's voice cut through Simone's final professional and personal reservations. "Of course, I'll help you."

"I shouldn't put you in this position. You've been so good with boundaries. Are you sure?"

Simone kissed Jeri's cheek and met her gaze. "There's no way I'm turning my back on you right now. You're at a critical point remembering the shooting. Where should we go?"

"Would my house be okay? I'd like to be in a familiar place."

"Perfect." Simone led a very wobbly Jeri through the bar and out the back exit to Jeri's car. As they pulled away, Simone saw Tom and a sexy butch entwined against the side of an old model Continental. How had she and Jeri met? Was this how they connected? She really didn't want to know the details.

Jeri opened the front door of her house and waved Simone in. "Excuse the mess. I wasn't expecting company."

The house was immaculate, no dirty clothes on the floor, no leftover containers littering the countertops, and no stack of liquor or beer bottles. "Looks good to me."

Jeri flopped onto the sofa and sighed. "Would you mind getting me a glass of ice water? I feel like I've run a marathon." She pointed to a cabinet beside the refrigerator. "Glasses. And there's Bushmills in the cupboard if you want."

Simone fixed two glasses of water while keeping an eye on Jeri. She was still pale and trembling. In some cases, unearthing lost memories could be as traumatic as the original event. "It's natural to feel tired." She handed Jeri her drink and sat down beside her. "Your brain has just had a pretty intensive workout." She sipped her water and waited, unwilling to push.

Jeri sat quietly drinking and staring at the fireplace until her trembling eased and her face again flushed with color. "I'm certain Vanoy charged me with a knife. The woman threw a flashbang, an explosive device, at my feet that temporarily deafened and blinded me. I can see their faces now. The woman yelled that he had a knife, but based on how I've been questioned, I assume the officers didn't find it."

"What could've happened to it?"

"In all the excitement, it would've been easy for the woman to take it and dive out the window. None of my assists saw her when they arrived. I don't know why she'd take the knife."

"And who were your assists?"

"The whole squad was there when I woke up. Carl and Randy were closest."

Simone shivered as she recalled the uneasy feeling with Randy at the coffee shop and his whispered words. She'd wanted to tell Jeri her suspicions tonight but thought sharing about Kay would reestablish their trust first. And then, Jeri had her flashback. "Anything else?"

Jeri drained her glass and looked at Simone. "This is going to sound crazy, but I'm not sure I shot the guy. It doesn't feel right. There's a missing piece."

Simone edged closer. "What do you mean?"

"I heard the gunshot, but it felt distant, not mine, if that makes sense. And the timing is mixed up with passing out. Why can't I remember that part?"

Simone pulled Jeri against her shoulder. "Don't worry about it right now. You're three-quarters of the way there. I call that progress. The rest will come. Try to relax."

"Will you be here?"

Simone felt Jeri's body tense against hers. Was Jeri afraid she'd push her away like she had after their brief kiss? If so, she needn't worry. Simone was too invested, too much in love to ever reject her again. *In love?* "I'll be right here."

Jeri sighed heavily and wrapped her arm around Simone's waist. "Thank you. And I'm sorry for being such a basket case lately. I'm usually a pretty stable and reliable person, even fun. I can provide character references."

Simone chuckled at Jeri's rare lightheartedness. "Can you?"

"My best friend, Vita Nix, has known me for twenty-five years." Jeri paused. "Well, maybe not Vita. She knows where all the bodies are buried. My neighbor, Mrs. Doyle, thinks I walk on water. You'd like her. She's very Irish."

"I'm sure I would." Without thinking, Simone kissed the top of Jeri's head and inhaled the outdoorsy fragrance of her shampoo. God, how she'd love to be in a cabin in the woods by a lake with the Jeri she'd met weeks ago—open, energetic, confident, and free of haunting memories and pending investigations. If only.

"Simone?"

"Uh-huh."

Jeri pulled away and made eye contact. "I'm sorry again about what happened after our kiss. That's not really me."

"Shush. I believe you. Rest."

Simone felt Jeri's body go slack against hers and hugged her tighter. "I've got you." But who would catch Simone if the angry Jeri returned and preferred the excitement of casual encounters to the challenge of a relationship? Or would she return? Maybe her memories would bring Jeri back to her life before the shooting.

She listened to Jeri's steady breathing and relaxed into the rhythmic rise and fall of her chest. It felt good, right, to comfort the one she loved. There was that word again. She rolled it around in her mind. Yes, she was in love with Jeri Wylder. Their talk tonight had been open and intimate, but how would Jeri feel when Simone revealed her suspicions about Randy? She tightened her arms around Jeri. Time to think about that later. She wanted to enjoy this moment as if it would be their last.

CHAPTER TWENTY-TWO

Jeri woke alone mid-afternoon covered in a blanket on her sofa. She'd run the gamut of emotions yesterday—relief at remembering most of the shooting, fear about the still missing bits, and intimacy and comfort in Simone's arms while she slept. During the night, she'd cried, Simone whispered soothingly, and the nightmares hadn't come.

Why did she leave without a word? Simone had shared a painful part of her past that brought them closer, but then they'd gotten sidetracked by Charlotte and Erica, and Jeri's flashback. She reached for her phone and saw Simone's text.

You looked so peaceful I couldn't wake you. Speak later?

Jeri's pulse quickened followed by a flush of heat. She wanted Simone—wanted to know her better, spend hours talking, learn about her childhood, all her past loves, and gradually hold and explore her body endlessly. Her feelings for Simone rang true with a certainty missing from the rest of her life since the shooting. Time to face facts. She was in love with Simone. No question. No doubt. She started to text back, but her phone rang. "Hello."

"Officer Wylder, this is Barbara in the criminal investigations division. Can you come down to the station to look at a lineup in an hour?"

"Is it about my case?" Detective Bowen in CID was handling the criminal part of the shooting, but she wasn't scheduled for another follow-up interview for two more days. Maybe they'd caught a break. Maybe someone was actually working her case even though she'd seen no evidence of it recently.

"I can't say. I was just told to notify you."

"On my way. Thanks." Jeri dressed and walked slowly to headquarters, replaying the recovered memories from last night and hoping the actual shooting would surface. No luck.

Detective Bowen met her in the reception area of CID. "Follow me, Wylder."

She buried her hands in her jacket pockets and followed, willing her jangling nerves to calm. "Can you tell me what this is about?"

He didn't respond until they entered a small viewing room with a two-way mirror and closed the door. "We located someone who might be connected to your case but need you to verify."

"Who is it?" Only one person, other than police, had relevant information about the shooting, unless another witness had come forward. "Never mind. Let's do this."

"You know the drill. Look at all the subjects carefully, but don't make any comment until I ask the question," Bowen said. "Are you ready?"

She blanked her expression, took a deep breath, and nodded.

Bowen tapped on the mirror, and lights came on in the adjoining room. Six women stood in front of the viewing window. Instead of looking for someone familiar, Jeri started on her right and worked her way down the line, studying faces, hair, build, and posture. She stopped at number three. Melony Wright. Jeri closed her eyes and reviewed the events of that night, confirming that she wasn't confusing her memory with the mug shot she'd recently seen. Definitely the same woman, just less wasted today. She opened her eyes, certain this was the woman she'd been searching for. She continued to the end of the line.

Bowen waited until Jeri looked at him again. "Do you recognize anyone, Wylder? If so, tell me how you recognize her."

"Number three. She was the woman in the room with Calvin Vanoy on Morehead Avenue the night he was shot."

"You're sure?"

The tight bundle of nerves at the base of her neck loosened, and her shoulders relaxed. "Absolutely. Who is she?" Jeri needed Bowen to say it, to confirm what she already knew.

"Melony Wright, Mel on the street. I wanted a positive ID before questioning her. I'll take it from here. Thanks for coming down." Bowen opened the door, but Jeri didn't move.

"Would you mind closing that again, please."

Bowen looked at her skeptically and did as she asked. "Yeah?"

"First, I want to thank you for not giving up on my case. I'm really grateful."

"It's my job and I take it seriously. Let's hope the girl supports your version of events."

"Yeah." Jeri hesitated for a second and then plowed ahead. "I have a favor to ask." If she told him about her dream or her gut feeling, he'd think she was nuts, but she questioned if she'd really shot Vanoy. The CSI had tested her hands for gunshot residue but wouldn't tell her the results. "I'd like to see the weapon."

"You mean *your* weapon, don't you?" He shook his head. "You want to help, I get that, but let us do our jobs. The weapon in evidence is the one you were issued the day you graduated from recruit school. So, please don't bring up a ghost gun at this point. It'll make you look desperate...and guilty."

"Please, Bowen. You're under pressure to clear this case, but it's my life and career on the line. If I could just look at the weapon you have in evidence. I have a hunch." It sounded better than I've had a dream. "I don't even need to touch it."

His expression changed from surprise to disbelief and finally a look of compassion softened the lines around his mouth and eyes. "I don't know what you hope to gain, but fine. One quick look. And you better not tell anyone I did this. Got it?"

"Agreed." She followed him to the evidence room where he secured her weapon from the clerk and held it out to her. "Would you turn it so I can look down the barrel?"

He shifted the Glock inside the plastic bag until the end of the barrel was visible.

Jeri felt like she'd been gut punched. How could this happen? *What* happened? She formed her next words carefully. "Something's wrong. My gun has a tiny nick on the end of the barrel. I dropped it on the sidewalk during requalification." Her heart pounded so loudly she could barely hear.

"That can't be. The serial numbers match. It's your gun."

"Did you run ballistics?"

Bowen looked everywhere but at her. "The request is in, but the lab is really behind right now." He gave her a sheepish look. "Sort of thought there was no rush. We ass—"

"You assumed the *entire* gun was mine since the serial numbers matched. Well, I'm thinking you should put a rush on those tests now. Every cop knows Glock barrels are interchangeable." She stared at him until he finally got it.

"Shit, what a rookie mistake. And I call myself a detective." He handed the gun back to the evidence tech and nodded for her to follow him outside to the parking lot. "I think you need to know something else." He checked the area to make sure they were alone. "Your body camera wasn't recovered at the scene. We have no idea where it is. And as you know, the camera footage has to be uploaded to the server before we have access."

"What?" Jeri felt like the world was closing in around her. "What about Randy's and Carl's cameras?"

"Randy's wasn't functioning because his battery ran down after six hours of off-duty work before his shift. And Carl never turned his on. The other officers arrived later."

"How convenient," she murmured. Cops were her friends, coworkers, and family, but she had a sick feeling that was about to change. Her squad and a dead man were the only people in the room when she woke up. Whatever happened while she was out, one or all of her guys knew the whole story. "I've been asking internal affairs to show me the footage for weeks to help with recall, and they never said a word. I thought it was because I'm not allowed to see it until the active investigation is over. What the hell is going on, Bowen?"

He shook his head. "I have no idea, but I'm damn sure going to find out. Nobody fucks with my investigation."

She nodded. "Then you'll have a lab tech check ballistics and then break the weapon down and dust the barrel for prints ASAP? I clean my gun before every shift. If that's mine, my fingerprints will be all over it. If not—"

"Some lowlife, bent cop framed you for the shooting. Because…" He stopped as if realizing he was about to say something he shouldn't.

"Because," Jeri finished for him, "my hand tested positive for GSR."

He nodded. "And gunshot residue can be transferred."

Chapter Twenty-three

Simone was almost home from work before she sent the text she'd rewritten a dozen times during the day. *Can I see you tonight?* Jeri had inhabited her mind all day—their exploration of Jeri's memories, sleeping on the sofa, and comforting her—the kind of intimacy that transcended sex. A couple of clients had commented on her distraction. Her usual pinpoint focus vanished when thoughts of Jeri popped up frequently, suddenly, and always with a jolt of emotion.

Jeri's reply came quickly. *Can't wait.*

Simone took a quick shower, changed into leggings and a bulky sweatshirt, and paced. Would her bad news dampen Jeri's upbeat mood? Simone didn't want to cause Jeri more trouble, but if her fears proved true, trouble and another rift were guaranteed. Her insides were such a tangle of nerves that she jumped when Jeri knocked. She opened the door, and Jeri's face read like a woman not at all happy.

"What's wrong?"

Jeri smiled but the attempt resembled a grimace. She gave Simone a hug that ended much too quickly and stepped back. "First, thank you for last night, for telling me about Kay, and especially for helping me through some scary stuff. I'm not sure what I would've done without you."

She took Jeri's hand, urged her inside, and closed the door. "Oh, I think Tom had things under control." She tensed at the memory of Tom's hands on Jeri when she walked into the restroom—not a scene she wished to experience again. She moved toward the sofa, unsure if she wanted to distance from Jeri or the memory. Without thinking, she blurted, "She's the woman you had, what did you call it, rough play with?"

Jeri glanced sheepishly around the condo before nodding. "About that."

"I don't need details. You said she helped you and that's good enough for me. I just sensed a connection when I saw you together. I'd rather hear what's going on today."

Jeri captured her hands and made her look at her. "But I want you to understand. Tom and I shared a bond we both needed at the time to get through our traumas. She told me about her family in Kentucky, and I talked about Vita and her Boston terriers mostly. Sex with a stranger isn't the best coping mechanism, but it worked for us. Sort of."

"I'm glad you had someone." But hearing Jeri talk about a bond with the sexy Tom made Simone almost squeamish. She tried to pull away, but Jeri held firm.

"You do understand, right?"

Simone forced the image of Tom and Jeri in the restroom from her mind and thought like a therapist. There were worse ways of coping. "Of course." She hesitated but had to know. "And now?"

"It's over, at least the sexual part. I'd like to be friends, but she's moving back to Kentucky, to her family. She needs their support, and fortunately, they want to help. I'm glad for her."

The tension that coiled Simone's insides released and she finally smiled. "I see. Would you like a drink?"

"No, thanks. I need to be totally sober for this." She clasped her hands behind her back, her posture rigid. "There's good news and possibly not so good news on the work front, none of which I should tell you. I'm sure it violates some departmental rule or regulation."

"O—kay."

"Would you mind if I hugged you again? I could really use another hug."

For the first time since they'd met, Jeri's expression of her needs sounded less like a cry for help and more like a girlfriend seeking intimacy. Simone opened her arms, and Jeri came to her. Jeri hugged her close, and Simone melted into her warmth, the need in her touch, and the way they matched curve to dip the length of their bodies. "You feel so good."

"I've needed you all day. When I woke up and you were gone..." Jeri's voice faltered, but she held fast, heat building between them.

"Sorry...work. I didn't want...to leave." Her words croaked out, thick with emotion. She gently led Jeri to the sofa. "Do you want to tell me what's happened? Generally, if that helps."

"I don't care about the damn rules anymore. I want to tell you everything." Jeri studied her for several seconds, and her eyes filled with tears. "They found the woman who was in the room with Calvin Vanoy when he was shot."

"That *is* good news."

"It could be, depending on what she says. If she verifies my version of what happened, great. If not..." Her voice trailed off. She turned Simone's hands over and kissed her palms before continuing. "And...there's a possibility I didn't shoot Vanoy."

"*What*? How much of a possibility? After all you've been through. Wouldn't they verify that as the first priority?" Jeri was practically vibrating with frenetic energy. What must she be feeling right now with the case changing so quickly? Simone could hardly contain her own emotions...and her hopes for their future. "Then who did—"

"If I'm right, someone I care about and consider a friend isn't. I'm not ready to name names. Naming makes it real, and real means I have to deal with it. And I can't deal with it until I have proof."

Simone squeezed Jeri's hands. "Maybe there's another explanation. Be optimistic." Jeri's reasons for optimism had been rare these past weeks, and Simone had been unable to help. All she could do now was love her and be there for her no matter what. "Can I do anything?"

Jeri edged closer on the sofa and pulled Simone to her. "I'm starting to feel things are turning in my favor, and maybe that angry beast inside is dying or at least calming." She stared into Simone's eyes, and her blue-gray irises turned dark with desire. "May I please kiss you, Simone Sullivan?"

Doubts lingered about Jeri's work situation and her future, but Simone's heart had no such reservations. "I wish you would."

Jeri cupped Simone's face and brought them together in a slow, deliberate dance of touching and not. She made eye contact, her gaze steady and full of need, her lids heavy. Anticipation surged through Simone and she licked her lips. "Please," she whispered.

"You are so beautiful."

Jeri kissed a light path across Simone's forehead, down her temples, the tip of her nose, her eyes, her chin, and finally paused at her mouth leaving a trail of gooseflesh and desire. Jeri's breath brushed Simone's lips, and she gasped. She'd imagined this tenderness from Jeri, and the reality took her breath. Jeri teased Simone's lips with the tip of her tongue before tentatively slipping inside.

When Jeri's mouth joined hers, Simone moaned and forced herself to savor each delicious second. This. This was what she'd wanted, needed for years—the slow burn of desire, building passion, a need so powerful she couldn't contain it. She slid her hand to the back of Jeri's neck as their kiss deepened and lost herself in the warm heat. Hunger flared.

Before reason took over, Simone guided Jeri backward on the sofa and stretched out on top of her. She wedged her knee between Jeri's legs and then stopped moving. Perfect. She knew they'd fit this way. She nestled her head into the dip of Jeri's shoulder, inhaled her fresh scent, and nibbled the side of her neck.

Jeri bucked, but Simone pressed her knee tighter against her crotch. "Please, lie still. Just give me a minute." Her breath came in ragged gasps, and pain stabbed her center. She memorized the fit of their bodies, the electricity surging between them, and a craving so intense it threatened to consume her. She claimed Jeri's mouth and poured her feelings into what could possibly be their last kiss. Once she told Jeri her suspicions, anything further was a crapshoot.

Jeri gripped Simone's hips and started rocking. "I want you... so much."

If she didn't stop now, she never would. "Jeri, wait." She kissed her again and sat back on her heels. "We need to talk."

Jeri groaned. "Really? Now? Did it ever occur to you that your profession could be an impediment to our relationship?" She waved her hand down her body. "In case you hadn't noticed, I need you right now."

"That makes two of us." Simone prayed that maybe this wouldn't be so bad. "I have to say this before we go any further." She took a deep breath. "The last thing I want to do is hurt you or cause you any more grief."

Jeri sat up on the sofa, fully focused on Simone. "Just say it. Rip off the bandage, whatever it is."

Simone hesitated, grappling for the right words. "I don't know how to tell you this."

"Have I done something wrong, again?"

"No, not at all."

"Something someone else has done...or said?" She studied Simone closely for several seconds and her eyes darkened. "Why don't I help you out. You can't get serious about a cop, a social nobody. Your friends and family will reject me like they did Kay. So, a fling is all we'll ever have. Am I close?"

Jeri's assumption and matter-of-fact delivery stunned her. "What?" She'd ignored other people's opinions since the day they'd met. "Jeri, no."

"But they wouldn't understand, would they?"

"Probably not, but—"

"Erica and Charlotte would have a field day with us at the gala. I can see all your rich society friends gawking at your rough-trade date."

"Jeri, where is all this coming from?" The turn of events caught Simone so off guard she scrambled to make sense of it.

"When I saw your friends in your condo, they did everything but sneer and step away from me like I was contagious, and at the club, their condescension was so thick I felt it."

Simone reached for Jeri, but she pulled back. "That's not what I wanted to talk about."

"Then what?" Her tone said she wasn't buying whatever Simone was selling.

Shock neutralized tact, and Simone blurted, "I think Randy Mardis attacked me outside my home." Jeri rose from the sofa so calmly that Simone wondered if she'd heard her. "Do you understand what I said?"

"I need you to stop right there." Jeri glared down at her. "If you wanted to get rid of me, you should've stuck with the friends and family plan. It made a lot more sense." Jeri turned and started toward the door.

"That's it? You don't want to hear why I suspect him?"

Jeri gripped the doorknob, started to open the door, but turned back to Simone. She processed everything Bowen had told her again. Hadn't she questioned her squad mates not an hour ago? But she wasn't ready to admit it aloud, especially not about Randy. "Fine. Tell me, but it better be good."

Simone wrung her hands and then motioned for Jeri to sit. When she didn't move from the door, Simone said, "I apologize for what I'm about to say because it's going to hurt you and that breaks my heart, but you need to hear it."

"I have no idea what to say to that." Simone was being sincere, open as usual, but Jeri wasn't over the shock of her suspicion of Randy and wasn't thinking clearly.

"It's okay. I know you don't want to hear this because Randy is your best friend, and the last thing you want to believe right now is that he betrayed you. My suspicion won't stand up in a court of law, but it's what I believe. You know how important instincts are, and I—"

"For God's sake, Simone, just say it."

"It's little things that add up. Those gloves he wears, the sound of his voice when he whispered to me in the café, and the words he used. It all felt so frighteningly familiar. And the way he pumped me for information about what you remembered of the shooting was beyond casual interest."

Jeri moved closer to Simone and stared into her green eyes, praying she was wrong, afraid she wasn't. "That's it? Really?" Then she recalled her conversations with Randy since the shooting. Every time he'd brought up the incident, asked what she remembered, urged her to make a statement, even if it wasn't entirely accurate. Was he afraid she'd recall something that would expose a cover-up?

Jeri's knees trembled, and she backed away from Simone and leaned against the doorframe for support. Was it possible? Would the forensic evidence support their suspicions? The next question was harder to ask. Why? "I can't believe it. Why would he..." Simone started toward her, but Jeri raised her hand for her to stop.

"I'm so sorry, Jeri. I had to tell you how I felt, but we should wait for real proof. I could be wrong."

Simone's comment struck Jeri as funny, probably a combination of frayed nerves and disbelief. She guffawed. "Really, Dr. Sullivan? You? Wrong?"

"It happens." Simone regarded her with concern. "Are you all right?"

"I can't remember the last time I felt all right and I'm far from it now." She stared at Simone for several seconds, unsure where this left them and unable to take on anything else at the moment. She needed to think, examine what she knew, suspected, and could prove.

"Please sit down, Jeri. Let's process what we know."

"I can't. No more *processing*. I need to think. Alone."

CHAPTER TWENTY-FOUR

J eri woke to protesters chanting outside her home, a constant since the chief released her name, but after the text from Detective Bowen this morning, the taunting didn't bother her as much. Today she'd face facts, and for the first time since the shooting, she had hope the facts favored her. Nothing was going to get in the way of her search for the truth, no matter where it led.

Mrs. Doyle and Toto were on their front porch when Jeri exited, and she raised her key ring with the four-leaf clover and said, "Wish me luck."

"It's yours, lass." She air toasted with her coffee cup, and Toto barked enthusiastically as she pulled out of the driveway.

Detective Bowen met her in the hallway outside the investigative division and nodded for her to follow. He led her through the building to the parking lot and leaned against the side of a car. "I don't want to risk being overheard."

The comment sent shivers through Jeri. "What's going on?"

"I have to handle my next move carefully."

Her nerves jangled and her mind went to worst-case scenarios. What if Wright's version of events conflicted with hers? What if her fingerprints were on the gun barrel and ballistics proved the bullet was fired from her weapon? And what if her body cam was never found…or if it was and provided further damning evidence. "Tell me."

"Melony Wright's statement jibes with your version of the shooting, as far as it goes."

Jeri blew out a long, relieved breath, but her respite only lasted until the end of his statement registered. "What does *as far as it goes* mean?"

"She confirmed Vanoy had a knife and charged you with it. She also admitted taking the knife, but she brought it in with her. So that's all good."

"But?" Jeri wanted to shake him so he'd get to the bad news before she had a heart attack or simply stopped breathing.

"After she tossed the flashbang, she has no idea what happened. She grabbed the knife when Vanoy dropped it, jumped through the open window, and ran. She can't tell us who shot Vanoy. The last thing she remembers seeing before the smoke is him charging you and you pulling your weapon."

"Fuck me."

"Not exactly." He placed his hand on her shoulder and squeezed. "I put a rush on the ballistics and fingerprint examinations."

Jeri held her breath for what seemed like an eternity. "And?"

He looked around to make sure no one was close before continuing. "Your fingerprints aren't on the barrel, but neither are anyone else's, at least not that we can make out. The prints are too smudged to make an identification. *But* the barrel currently in the slide of your weapon definitely fired the bullet that killed Vanoy, and according to you, it's not yours."

She placed both hands against the side of the car to steady herself. "That doesn't really help." The last few weeks she'd felt like a dead man walking just waiting for execution day. She took several seconds to let the news sink in. Her muscles relaxed all at once, and her legs felt wobbly. Before she could stop herself, tears streamed down her cheeks. She roughly wiped at her face before looking up at him.

Bowen unlocked the car and guided her into the front seat. "I know it's not what you wanted to hear."

"Understatement. It's like I've been living somebody else's life since the shooting. I don't recognize myself or understand what I'm doing or why I'm doing it most of the time." She dried her face on her sleeve. "If I could remember the last part of the incident before I was struck or fell or whatever the hell happened, I could clear my name."

"The forensic evidence can still help with that."

"How?" Jeri asked as she composed herself and exited the car.

"I have to question the other officers who were on the scene and run forensic tests on their weapons. If your fingerprints are on the barrel of a weapon one of them has, and the ballistic pattern of that barrel is from your gun, one of them stitched you up."

Simone's suspicions returned, but Jeri refused to voice them. The only way she'd believe one of her squad mates betrayed her was to have solid forensic proof. "That'll cause a stink."

"Yeah, I'm not looking forward to opening that line of questioning."

"Damn, I wish we had that body camera." Like many of her peers, Jeri had initially been skeptical of the cameras, but the footage had cleared officers of wrongdoing and brought justice to others, proving the cameras' worth many times over.

Bowen glanced back toward the building, then at the darkening sky. "Yeah. I was hoping Wright could tell us what happened to it."

"So, where does that leave me with internal affairs? Will you forward this information to them or should I tell them?"

He pointed at her. "Say nothing to *anyone* until I've interviewed the rest of your squad and run the necessary tests, filed my report, and forwarded it to IA. Got it?"

"Please hurry. I'm getting tired of being the bad guy." Jeri shouldn't give him a hard time, because he was trying to help, something not many in the department were interested in right now. They just wanted to close the case, end the adverse publicity, and move on. She shook her head, unable to accept that anyone on her squad would let her take the fall for something she didn't do. She looked at Bowen and forced herself to think like a cop. "You should probably approach them at the same time and not allow any phone contact before questioning. We're a close-knit group, and Randy and Carl have known each other since high school."

"Thanks. I'll keep that in mind."

"When will you do it?"

"At evening lineup, in an hour. I've asked the off-duty coordinator to secure fillers for the squad. You've been through enough, and the sooner we clear your name, the better."

Jeri offered Bowen her hand. "Thank you for believing in me. I'll be there."

"That's not necessary."

"I have to see the looks on their faces when you pull them aside."

"See you then. I've got a stop to make at the jail before I'm ready to interview these guys. If I'm lucky, I won't need to talk to all of them."

"What does that mean?"

He waved her off. "Wait for it, Wylder."

When Bowen went back into the station, Jeri stared at the sky letting his news spin over and over in her mind. If a fellow officer swapped her gun barrel, did he also take her body camera, and if they found it, would the video prove her innocence beyond a doubt or damn her further? She closed her eyes and relived the shooting again, but the last few seconds remained a blur. Patience. Before the night was over, she'd have her answers.

What she really wanted right now was to see Simone, but she had only an hour before evening lineup. One hour wasn't nearly enough time to apologize for her mistakes, sufficiently grovel, and beg for forgiveness before telling Simone she was in love with her. A confession like that needed time and finesse. She palmed her cell and did the next best thing.

Sorry I haven't gotten back to you. A lot happening. Sorry about last night too. You might be right. Talk later? She held her breath and waited for a reply.

I'd love that. Anytime. Not a school night.

Jeri started to type I love you, but texting wasn't the proper way to deliver words that meant so much. Simone deserved to see her face because she read people for a living, and Jeri needed her to know she was sincere. After tonight, maybe she and Simone could return to the charged anticipation of their first meeting and enjoy the easy banter they'd shared at Green Bean. She wanted to say so many things to Simone, wanted to know everything about her, and the possibility now felt real. One more hurdle and her life could return to normal...better than normal with Simone. If Simone would have her.

She walked back to her vehicle wondering why she hadn't believed Simone last night or her own instincts. If Randy, or any other member of her squad, was capable of framing Jeri for a shooting, he'd certainly be capable of assaulting Simone. The troubling question was why. She'd worked with those guys for years, fought beside them on the job, and helped them personally on more than one occasion. Why would any one of them set her up?

CHAPTER TWENTY-FIVE

Simone checked her phone after each client hoping to hear from Jeri, but at five o'clock, she was convinced she was being ghosted. She'd hoped Jeri would give her theory some thought and at least admit it was possible. She should've expressed her suspicions about Randy more carefully, but was there really a delicate way to tell someone their best friend was possibly a criminal? When the someone was Jeri, probably not. She'd been through too much lately to see things clearly, especially when it came to the shooting.

She packed her bag and started toward the elevator but spotted Cleaves and ducked into the stairwell. The last thing she wanted right now was another vague conversation and condescending look from him. She was almost home when her phone pinged with a text.

Meet us at Zeto for wine?

Charlotte's message clearly included Erica, and Simone checked herself before answering. She hadn't spoken to Erica since their exchange about Jeri at the bar and wasn't sure she wanted to. Why should she? *Because you love Jeri*, her conscience replied. She texted back. *See you in 15.* She darted upstairs, dropped off her bag, changed clothes, and walked into the bar precisely on time.

"Hey, girl." Charlotte rose to give Simone a hug. "Glad you could make it."

"Me too. I needed this." She glanced sideways at Erica but didn't acknowledge her.

"We probably need to talk," Erica said, waving for Simone to join them.

"Probably a good idea." Simone took the seat across from Erica so she could watch her reactions and gauge her comments and responses. "I'm listening."

Erica knocked back a shot of wine and wiped her mouth before starting. "I'm really sorry for acting like such a bitch." Charlotte nudged her, and Erica shot her a hard stare. "About Jeri."

"Okay."

"I have no right to judge who you date, and God knows I can be abrasive about it. I was wrong about Kay and thought I'd learned my lesson, but the truth is, I worry because you're so compassionate and kindhearted. I'm afraid someone will take advantage of you. Probably unnecessary, but true."

"I *can* take care of myself," Simone said. "I did it for quite a while after Kay."

Erica hung her head. "I know, and that's my fault too for siding with your parents and leaving you alone to deal with everything. I've tried to be a good friend since, maybe a little overbearing, but I promise I'll never interfere again. If you like Jeri, that's great. I just want you to be happy."

"Me too," Charlotte added.

Erica sat back in her chair, waiting for Simone to make the first move. It had been a longstanding tradition that the injured party decided when the exile over hurt feelings ended.

Simone wanted to finally forgive and forget the past, so she chose to believe Erica was sincere. She nodded, raised her glass, and said, "Let's drink."

Charlotte already had another bottle of red breathing on the table with three glasses. "Hope this will be okay. I've wanted to try it for some time."

Simone grinned. "I'd prefer whiskey, but this will do. So, what's going on with everyone?"

Charlotte glanced at Erica before taking off. "Well, I've been shopping for a new dress for the GGF gala and I want both of you to help me choose from three I have on hold. I'm thinking about donating some of my old formals to the auction."

Erica laughed. "Really? You're not the Queen, Charlotte, or even a princess. Who'd want your castoffs?"

"Hey, it's not about me. Some of those gowns have history. I wore the gold one to Obama's inaugural ball, the silver one to the governor's last gala, and the lavender one I've had since college graduation when—"

"Not the lavender lesbian deflowering gown?" Erica pressed the back of her hand to her forehead and feigned fainting.

Charlotte blushed, and her pale complexion turned bright red. "The very one. Tell me that won't bring a nice chunk of change."

"Only if you share the story," Simone said and winked.

Erica shook her head. "Whatever. Leave it to the junior sister to come up with unique ways to contribute. You do us proud. And of course, she's the first outfitted, bejeweled, corsaged, and ready to dance." She raised her wine glass for a toast. "I'm not sure if I'm going frocked or suited this year. The jury is still out, depending on my date."

Simone was about to say she didn't have a date yet when her phone chirped with a text. She held up her finger and looked at the message she'd been hoping for all day.

Sorry I haven't gotten back to you. A lot happening. Sorry about last night too. You might be right. Talk later?

She reread the message several times. Did *you might be right* refer to Randy? She'd never wanted to be wrong about anything so badly. Jeri would be devastated. Simone's chest tightened, and she took a gulp of wine before typing back. *I'd love that. Anytime. Not a school night.*

"Are you okay, Simone?" Charlotte asked. "You look weird."

"I'm fine now." She placed her phone face up beside her in case Jeri replied.

"So…how's it going with Jeri?" Erica asked.

"Good, really good. I think the shooting case is almost over, so she'll be doing what she loves again." Simone reconsidered what she was about to say and then blurted, "I'm going to ask her to the gala."

Charlotte and Erica stared and neither spoke for several long seconds. Charlotte's expression softened first and she said, "That's great."

Erica nodded but her eyes bulged with surprise.

"I'm in love with her." The words rolled off her tongue so easily she wondered why she hadn't said them sooner, to Jeri. She should've told Jeri first. "I'm totally in love with her." Simone's body warmed and tingled with the realization and the urge to tell Jeri.

Charlotte shrieked, and Erica's mouth hung open.

"I know you don't approve, but I can't worry about that anymore. I've never been more certain of anything. Ever."

Erica met Simone's gaze. "You've got that look we all hope to have someday. I'm happy for you. Really."

"And I'm over the freaking moon. That woman is *so* hot." Charlotte hugged Simone and wiggled against her, giggling the whole time. "Can I have just one dance with her, please?"

Simone held her at arm's length. "Not if you're going to shimmy like that."

"I'll behave." She crossed her fingers and raised her eyebrows. "Maybe."

Erica slid closer to them. "Don't worry, Simone, I'll chaperone our little sister." She raised her glass again. "Here's to love. May we all find it someday."

"Cheers." The doubt that had haunted the edges of their friendship since Kay finally faded, and Simone felt better. They finished the bottle before Simone excused herself and headed home.

She'd just closed and locked her door when she got Jeri's next text telling her she was sixty minutes out. Simone took a short shot of Jameson's to the bathroom, drew a hot bubble bath, and settled in. While she soaked in the foamy suds, she imagined scenario after sexy scenario of Jeri's arrival.

She'd held back physically for so long, and now her body hummed with excitement and anticipation. Jeri's ordeal was almost over, and Simone could finally shed her reservations. However tangentially, those doubts had separated them as definitively as a brick wall. She emptied her whiskey glass, toweled dry, and slid into a pair of silk pajamas, the fabric arousing her body even more. In the living space, she turned the gas logs on and threw a light blanket over the back of the sofa. Perfect. The stage was set, and she was so ready.

When the knock sounded at her door, Simone jumped. Now that the moment had arrived, she was unexplainably shy and uncertain. Did Jeri share Simone's feelings of love or was her interest merely casual? Was there hope for a future together? Could they overcome their differences? She took a deep breath and moved slowly toward the door. Only one way to find out. She opened the door and her body tensed. "Randy? What are you doing here?"

"I need to talk to you."

The last time he'd said those words, he'd tried to con her into a conversation about Jeri. That wasn't happening again. "I'm sorry. I'm expecting someone. You need to go."

"I'm afraid I have to insist." He pushed past her and closed the door behind him.

Chapter Twenty-six

Fifteen minutes before showtime, Jeri walked into the lineup room. Everyone stared, and she played it off, cutting up as usual. "What's up, guys? Forget me so soon?"

"What the actual fuck are you doing here?" Carl asked. "You cleared for duty?"

"Nah, just missed your ugly mugs." She glanced around the room. "Where's Randy?"

"Called out sick," Carl said. "Told him I was in the mood to make a few arrests tonight, so he probably couldn't take the pressure to keep up." Carl whipped his aluminum alloy baton from the holder, snapped his wrist, and the six-inch expandable device locked into a twenty-one-inch weapon. "Think fast, Wylder." He rushed toward her and feigned hitting her on the head but drew back at the last second.

The hairs on Jeri's arms and the back of her neck bristled, and she broke out in a cold sweat. *It can't be.* She stumbled backward and dropped into a chair, suddenly in that other room on Morehead Avenue. And she remembered. Smoke billowed around her, and Vanoy rushed her with a knife. She saw it clearly, drew her weapon, and pointed. Someone fired a shot, but not her. She glanced right, and Carl charged her with his ASP cocked. A sharp blow to her head, excruciating pain, and then darkness.

"Hey, you all right? I was joking," Carl said.

She pulled for breath and realized she was hyperventilating. "Good. I'm...good." She couldn't get away from him fast enough.

"Have to go." She barreled down the hallway to the exit nearly bowling over officers in her path. Detective Bowen pulled into the parking lot as Jeri got to her car, and she ran to him. "Carl knocked me out. Not sure who shot Vanoy though."

"I think I do. Talk later?"

"Yeah. Thanks." Cops were supposed to look after each other. The thin blue line was real, or so she'd thought. Now she wondered if it was necessary as she'd been told or just a way to cover up misconduct. Was Randy part of the deception, of setting her up? If so, she had to know why. The idea of his betrayal made her tremble with grief and rage.

She needed to see Simone, to ask her advice, and take a few minutes to focus before confronting Randy. Or maybe she should get the Randy business behind her and go to Simone with everything settled. Before she could decide, her phone rang.

"Hey, partner, it's Randy. I need to see you."

"Yeah, me too, but I have something else to do first."

"I'm with Simone. You should probably come to her place now."

"You're what?" The worse-case scenarios spun through her mind, and she blurted, "If you hurt her, I'll kill you with my bare hands. Do you understand?"

The line went dead.

The drive to Simone's passed in a tortuous slow-motion crawl. She weaved her vehicle between incompetent and dangerous drivers, crossed the center line, and ran stoplights, but none of that mattered. Randy had Simone, and all Jeri could think about was the ways he could hurt her if he chose. She brushed tears from her cheeks, refusing to give in to her feelings.

She slid her vehicle to a stop in front of the Madison, bailed out, and ran up the four flights of stairs. When she reached Simone's door, she paused to catch her breath and tried to plan her approach, but her mind blanked. There was no plan except to make sure Simone was okay. She pulled the Walther from her ankle holster and knocked.

Randy opened the door and stood aside. "It's about time."

Jeri grabbed him by the belt, pushed him against the wall, and shoved her gun under his chin. "What the hell are you playing at?"

Randy's eyes bulged and his Adam's apple bobbed. "Can we… talk?"

Jeri glanced at Simone sitting on the sofa in her pajamas, feet propped on an ottoman, sipping whiskey from a rocks glass. "Are you okay?"

"So far. I'm just a little confused by Randy's late-night visit. He wouldn't tell me why he was here until you arrived." She pointed. "Would you mind putting that thing away?"

Simone's calm tone and steady gaze soothed Jeri. She looked at Randy again, saw no threat in his eyes or demeanor, and lowered her weapon. "Sorry?"

"You might want to hold off on that." He straightened his clothes and lumbered to a chair opposite the sofa. "Have a seat."

"Just tell me what the hell is going on." Jeri was too hyped to sit so she paced behind Simone and waited. "Hurry up, damn it."

"Let him take his time," Simone said, reaching for Jeri's hand. "I have a feeling this isn't good news."

"Understatement." Randy looked at them both before leaning forward and burying his face in his hands. "I shot Calvin Vanoy." His shoulders jerked up and down as he sobbed quietly.

Jeri felt like she was on a roller coaster, up and down emotionally so frequently that nothing made sense. She came around the sofa and dropped down beside Simone, who wrapped an arm around her shoulder. She started to ask why, but Simone shook her head and mouthed *wait*. It was one of the hardest things she'd ever done. Every part of her wanted to scream that they'd been like siblings so what could've made him do such a despicable thing, but she clenched her fists and waited. Eventually, Randy spoke, his voice quiet and strained.

"I got there just before the flashbang went off. I don't think you even realized I'd arrived. Vanoy charged with the knife, and you hesitated. I thought he was going to kill you."

She had hesitated, unsure if Vanoy would stop, unsure of her target in the heavy smoke. Jeri started to say thank you but had to know the rest. "And then?"

Randy wiped his face and finally made eye contact. "Carl arrived. He saw what had happened and cold-cocked you with his baton. I swear, Jeri, I had no idea what he was doing." Randy waited a few seconds before continuing. "He grabbed my weapon, took the barrel off, and rubbed it on your hands before switching it for yours."

Their damn leather gloves. Of course, neither of them would've tested positive for gunshot residue. Why hadn't she thought of it sooner? Because she didn't want to believe any of this, at all.

"He was moving so fast, and I guess I was in shock or something. Then he turned off your body camera and stuffed it in his pocket. By that time, the woman was gone with the knife, and the rest of the squad arrived a few seconds later while you were still out."

Jeri felt her body grow warm as her anger built, but Simone squeezed her hand and told her to breathe. How could she breathe when her best friend had betrayed her so completely? He'd left her hanging all these weeks, facing possible criminal and administrative charges for things she hadn't done. He'd let her believe she killed someone and said nothing while she struggled with grief and guilt. She'd waited long enough. "Why?"

Randy shrugged. "Carl and I grew up on the rough side of Jersey. We saved each other's lives more times than I can count since we were teenagers. He left his family and friends to move here after I joined the force."

"So, why did you two set me up? Why not just tell the truth? You were protecting me."

"If I got sidelined on administrative leave, I wouldn't be able to work extra duty. I couldn't afford that, Jeri. Side jobs pay for my mom's in-home care. I couldn't give her round-the-clock staff on my salary alone. Carl thought it through quicker and covered for me."

"But you went along and threw me under the bus. Well-intentioned or not, you lied and broke the law." When she looked at Randy, he seemed a stranger. Could a friend really do such a thing? The dull ache and deep sense of loss she felt said yes. Would the pain ever go away?

"We thought you'd give your statement, be cleared, and that would be the end of it. The amnesia screwed everything. I'm really sorry, Jeri. Please try to understand."

"It's a little late for sorry and understanding, don't you think? You really believed I'd lie for you? That I'd cover evidence tampering?" He nodded, and she asked, "Does Carl still have my body camera?"

"Yeah." The word was barely audible as Randy stood and started toward the door.

"Where you going?"

"To turn myself in to Bowen. Carl texted that he was rounding up the whole squad, so I have to put an end to this. I'll make it right, Jeri. I swear. And again, I'm sorry."

Jeri looked at Simone for some indication of what she should do next, but when she did, she knew. "I have one more question before you go." She didn't wait for a reply. "Did you attack Simone on the street in front of the Madison?"

Randy shook his head. "Carl. If her property wasn't redeveloped, my uncle Finelli's company would lose the job, and I'd be out of more work. Another example of Carl doing the wrong thing to help. When he told me, I was pissed." He glanced at Simone. "I'm really sorry he did that."

"Did Carl also leak my address to the protestors and break into Simone's loft?"

Randy couldn't look at her but nodded as he reached for the doorknob. "I should go." When he opened the door, Bowen and a uniformed officer were waiting. "How?"

"Pinged your cell phone," Bowen said. "Randy Mardis, you're under arrest for obstructing justice, filing a false report, destroying evidence…and anything else I can think of on the way to jail. Put your hands behind your back."

Bowen cuffed Randy and handed him off to the uniformed officer before turning back to Jeri. "You have a follow-up interview with IA at ten tomorrow. Stop by my office before and I'll fill you in on the details. I think we can wrap this investigation up and clear you by lunchtime."

"Sounds great. Thanks, Bowen." Jeri closed the door and felt Simone behind her.

"Well, that certainly wasn't how I thought we'd spend our evening."

She turned into Simone's arms. "Oh, really? What did you have planned?"

"Some of this." Simone hugged her close and nuzzled the side of her neck. "A lot of this." She kissed Jeri and eased her leg between Jeri's. "And other things better discussed in another room." She slid her arm around Jeri's waist and guided her toward the bedroom.

CHAPTER TWENTY-SEVEN

S imone felt the muscles in Jeri's body relax as she led her to the side of her bed. The shock would be wearing off soon and giving way to realization and possibly more questions. Was she being too hasty? Did Jeri need to process what Randy had told her and how she felt about it before taking another emotional plunge? She forced her baser instincts from a gallop to a slow walk and asked, "Are you okay? Do you want to talk about what's happened today?"

Jeri sat on the side of the bed and pulled Simone between her legs. "That's so you, and I appreciate the offer, but talking is the last thing I want right now." She glanced up and smiled. "Maybe later?"

"If you're sure." Simone raked her fingers through Jeri's short hair and lightly brushed her thumb across Jeri's lips. "So...tell me. What do you want?"

"To hold you, naked...and then we'll see." Simone reached for the top button of Jeri's shirt, but she stopped her. "This may sound weird, but can we pretend we've been together for years and are just getting ready for bed like any other night?"

Simone chuckled though her body ached for connection. "Performance anxiety?"

Jeri cocked an eyebrow in a *seriously* look. "I've just gotten some of the best and worst news of my life and I don't want to clump my feelings about you or us in with anything else. You deserve better."

Simone touched Jeri's face. "That's the most beautiful thing anyone has ever said to me, and I understand completely." She unbuttoned her pajama top and let the silk garment fall to the floor. Jeri licked her lips. "If we're going to pretend we've been together for years, you need to stop giving me that look. It's like a lightning bolt shooting through me."

"You're just so unbelievably beautiful." Jeri stood and peeled her clothes off without breaking eye contact. She folded the bedcovers back and waved Simone in before joining her. Jeri opened her arms, and Simone moved to her without hesitation. "Lightning, huh?" Jeri traced Simone's brows, cheekbones, and finally her lips with the tip of a finger, every touch stoking the fire inside. "Does that mean you like me now?"

Heat blossomed between them, and Simone ached and wanted. She wrapped a leg over Jeri and trailed her fingers across her breasts, reveling in the way her nipples puckered and Jeri squirmed against her. "I liked you the moment I saw your little victory dance on my lawn after arresting the arson suspect, but life sort of got in the way. Now…"

"Now what?" Jeri hugged her tighter.

"I need to tell you something."

Jeri placed a finger over Simone's lips. "May I please go first?"

Jeri gazed at her with those blue-gray eyes, and Simone's heart stopped. All she could do was nod.

"I'm in love with you, Simone Sullivan." Her stare was unwavering. "I've never said those words to anyone else in my life. But like they say in the movies, 'Saying I love you is like a gun fight. If you draw first, you better not miss.'" Jeri paused, and her eyes widened. "Did I miss or misread our situation?"

Simone felt her heart would explode from the joy of the words she'd waited so long to hear and believe. The tears pooling in Jeri's eyes, and the slight quiver of her bottom lip told Simone everything she needed to know. She cupped Jeri's face and set her feelings free. "My darling, you've read things exactly right. I love you so much." She allowed her confession to sink in before lowering her mouth over Jeri's and claiming her. Their kiss deepened, and Simone felt she'd never be able to stop until she remembered Jeri's request and pulled back breathless. "So…sorry. You *just* wanted to hold me."

"That might've been a bit optimistic first time out." Jeri kissed her again and pressed their bodies so close Simone gasped. "Renegotiate?"

"Yes, please."

"Can I kiss you again?"

"You can do whatever you'd like. I'm yours."

"Never thought I'd hear those words from you." She kissed Simone again, pressing, exploring, and wanting. Then she pulled back and said, "Look at me. Don't close your eyes no matter what happens."

When their gazes met, Jeri's irises turned deep blue, and her pupils dilated. "It's like gazing into your soul," Simone said.

"I couldn't do this with anyone else, couldn't bear for them to look too closely."

"Thank you for letting it be me."

"I want to do everything with you. May I try something?" Jeri captured Simone's wrist and waited until she nodded. Jeri brought Simone's hand between her legs. "Just hold me." Then she put her own hand between Simone's knees and slid it up to her sex.

Heat poured from her center, and she felt Jeri's pulse in the palm of her hand mirroring her own insistent throbbing. As if by unspoken agreement, they languidly rocked against each other. Simone panted softly with each touch and closed her eyes.

"Look at me, Simone. Ple…ase." Jeri's voice choked with emotion.

"Sorry. You just feel so good." She opened her eyes and saw tears running down Jeri's face. Her nurturing gene kicked in. "What's wrong, my love?"

"I love you so much. Never thought I'd find you." She blinked hard and licked her lips. "I need you. All of you. Your gorgeous, tempting body. Your brilliant and witty mind. And especially your beautiful, nurturing nature."

The words released something inside Simone, and she hugged Jeri closer, letting their desire set the pace. Jeri's thrusts became more urgent, and Simone met her each time until the pressure inside threatened to overpower her. "I'm close."

Jeri's eyelids flagged and she breathed harder. "Me too. Keep looking. I want us to see each other when we come together the first time." She pressed a finger inside Simone. "Now you."

Simone did the same and within seconds, Jeri's sex pulsed in orgasm.

"Yes," Jeri cried. "Oh, yes."

The sensation of being drawn farther into Jeri tipped Simone over the edge. They panted in sync with each contraction, their gazes locked, kissing and quickly parting for air. "Jeri, I love you."

When the final tremors subsided and they separated, Jeri eased Simone's head against her chest. "I've never felt anything so powerful in my life. And now I'll have the image of you looking at me when you come. Forever."

Simone play punched her. "Way to make a girl feel self-conscious, Wylder."

"I hope not because it was beautiful, just like you." She nestled closer, entwining their legs. "This is a totally douche male thing to say, but I'm exhausted."

"I'm not surprised. You've had a wild ride for weeks, got more emotional news this evening, and of course, this." She stroked the side of Jeri's face. "Rest. We'll continue later."

Jeri's eyes fluttered shut. "Thanks. I love you."

Simone kissed the side of Jeri's neck and pulled the covers over them. "I love you too."

Chapter Twenty-eight

"Do you submit?" Jeri looked up from between Simone's legs and grinned, pleased with herself and Simone's ear-splitting orgasm.

Simone propped on her elbows, cheeks red, chest heaving for breath. "If it means…you're going to stop…doing that, never. You'll have to sex me into submission often."

Jeri slid off the bottom of the bed, and Simone groaned and reached for her with both hands. "As much as I'd like to take you up on that offer, I have to see another shrink now."

"Two-timer."

"Hardly. I asked Cleaves for an emergency meeting so I could check him off my list. I can't wait to see his face when I tell him I remember everything." She stopped at the bathroom door. "Would you like me to fill him in on the last fourteen hours too?"

Simone tossed a pillow at her.

"Oh, you'd like to brief him yourself?" Simone threw another one harder, and Jeri ducked. "Got it. No sharing with Cleaves."

"I'm so glad you were finally able to open up to him and make progress. You're amazing."

Jeri showered quickly and came out toweling off. "Amazing, you say? Anything else?"

Simone tugged on the towel in Jeri's hand and drew her closer. "Hot, tempting, enthusiastic," she said, trailing her finger down Jeri's body as she spoke, "an expert with your hands and—"

"Okay, so I'm perfect." Jeri grinned while she dressed, and then kissed Simone good-bye, once, twice, and again. "We *have* to stop, or I'll never get out of here."

"Would that be so bad?" Simone tried to pull her back into bed.

"Not at all, but I have things to do…so we can start our life together with a clean slate. Can you meet me at the station at nine? Bowen is going to update me, and I'd like you there."

"Are you sure?" Simone followed her naked to the front door.

"Totally. I want to share everything with you." She slapped Simone's bottom and rushed out before she caught her. "Love you."

An hour and a half later, Jeri closed Cleaves's office door for the last time. To say he'd been surprised by her revelations would be an understatement, and it gave her a great deal of pleasure. He assured her his FFD report would be on the chief's desk before the end of the day.

When she pulled up to the station, Simone was talking to a young female officer in the parking lot. Her jeans and cashmere sweater clung to her the way Jeri had last night and this morning, barely allowing her room to breathe. Her heartrate trebled and her center ached. A surge of desire and unexpected jealousy claimed her as she watched their interaction.

Without prompting, Simone suddenly looked at her as if they were tethered, waved, and gave her a smile so open and genuine that Jeri's eyes filled with tears. Her world righted again. Her time with Simone had been real, and their future could actually happen. She forced herself to walk slowly to Simone's side but stopped short of touching her.

Simone took Jeri's hand and pulled her close, and Jeri's heart swelled with love and pride. Leave it to the shrink to establish the boundaries. "Darling, do you remember Officer Thompson? She said you helped her out in recruit school."

Jeri shook hands with Thompson and said, "I believe that debt has been paid in full. She got me out of a tight spot recently."

"Sounds like a story I need to hear." Simone nodded to Thompson and allowed Jeri to lead her into the station.

Detective Bowen guided them into a small interview room with no viewing windows, waited until they were seated, and glanced between Simone and Jeri.

Simone nudged Jeri, and she said, "Sorry. This is Simone Sullivan. She's with me."

"Okay, I'll get to it. A lot has happened overnight. First, I interviewed the arsonist who tried to set fire to the Madison Building, which I think you own, Ms. Sullivan."

"Damn, I intended to do that, but...anyway, why did you decide to talk to him?"

"Just a hunch. There were too many things that seemed unrelated, and I don't believe in coincidences. The shooting at the abandoned house, sudden increase in crime in the area, attempted arson, the assault on Ms. Sullivan, and certain cops working extra duty with the construction company in charge of the redevelopment project."

"And?" Jeri's shoulders ached and her back strained against the rigid chair. She clasped Simone's hand and brought it to her lap, needing the comfort and stability of her calm presence.

"Anton Finelli was going to lose his job if the Fisher Park project didn't go through. He paid Carl to find someone to torch the Madison after his nephew, Randy, refused to cross that line. You know Carl assaulted Ms. Sullivan, but he also broke into her condo, and paid graffiti artists to tag her place on several occasions."

"If I'd gone back and interviewed the arsonist like I planned, this could've been over much sooner." Jeri shook her head. She'd skipped over the weakest link, and the chain had held.

"Don't beat yourself up. You've been a little distracted. Besides, light duty equals no real police work," Bowen said.

"Why was Carl so invested in this project?" Simone said. "What's the connection?"

Before Bowen could respond, Jeri said, "Randy."

Bowen nodded. "Apparently, their friendship goes way back. Randy took a couple of juvie wraps for Carl, they worked together on the New Jersey State Police, and Carl followed him to North Carolina. The shooting coverup was all about protecting Randy."

Jeri sat quietly letting the information sink in and jibe with the facts she already knew. "Guess it makes sense."

"In a twisted sort of way, I can understand it," Bowen said.

"Makes sense? Understand it?" Simone glared at Jeri and Bowen like they were prey coming after her cubs. "Seriously? These *cops* tried to destroy the woman I love, and you two somehow get why they did it? They covered up the death of a man for weeks, denying his family the truth. If this is some of that thin blue line bullshit, I won't have it." Her eyes flashed with anger and disbelief.

"I don't condone it at all. I just get it as a motive," Bowen said, but Jeri could see Simone wasn't hearing him.

"It's all right, babe." Jeri patted Simone's hand and tried to calm her. "Aren't you supposed to be the sensitive, understanding one?"

"Not about this. Never about anything or anyone that hurts you."

"And I love you for that, really." She leaned over and kissed Simone on the cheek and whispered. "I have to hear all of it, but you don't if it makes you uncomfortable. Do you want to wait outside?"

Simone pulled a couple of heavy breaths to compose herself. "Thanks, but I'm good." She smiled apologetically at Bowen. "I'm very protective of the people I love."

"Totally get that. Wylder's lucky to have you."

"Yes, I am," Jeri said, squeezing Simone's hand. "The only other question I have is—"

"About the body camera?" Jeri nodded, and Bowen continued. "Carl took it, turned it off, and kept it. Thank God he didn't destroy it, because the footage cleared you completely. It shows the shot came from Randy's gun, and Carl knocking you out with his ASP."

Simone flinched, and Jeri shot her a quick smile to comfort her.

"And then Carl swapping the barrel of your weapon with Randy's. The final nail in his coffin is the forensic evidence. The weapon in Randy's possession has your fingerprints on the barrel, which means it belongs to your weapon, and the ballistics test matched his barrel, which is now on your gun frame but should be on his. Forensics don't lie."

Jeri's back and shoulder muscles released, and she collapsed against the chair. "Wow." She was almost afraid to ask the next question. "Is it finally over?"

"Almost." Jeri tensed again, and Bowen waved his hand toward her. "Relax, soldier. I've already sent the body cam to IA, and they're expecting you as soon as we finish. When they see the footage and hear your final statement, then it'll be over."

Jeri stood, pulled Simone into her arms, and hugged her. Tears threatened and finally fell when she turned to shake Bowen's hand. "I can never thank you enough."

"No need. It's my job, and in this case, my pleasure. Good cops have to stick together to weed out the bad." He smiled at Simone and said, "Well, I'll leave you to it."

When the door closed behind Bowen, Simone grabbed Jeri and held her close. "You're totally vindicated and finally free."

"After the IA interview."

Simone flicked her fingers in the air. "A formality. How would you like to celebrate?"

Jeri backed her against the door and kissed her lightly, then more hungrily. "How about picking up where we left off this morning?"

Simone grinned and tugged the waist of her jeans.

"Too thirsty?"

"Never." Simone slid her knee between Jeri's legs and lifted until she brushed her center. "I have two tiny favors to ask first. They're dangerous but absolutely vital to our future."

Jeri moaned and pulled back to look at Simone, the only woman she could imagine spending the rest of her life with, revealing her secrets to, and coming home to every night. "I'd walk through fire for you."

"Close." Simone grinned. "Have dinner with my brother, his wife, and my parents tonight?" With the announcement of the final guests, Simone pressed her knee firmly against Jeri's crotch.

Jeri groaned and doubled over. "Damn, woman, you sure know how to get your way." The bomb finally registered. "Wait. *Your parents?*"

"They've been out of the country for two years, so Andy and I planned a welcome home meal, before *we* happened."

Jeri's pulse quickened. "From first sex to parents in less than twenty-four hours has to be a new world's record. Are you sure you want to do this now?"

"Totally sure, unless you're uncomfortable with it. I want you to share every part of my life, and they need to accept you or lose me. Their choice, and the sooner I know the better."

"Ouch. A little harsh." Jeri nuzzled the side of Simone's neck.

"I gave up someone I loved when I was a teenager because I was afraid to stand up to my parents and friends. I won't do it again."

She cupped Simone's face and met her gaze. "I'm with you. Should I wear my uniform, complete with Kevlar vest?" Simone smiled, kissed her, and Jeri added, "After that request, I'm afraid to ask about the other favor."

"Be my date to the Guilford Green Foundation gala tomorrow night?"

Jeri felt like her heart would burst. The gala was a big deal, and she'd purposely not gone until she could sport the woman she loved on her arm. Now was the time for all things couple-y. "Can I wear a tux? 'Cause I'm just saying, I look hot in a properly tailored tux." She waved her hands down her body, rested them on her hips, and gave a seductive thrust. "You'll have to beat the women off me."

"And vice versa because I rock an evening gown like no one you've ever seen." Simone twirled and feigned wilting in Jeri's arms. "I'll need a Princess Charming to keep me safe."

Jeri started to kiss Simone again, but stopped. "Just to keep the rest of the attendees safe, let's stick together. We wouldn't want anyone to hurt themselves trying to get our attention."

"Agreed." Simone spun out of Jeri's grasp and squeezed her ass. "Go give your final statement to those internal affairs guys and meet me at—"

"My place? You're entirely too loud for condo living. Bring enough clothes for the weekend, not that you'll need them beyond the mandatory public appearances. I plan to keep you naked and screaming the rest of the time."

"I look forward to it." Simone kissed Jeri again and her expression turned serious. "Jeri?"

"Yes, love."

"Are you sure you're okay being in a relationship with a fancy girl who has rich parents and attends ritzy galas in lavish gowns?"

"As long as you're okay being with a woman who has no parents and may or may not be a cop, or even employed at all, soon."

Simone moved closer to Jeri again and looked into her eyes as if trying to gauge if she was joking. "What? You're going to quit?"

"Possibly." Saying it aloud wasn't exactly what she'd planned, but she'd been thinking about it ever since the shooting, so might as well warn Simone now. "I've been weighing my options. I never realized how much killing someone, or even thinking I'd killed someone, would affect me. Maybe I don't want to do this kind of work anymore. And if I can't trust my coworkers, I'll never feel really safe on the street."

"Give it some time, Jeri. You might feel differently when you've had time to process." She encircled Jeri's waist and pulled them back together. "And just so you know, I'm totally fine with whatever you decide to do." She grinned and her green eyes sparkled. "But just because I'll be a trust-fund baby someday, don't expect to be a kept woman."

"Not my style." Simone leaned in and kissed her so deeply that Jeri felt herself grow wet. When the kiss ended, Jeri studied the face of the woman she loved, memorizing how it looked at this moment, certain she'd be happy to see it every day for the rest of her life. "Okay, then, let's start fitting our lives together."

About the Author

A thirty-year veteran of a midsized police department, VK Powell was a police officer by necessity and a writer by desire. Her career spanned numerous positions including beat officer, homicide detective, vice/narcotics lieutenant, captain, and assistant chief of police. Now retired, she devotes her time to writing, traveling, and volunteering.

VK can be reached on Facebook at @vk.powell.12 and Twitter @VKPowell.

Books Available from Bold Strokes Books

A Turn of Fate by Ronica Black. Will Nev and Kinsley finally face their painful past and relent to their powerful, forbidden attraction? Or will facing their past be too much to fight through? (978-1-63555-930-9)

Desires After Dark by MJ Williamz. When her human lover falls deathly ill, Alex, a vampire, must decide which is worse, letting her go or condemning her to everlasting life. (978-1-63555-940-8)

Her Consigliere by Carsen Taite. FBI agent Royal Scott swore an oath to uphold the law, and criminal defense attorney Siobhan Collins pledged her loyalty to the only family she's ever known, but will their love be stronger than the bonds they've vowed to others, or will their competing allegiances tear them apart? (978-1-63555-924-8)

In Our Words: Queer Stories from Black, Indigenous, and People of Color Writers. Stories Selected by Anne Shade and Edited by Victoria Villaseñor. Comprising both the renowned and emerging voices of Black, Indigenous, and People of Color authors, this thoughtfully curated collection of short stories explores the intersection of racial and queer identity. (978-1-63555-936-1)

Measure of Devotion by CF Frizzell. Disguised as her late twin brother, Catherine Samson enters the Civil War to defend the Constitution as a Union soldier, never expecting her life to be altered by a Gettysburg farmer's daughter. (978-1-63555-951-4)

Not Guilty by Brit Ryder. Claire Weaver and Emery Pearson's day jobs clash, even as their desire for each other burns, and a discreet sex-only arrangement is the only option. (978-1-63555-896-8)

Opposites Attract: Butch/Femme Romances by Meghan O'Brien, Aurora Rey, Angie Williams. Sometimes opposites really do attract. Fall in love with these butch/femme romance novellas. (978-1-63555-784-8)

Swift Vengeance by Jean Copeland, Jackie D, Erin Zak. A journalist becomes the subject of her own investigation when sudden strange, violent visions summon her to a summer retreat and into the arms of a killer's possible next victim. (978-1-63555-880-7)

Under Her Influence by Amanda Radley. On their path to #truelove, will Beth and Jemma discover that reality is even better than illusion? (978-1-63555-963-7)

Wasteland by Kristin Keppler & Allisa Bahney. Danielle Clark is fighting against the National Armed Forces and finds peace as a scavenger, until the NAF general's daughter, Katelyn Turner, shows up on her doorstep and brings the fight right back to her. (978-1-63555-935-4)

When in Doubt by VK Powell. Police officer Jeri Wylder thinks she committed a crime in the line of duty but can't remember, until details emerge pointing to a cover-up by those close to her. (978-1-63555-955-2)

A Woman to Treasure by Ali Vali. An ancient scroll isn't the only treasure Levi Montbard finds as she starts her hunt for the truth—all she has to do is prove to Yasmine Hassani that there's more to her than an adventurous soul. (978-1-63555-890-6)

Before. After. Always. by Morgan Lee Miller. Still reeling from her tragic past, Eliza Walsh has sworn off taking risks, until Blake Navarro turns her world right-side up, making her question if falling in love again is worth it. (978-1-63555-845-6)

Bet the Farm by Fiona Riley. Lauren Calloway's luxury real estate sale of the century comes to a screeching halt when dairy farm heiress, and one-night stand, Thea Boudreaux calls her bluff. (978-1-63555-731-2)

Cowgirl by Nance Sparks. The last thing Aren expects is to fall for Carol. Sharing her home is one thing, but sharing her heart means sharing the demons in her past and risking everything to keep Carol safe. (978-1-63555-877-7)

Give In to Me by Elle Spencer. Gabriela Talbot never expected to sleep with her favorite author—certainly not after the scathing review she'd given Whitney Ainsworth's latest book. (978-1-63555-910-1)

Hidden Dreams by Shelley Thrasher. A lethal virus and its resulting vision send Texan Barbara Allan and her lovely guide, Dara, on a journey up Cambodia's Mekong River in search of Barbara's mother's mystifying past. (978-1-63555-856-2)

In the Spotlight by Lesley Davis. For actresses Cole Calder and Eris Whyte, their chance at love runs out fast when a fan's adoration turns to obsession. (978-1-63555-926-2)

Origins by Jen Jensen. Jamis Bachman is pulled into a dangerous mystery that becomes personal when she learns the truth of her origins as a ghost hunter. (978-1-63555-837-1)

Pursuit: A Victorian Entertainment by Felice Picano. An intelligent, handsome, ruthlessly ambitious young man who rose from the slums to become the right-hand man of the Lord Exchequer of England will stop at nothing as he pursues his Lord's vanished wife across Continental Europe. (978-1-63555-870-8)

Unrivaled by Radclyffe. Zoey Cohen will never accept second place in matters of the heart, even when her rival is a career, and Declan Black has nothing left to give of herself or her heart. (978-1-63679-013-8)

A Fae Tale by Genevieve McCluer. Dovana comes to terms with her changing feelings for her lifelong best friend and fae, Roze. (978-1-63555-918-7)

Accidental Desperados by Lee Lynch. Life is clobbering Berry, Jaudon, and their long romance. The arrival of directionless baby dyke MJ doesn't help. Can they find their passion again—and keep it? (978-1-63555-482-3)

Always Believe by Aimée. Greyson Walsden is pursuing ordination as an Anglican priest. Angela Arlingham doesn't believe in God. Do they follow their vocation or their hearts? (978-1-63555-912-5)

Best of the Wrong Reasons by Sander Santiago. For Fin Ness and Orion Starr, it takes a funeral to remind them that love is worth living for. (978-1-63555-867-8)

Courage by Jesse J. Thoma. No matter how often Natasha Parsons and Tommy Finch clash on the job, an undeniable attraction simmers just beneath the surface. Can they find the courage to change so love has room to grow? (978-1-63555-802-9)

I Am Chris by R Kent. There's one saving grace to losing everything and moving away. Nobody knows her as Chrissy Taylor. Now Chris can live who he truly is. (978-1-63555-904-0)

The Princess and the Odium by Sam Ledel. Jastyn and Princess Aurelia return to Venostes and join their families in a battle against the dark force to take back their homeland for a chance at a better tomorrow. (978-1-63555-894-4)

The Queen Has a Cold by Jane Kolven. What happens when the heir to the throne isn't a prince or a princess? (978-1-63555-878-4)

The Secret Poet by Georgia Beers. Agreeing to help her brother woo Zoe Blake seemed like a good idea to Morgan Thompson at first...until she realizes she's actually wooing Zoe for herself... (978-1-63555-858-6)

You Again by Aurora Rey. For high school sweethearts Kate Cormier and Sutton Guidry, the second chance might be the only one that matters. (978-1-63555-791-6)

Coming to Life on South High by Lee Patton. Twenty-one-year-old gay virgin Gabe Rafferty's first adult decade unfolds as an unpredictable journey into sex, love, and livelihood. (978-1-63555-906-4)

Love's Falling Star by B.D. Grayson. For country music megastar Lochlan Paige, can love conquer her fear of losing the one thing she's worked so hard to protect? (978-1-63555-873-9)

Love's Truth by C.A. Popovich. Can Lynette and Barb make love work when unhealed wounds of betrayed trust and a secret could change everything? (978-1-63555-755-8)

Next Exit Home by Dena Blake. Home may be where the heart is, but for Harper Sims and Addison Foster, is the journey back worth the pain? (978-1-63555-727-5)

Not Broken by Lyn Hemphill. Falling in love is hard enough—even more so for Rose who's carrying her ex's baby. (978-1-63555-869-2)

The Noble and the Nightingale by Barbara Ann Wright. Two women on opposite sides of empires at war risk all for a chance at love. (978-1-63555-812-8)

What a Tangled Web by Melissa Brayden. Clementine Monroe has the chance to buy the café she's managed for years, but Madison LeGrange swoops in and buys it first. Now Clementine is forced to work for the enemy and ignore her former crush. (978-1-63555-749-7)

A Far Better Thing by JD Wilburn. When needs of her family and wants of her heart clash, Cass Halliburton is faced with the ultimate sacrifice. (978-1-63555-834-0)

Body Language by Renee Roman. When Mika offers to provide Jen erotic tutoring, will sex drive them into a deeper relationship or tear them apart? (978-1-63555-800-5)

Carrie and Hope by Joy Argento. For Carrie and Hope loss brings them together but secrets and fear may tear them apart. (978-1-63555-827-2)

Death's Prelude by David S. Pederson. In this prequel to the Detective Heath Barrington Mystery series, Heath discovers that first love changes you forever and drives you to become the person you're destined to be. (978-1-63555-786-2)

Ice Queen by Gun Brooke. School counselor Aislin Kennedy wants to help standoffish CEO Susanna Durr and her troubled teenage daughter become closer—even if it means risking her own heart in the process. (978-1-63555-721-3)

Masquerade by Anne Shade. In 1925 Harlem, New York, a notorious gangster sets her sights on seducing Celine, and new lovers Dinah and Celine are forced to risk their hearts, and lives, for love. (978-1-63555-831-9)

Royal Family by Jenny Frame. Loss has defined both Clay's and Katya's lives, but guarding their hearts may prove to be the biggest heartbreak of all. (978-1-63555-745-9)

Share the Moon by Toni Logan. Three best friends, an inherited vineyard and a resident ghost come together for fun, romance and a touch of magic. (978-1-63555-844-9)

Spirit of the Law by Carsen Taite. Attorney Owen Lassiter will do almost anything to put a murderer behind bars, but can she get past her reluctance to rely on unconventional help from the alluring Summer Byrne and keep from falling in love in the process? (978-1-63555-766-4)

The Devil Incarnate by Ali Vali. Cain Casey has so much to live for, but enemies who lurk in the shadows threaten to unravel it all. (978-1-63555-534-9)